For my good buddy Jim

AFTER THE WIND

Roger,

ROGER L. CONLEE

Pale Horse Books

Two 20th-century milestones form the background of this historical novel: the tragic Korean War and the death of the flamboyant newspaper mogul William Randolph Hearst. Although this is a work of fiction, the scramble for the Hearst fortune after his death and the early months of the war in Korea are described accurately. Except for known historical figures such as Hearst, the characters and dialogue are products of the author's imagination. Any resemblance to living persons is entirely coincidental.

Library of Congress Control Number: 2017916598
ISBN: 978-1-939917-22-5

Cover Design: Mark A. Clements

Other novels by Roger L. Conlee:

- *Deep Water*
- *Dare the Devil*
- *Fog and Darkness*
- *Souls on the Wind*
- *The Hindenburg Letter*
- *Counterclockwise*
- *Every Shape, Every Shadow: A Novel of Guadalcanal*

All are available through PaleHorseBooks.com, as well as Amazon and Barnes & Noble.

www.palehorsebooks.com
www.RogerLConlee.com

"Yet when I surveyed all that my hands had done . . . ,
everything was meaningless, a chasing after the wind."

— Ecclesiastes 2:11

CHAPTER ONE

August 14, 1951.

They stole him from me," cried the hysterical voice. "They stole him from me."

Jake Weaver recognized the voice. Marion Davies. One-time actress and longtime mistress of William Randolph Hearst, the owner of Weaver's newspaper, the *Los Angeles Herald-Express*.

"Stole whom, Miss Davies?" Jake knew the answer. There'd been a death watch for a week now at the Hearst mansion on Beverly Drive.

"My Willie. He died today." Sobbing, having trouble getting the words out.

"I'm so sorry, Miss Davies."

"I was asleep upstairs, Mr. Weaver. I'd been sitting up with Willie for so long, for so many days, the doctor insisted I take a sedative. When I woke up the place was quiet. I asked the nurse where he was. She said he was dead. His body was gone, whoosh, just like that. They took him. He belonged to me and I to him. And now he was gone."

Jake knew that Hearst's son, William Junior, had been staying in the guest house along with Richard Berlin, president of the Hearst Corporation, part of the death watch.

"The nurse said they told her not to bother me, not to

even wake me up when the hearse came to take him off to the mortuary." That's really cruel, Jake thought bitterly.

Jake liked Miss Davies. He felt her pain like a nail to the chest. He himself had visited Hearst three days ago. Unable to get out of bed, wasted away to about 120 pounds, the old man had feebly placed a hand on Jake's head as if bestowing a papal blessing.

"You . . . were always . . ." The words coming slowly, so softly Jake had to strain to hear them. ". . . my favorite bloodhound."

Hearing that, Jake couldn't help the tear that began to trickle onto his cheek. He'd worked for this American journalism giant for fourteen years. He'd covered a war for him, risked his life in Nazi Europe for him, led a crusade against the underworld for him.

"You didn't even get to say goodbye, Miss Davies? I'm sorrier than I can say."

"What can I do, Mr. Weaver?" Pitiful desperation in her voice. "What can I possibly do?"

Jake knew that Bill Hearst, Richard Berlin, and Millicent Hearst, who'd refused all these years to grant her husband a divorce, would fight Davies for control of the Hearst fortune. His will had been vague on that, or so he'd heard from newspaper gossips. He also was aware of California's community property laws.

Marion Davies had been the old man's faithful companion for three decades. There'd never been any doubt that her love for him was real. She was no gold-digger. Miss Davies had made a lot of money in Hollywood and had invested it well. She'd even lent Hearst a million dollars during the Depression before his news empire's remarkable recovery during World War II.

Jake knew that now she could get royally stiffed on this.

He had been the *Herald-Express* military writer for nine years but recently was bumped up to assistant managing editor. He still kept his hand in, though, writing the occasional news story.

Jake felt humbled that the spunky one-time actress had turned to him in her desperation. Over the years they'd developed a rapport and she'd sometimes asked his advice on small things such as what to give W.R. for his birthday.

He knew that the Hearst sons and their mother Millicent had been circling for days waiting for the old man to breathe his last. Now the birds of prey had pounced.

"I'll see what I can do, Miss Davies," Jake said. "I'll see what I can do."

CHAPTER TWO

August 1930.

Kenny Nielsen hated caves. The very thought of them made him tremble, his forehead go clammy. That hadn't been the case for the first nine years of his life, though. Then, as a ten-year-old, he and his three good buddies — Mikey, Richard and Peewee — decided to explore a cave.

In their hometown of Galesburg, Illinois, this Fearless Foursome, as Kenny had nicknamed them, did things like that. They would go out and romp through Mr. Cunningham's pasture, daring the bulls to charge them. Sometimes the bulls did, and the boys would run like crazy.

They would steal apples in farmer Wagner's orchard, hoping old man Wagner wouldn't be nearby with that big shotgun of his. When swimming at Lake Storey they'd stay under water to see who could hold his breath the longest. It was usually Mikey who could.

They sometimes teased Peewee, the youngest of the four, over the crush he had on Betty Jo, the cute redhead who lived on his street. Mikey once said, "Why don't you do something about it, Pee? Go up and kiss her on the mouth. She'll probably faint right into your arms and you can feel her up."

"Shut up, Mikey. I don't see you getting anywhere with girls."

9

At the Santa Fe tracks they occasionally hopped on the side of a freight car — if it was moving slow enough — and hang on for a block or two before jumping down. They rode their bikes out to the airport to watch the biplanes take off and land on the grassy airstrip, and pretend they were Charles Lindbergh soaring over the Atlantic.

On hot days they sometimes went to the big icehouse on Main Street, chipped off some chunks of ice and rubbed them on their faces.

The Fearless Foursome's days and nights seemed to last forever that golden Galesburg summer of 1930. The balmy evenings seemed more full of fireflies than ever before or since, and the cicadas in the maples and elms would squeak their one-tone songs for all they were worth.

There would be one last big adventure that summer, before it all had to end with starting fifth grade at Silas Willard Elementary, their red-brick schoolhouse on East Fremont Street. And that adventure would be the exploration of the cavern at St. Louis Canyon, out near Utica.

They'd start out early, taking along lunches in knapsacks, in Kenny's case a white-bread bologna sandwich and a red apple.

"You be careful today, Kenneth," his mother told him. "No tomfoolery now."

"Sure, Mom," he replied, and she kissed him on the forehead. He hopped on his bike and rode out to Lincoln Park to join up with Mikey, Richard and Peewee.

Twenty-one years later, lying in his bed at Balboa Naval Hospital in San Diego, California, Lieutenant Colonel Kenny Nielsen, USMC, remembered it all. It made him shiver.

CHAPTER THREE

Jake Weaver got out his notepad and made a list of things to find out. First, would there be an autopsy on old man Hearst's body?

Cynical reporter that he was, Jake wondered if there'd been any foul play in Hearst's demise. Young Hearst and Richard Berlin had been right there on the property for more than a week. What could they have gained by hastening the old man's death? He couldn't have lasted much longer in any case. And yet maybe they'd wanted to get it over with as soon as possible for reasons Jake couldn't imagine.

After his question about the autopsy, the list grew.

- What mortuary was Hearst taken to?
- What were the funeral arrangements?
- Who was Marion Davies' attorney and how good was he?
- Could Jake somehow sneak a peek at Hearst's will?
- What was in the trust Hearst had set up for Miss Davies?

Jake would talk this over with his German-born daughter Ilse, a senior at UCLA and editor of the college newspaper. The clever young lady was a great reporter. They'd collaborated on a story that had been a sensation, revealing that Standard Oil of New Jersey made millions from Nazi Germany in illegal profiteering during World War II.

Ilse would probably ask why he was looking into this

and were he and Marion Davies friends? And Jake would say that sometimes an underdog just needed help.

Ilse had moved out and taken an apartment, but she came over for dinner that night with her father and stepmother. As they sat around the table, Jake's wife Valerie, who worked in rocket design at Lockheed, said, "I was sorry to hear Mr. Hearst passed away, though I'm not surprised. He was very ill, wasn't he?"

"Yeah," Jake replied. "He'd had one foot in the grave for the past month."

At 37, Valerie was five years younger than Jake. They'd been married for almost nine years. As was Jake, she was on her second marriage. Her husband had been killed in a car crash in Illinois. Grieving, trying to put sad Midwestern memories behind, she'd moved to L.A. during the war.

She put down her wine glass and brought up the question of possible foul play by the Hearst sons or their mother in the old man's passing.

Jake said he'd thought about that too but didn't think it likely, since W.R. was already clearly at death's door. He then told about the call he'd got from Marion Davies.

Ilse sipped some Sonoma pinot noir, set the glass down, and said, "Did she ask for your help, *Vati*?" Jake was pleased that even as a young adult she still called him by the German word for daddy. Then and now, daddy's girl.

"Ask me? Not exactly, *Liebchen*," he answered, "but I do want to help her."

"Are you friends with her?" Ilse asked as he'd expected she would.

"Not close, but we've known each other a long while. She deserves to get her fair share of Hearst's money."

"Then I'd like to help too if I can," Ilse said.

With a worried look on her face, Valerie put in, "Hearst

12

Junior will be in charge of the papers now, won't he? Helping Miss Davies could put you in bad with him."

Yeah, it could, Jake admitted to himself.

CHAPTER FOUR

August 1930.

After their long ride to St. Louis Canyon, the boys stashed their bikes and lunches out of sight behind some wild buttonbush and clambered up to the opening, pretending they were a patrol behind German lines in the Great War. Mikey's idea.

In those days, very few caves were closed off or watched over by any uniformed officials. The opening in the rocky hillside was a black hole maybe twenty feet wide and seven high. To young Kenny Nielsen it looked ominous. It was like the mouth of some huge dragon.

Mikey, always the most fearless of the foursome, went in first. "Come on, men," he called out. "Follow me." Kenny went next, then Richard. Peewee brought up the rear.

Mikey carried a flashlight — the others hadn't thought to bring one. The ground beneath their feet was damp and a little slippery. They crept ahead slowly. In the jerky, eerie light of Mikey's flash, stalactites hung from above like jagged gray knives. Kenny wondered if there were any snakes in here. He prayed not.

The cavern soon narrowed. The overhead grew lower.

Kenny listened for sounds but could hear nothing but their own footsteps, faint on the moist soil.

Before long, Mikey's light swept onto some curious drawings along the left wall. Stick figures, walking or dancing, pointing every which way. "Look at this, men," he said. "Codes put here by Hun soldiers." Kenny thought they'd been drawn eons ago by Sauk or

Potawatomi Indians. He said so, but Mikey retorted, "Come on, Corporal, you know there aren't any Injuns in France."

"They give me the creeps," Peewee said in a weak voice. "I'm gonna go on back and wait for you guys outside."

"No, Private, you stick with the patrol," Mikey said. "You leave now and I'll put you on report. Forward, men."

As they crept ahead, the cave continued to narrow. The rock ceiling grew lower. And wetter. Kenny knew they were close to the Illinois River. The water table here was high. A few droplets began to fall on their heads.

"Hey, give me some light back here, Mikey," Richard complained. "Don't hog it all for yourself. I keep stumbling on rocks."

Mikey reached up and broke off a stalactite that hung in his way. "Ouch. That cut my finger a little. Probably sniper fire. Guess I just earned a Purple Heart."

On they stepped, cautiously. Peewee reached forward and put a hand on Richard's shoulder.

Stalagmites began to appear, rising from the ground as if searching for their cousins up above. Kenny stumbled on one and felt a small pain in his right leg. "Just got cut a bit," he said. "I earned a Purple Heart too." He reached down and felt a rip in his jeans. Mom wouldn't be happy about that. He knew that later she would get out her sewing kit and mend it.

"Step carefully, men," Mikey said. "These are mines laid here by the Huns."

"The Huns?" Richard said sarcastically. "Give me a break."

Mikey's light showed an opening about four feet high in the right wall, a side tunnel. The light revealed nothing in there but more stalactites and stalagmites. He swung the light ahead and they continued their slow trek onward.

They eventually reached a spot where a limestone rockfall partially blocked their way. Mikey's light showed an opening about three feet high above the rubble and below the cavern roof.

"You crawl over there first, Richard," Mikey said, "and be careful. There might be Germans on the other side, just lying in wait for us."

A frightening thought occurred to Kenny. What if they found a skeleton over there? White bones and a skull leering at them, grinning at them. He'd piss in his pants.

"Not me," Richard said. "I'm not going in there. Looks dangerous to me."

"You gotta be brave, Richard. War is a serious business."

"More than you know, Mikey," said Lieutenant Colonel Nielsen in his hospital bed. That darn memory of his. "More than you'll know for fourteen years anyway — till the day you reach Omaha Beach."

CHAPTER FIVE

Jake knew that Ed Franklin, the chief attorney for both Hearst papers in L.A., the *Herald-Express* and the *Examiner*, had drawn up the trust W.R. had set up for Marion Davies. Franklin had appeared in court with Jake a couple of years before when he'd been charged with trespassing by the mobster Jack Dragna.

Hoping to learn about that trust, Jake called and made an appointment to see Franklin. On Tuesday morning he went to his office in the *Examiner* building on Broadway, walking the five blocks from his own paper's building on South Trenton.

Jake knew that Franklin was fond of Miss Davies but he had no idea how the man felt about William Junior or where he stood with corporate president Richard Berlin and the elderly widow Millicent Hearst. Probably fond of his job, it was certainly possible that Franklin was snugly in their pockets.

As he approached the Spanish-Moorish *Examiner* building with its Islamic arches and bulbous domes, he thought it would look at home in San Diego's Balboa Park or Hearst's castle at San Simeon. The word simplicity had never been in old man Hearst's vocabulary.

Jake entered and climbed the elaborate staircase to Franklin's third-floor office. Block letters on the pebbled glass read EDWIN P. FRANKLIN, ATTORNEY AT LAW. He found Franklin in conversation with a young female attorney Jake had met but whose name slipped his mind. They both stood, Franklin from behind a big cherrywood desk and the woman from a facing chair.

He noted with approval her short brunette hair, blue eyes and perfect nose. Jake recalled that his wife Valerie often said, "You sure check out the young women, don't you?" He usually answered, "They don't compare with you, darlin'," but the unspoken response was, "Don't all men?"

"Hello, Jake," Franklin said. "Have you met my assistant, Amy Noonan?" Ah, that was her name.

She stepped forward and offered her hand. Jake took it and said, "Sure have. Nice to see you again, Miss Noonan."

"It's Amy," she said.

"Amy it shall be," Jake replied.

Franklin asked if he'd care for some coffee. When Jake declined they all sat, he and Amy facing Franklin behind his desk. The man had thinning brown hair with some gray showing, an ample nose, and wore black-rimmed glasses. Two framed photos sat on the desk, one a close-up of a woman and the other of the same woman along with two young boys. Obviously the wife and kids.

They chatted awhile about the L.A. Rams and what kind of season they might have. A football fan, Franklin said he wondered if Norm van Brocklin splitting time with Bob Waterfield at quarterback was such a good idea. Then, "Well, Jake, what brings you here? Problems with our underworld again?"

"Nope, I'm copacetic with those fellas these days. I was wondering, you drew up that trust W.R. set up for Marion Davies, didn't you?"

"Yes I sure did. Why do you ask?

"Miss Davies called me. She's pretty upset, understandably so. I wonder if I could take a look at it."

"Did Jack Campbell" – meaning the *Herald's* managing editor — "ask you to do this?"

"Oh no, I'm not after a story here. I like Miss Davies and hope she'll be taken care of in all this." Amy Noonan shot Jake a look he couldn't decipher.

"Sorry," Franklin said, "but I cannot do that, Jake. Attorney-client confidentiality, you know."

"But in this case the client is dead," Jake said.

"The principle still applies. The trust affects a lot of people."

"What harm could it do, Ed? I'm not gonna write about it."

"Nevertheless, I can't do it, Jake. Legal standards apply. I hope you understand. Is there anything else I can do for you today?"

Disappointed, Jake said, "Nope. That's all I had."

"Then you've wasted a trip over here. I could have told you this by phone."

"No problem, Ed. It's a nice day for a little walk." He wondered if Franklin would tell William Junior about this. He hoped not. "Thanks just the same."

Turning to Miss Noonan, Jake said, "Sure nice to see you again, Miss, I mean Amy."

Moments later as he walked down the hall toward the stairway, Jake was thinking, "Damn Franklin's stubborn hide" when he heard heels clacking on marble behind him. He turned.

"Jake, wait up," Amy Noonan said. "I like Miss Davies too. She's always been nice to me. Maybe I can help you out."

21

CHAPTER SIX

August 1930.

I'll do it," Peewee said. The youngest of the Fearless Foursome always had to work hard to prove himself, Kenny thought, especially after he tried to chicken out earlier. Staring at the opening, Peewee said, "I'm going in there."

"Hey, I would've done it," Richard said, trying to redeem himself, as Peewee crawled up the rocky rubble. Peewee peered in for a long moment, then shrugged and climbed in.

Kenny heard the sound of a splash. "Geez, there's water in here," Peewee called out. "Gimme some light, Mikey."

Mikey crawled to the gap and shone the light in. Kenny wanted to ask, "See any skeletons in there?" But he didn't.

"There's half a foot of water down there," Peewee said. "My feet are soaked. I better come back out."

"Hold on, Private," Mikey commanded. "What else can you see? Any sign of the enemy?"

"Nope, nothin' else. Just more of these spikey things hangin' down. The tunnel keeps going, but the top's only four or five feet high. Can't even stand up and I'm not gonna go crawling around in this water. It's kinda like a little creek. I'm coming out."

"All right," Mikey said, and Peewee soon reappeared, his eyes wide as silver dollars. When he'd climbed back down, Kenny saw his sneakers and the cuffs of his jeans dark with wetness. And something else. Peewee shivered.

"Good recon, Private," Mikey said, slapping Peewee on the shoulder. Peewee smiled.

"Okay, we'll head back and reconnoiter that side tunnel," Mikey said.

In the wavering light, Kenny noticed something glittering on top of one of Peewee's wet sneakers, something that looked like it didn't belong. Pointing, he said to Mikey, "Shine your light down there."

Kenny reached down for the gizmo, whatever it was. "Whatcha doing?" Peewee wanted to know.

Kenny picked up a small round disk about the size of a quarter, but heavier. "Put your light on this," he said.

He and Mikey looked closely. The object bore what looked like an eye — yes, definitely an eye. Someone, probably long ago, had done some intricate design work, cutting that image onto what appeared to be a silver surface. The iris and pupil were very lifelike. They seemed to bore into Kenny. They made him tremble.

"Some kind of a German thing," Mikey said. "Probably a soldier's good-luck piece."

"Oh baloney," Kenny said. "You and your Germans. I think that's a Potawatomi talisman." He had to admit it gave him the creeps. "When we get back to town we can take it to the historical society and see what they say."

"Talisman?" Mikey said. "Where do you get big words like that?"

"Hey, that's mine," Peewee said. "Finders keepers."

"That's right," Kenny agreed. "It was your foot that found this. But we do need to show it to the history folks when we get back." He handed it over to Peewee, who shoved it in his pocket.

"Hope it's valuable," he said.

"Okay, okay, it's Peewee's," Mikey put in. "But now let's go back and check out that side tunnel before my batteries run down."

Just then his light dimmed a little.

CHAPTER SEVEN

With an odd little grin — was it conspiratorial? —Amy Noonan told Jake, "That's good if you're trying to help Marion Davies. I like her too. Miss Davies is a nice lady and she's not likely to catch a break from the Hearst clan."

"No, probably not," Jake agreed.

Amy Noonan took him by the arm, a surprising gesture but one Jake liked. He caught the scent of her perfume. Jasmine, maybe. He noticed she wore no ring. *Now why did I look at that?* He was glad his wife Valerie couldn't see him now. He was very much in love with his wife.

"Come on down to my office," Amy Noonan said. "I'll show you a copy of that trust. Don't ever tell Mr. Franklin I'm doing this."

"I sure won't." Although grateful, Jake worried that Amy could get in trouble over this.

She led him down the hall in the opposite direction of Franklin's office, opened a door and showed him in. Her room was smaller than Franklin's. A vase held some flowers — mums and dahlias, Jake thought. A photo of Yosemite Valley hung on a wall and a window looked out on the Red Line trolley tracks.

Amy went to a metal filing cabinet, sorted through some files and finally pulled one out. Returning to the desk she said, "I can't let this out of here but you can read it and make all the notes you want."

She then went to the door and pushed down the latch,

locking it. "Just in case Mr. Franklin or anyone else stops by," she said.

Clever lady, Jake thought. He also wondered why she was doing this risky thing. He sat in a chair facing the desk and opened the file. Amy lightly touched his shoulder for a second before sitting in her own chair.

This woman looks like she's about 26 or '7, Jake thought, and I'm 42 — and married. *Oh, stop that. What's the matter with me? Start reading this file.*

CHAPTER EIGHT

The Fearless Foursome went back several yards to the opening of that side tunnel. Mikey's light was shining brightly again. "Kenny, go in there and see what you can find," he said.

Kenny didn't want to, but there was no way he was going to look like a coward in front of these guys. "Okay, and be sure to give me some light." As he crept in cautiously, he recalled his mother saying "No tomfoolery now." *This is beyond tomfoolery, Mom.*

Kenny took several steps into the gloom, the light eerily throwing his shadow ahead of him. That shadow, shaky and quivering, looked every bit as uneasy as he was.

The cave top was a few feet above his head. The sides were narrow; he could easily reach out and touch them. Below, the floor felt soft and squishy with each step.

"Whatcha you see in there?" Mikey asked.

"N-nothing, absolutely nothing." Gee whiz, Kenny thought, this is crazy, walking in here with only a little light many yards behind me. And that light growing more distant with each step. What the heck was he doing in here? They should have done something else, something above ground, like going out to the airport.

Then he slipped and fell — into water. His hands braced his fall. Damn, they were wet and so was his shirt front.

The pool of water was a foot deep, maybe more. Suddenly Kenny felt something slithering around in there. Blind terror gripped him. What are these? Snakes? Eels? He knew there were some river eels in Illinois. His father had once caught one when fishing in the Spoon River.

Whatever they were, one of them began squirming up his arm. His heart stopped — Kenny was sure of it. He jumped to his feet, banged his head against the side wall — *ouch!* — and shook the slimy thing off. He took a step back.

That's when Mikey's light dimmed again and then blinked out.

CHAPTER NINE

Jake felt some satisfaction, having read the trust Hearst had set up for Marion Davies and making notes.

"I appreciate this," he told Amy Noonan. "But why are you doing this risky thing for me?"

"I always thought I'd like to be a reporter. I've noticed that at present the *Herald-Express* doesn't have anyone covering the courts like the *Times* and *Mirror* do. Having an actual attorney covering the courts could be a big plus for your paper, couldn't it?"

"Interesting notion, Amy." News writing was much different than legaleze, but maybe she could pull it off if she didn't mind a pay cut. Reporters didn't make near what attorneys do. "I'll give that some thought," he said. "Meanwhile, thanks a lot for letting me see this."

He got up and left her office. Starting down the hallway, who should he see approaching but Ed Franklin with a surprised look on his face. *Uh-oh. Should have met with Amy somewhere else, not in her office. Dumb me.*

"Jake, you still here?" the attorney asked. "Thought you left an hour ago."

"Well, Ed, I was in the city room down there shooting the bull with some of my reporter pals."

With a skeptical look, Franklin said, "I see. Well, it was good seeing you today."

The *Examiner*'s city room occupied the floor below and Franklin would wonder why he was back on this level again. Suspicion had surely been raised.

"Plus, I wanted another look at the art deco sconces on the walls up here," Jake contrived. "Real interesting stuff. Well, so long, Ed."

Jake doubted that Franklin bought any of that. Too bad he couldn't have come up with a better story. Worry followed his every step as he hiked back to the *Herald-Express*.

CHAPTER TEN

"My batteries died." Mikey's voice came faintly to Kenny, the three other boys being fairly far away from this side tunnel. "We're going on out now. We'll go slow and do it by feeling the walls. That's what you gotta do too. Guide yourself on out feeling the walls."

Kenny had never known darkness as black as this. Even on the darkest moonless nights he could make out shapes by starlight. That was true even the night Galesburg had a power outage and the streetlights were out. This was far worse. He couldn't see a thing, not a blessed thing.

Kenny said "Okay" but his throat was so tight it came out weakly. He doubted the others heard him.

He reached out and touched a wall. It felt cold and rough to his fingers. He took one slow step, then another. He was headed in the right direction, wasn't he?

Another slow step. Water! He stepped in water. Had there been another little pool when he'd come in here? He couldn't remember. Or was he back with the eels again? His heart thumped in his chest. *Boom boom boom.* Utterly disoriented now.

Feeling the wall again, totally blinded, Kenny tried to walk a little faster. Going toward his pals, he hoped, he prayed.

"Mikey," he called out. "Mikey, can you hear me?" No answer, the limestone swallowing up his voice.

Well, crud, keep moving, he told himself. He would reach the place where this side tunnel connected to the main chamber

31

pretty soon. Wouldn't he?

On he went, one careful step at a time. His head bumped hard against something. A stalagmite? Or was it the ceiling of this thing, lower now? It wasn't this low before. If it really *was* lower, he was going the wrong damn way.

Another step. Another bump on the head. Was forced to crouch. Yeah, he was going the wrong way. As he began to turn around his head bumped yet again and he heard a rumble directly above. Then a crashing sound. Rocks began falling on his head and shoulders. The ceiling was giving way. His head must have jarred something loose. Rocks pressed down, tossing him to the ground. The noise abated and the rockfall stopped.

He lay there feeling that weight on his back, butt and legs. It was like being pinned by sacks of cement. He was trapped.

Was there any possible way to get out of this? None that Kenny could think of. He tried to wriggle and found he could move his shoulders just a little. Did a rock or two fall off him? Naw, probably just his imagination. He tried to squirm forward or even backward. Just couldn't. Hope dwindled. Was this it? The end of the line? Was he going to die here?

Eventually he began to mull over some things he'd probably never get to do again. The fun he used to have around the neighborhood playing games like hide and seek, and kick the can. Playing baseball with his buddies in the vacant lot over on Seminary Street. How he'd enjoyed the civics and history lessons in Mrs. Conger's fourth-grade class, especially her stories about Illinois' own Abraham Lincoln, who'd debated Stephen Douglas right here in Galesburg. How he'd done well in the spelling bees she used to conduct.

All of that was over. Yeah, he was going to die here. Would never see his mother again, or play ball, or see Jacquelyn Lundquist, the classmate he was sweet on. He began to cry, great sobs of fear and self-pity racking his chest.

He hadn't prayed a lot, except in Sunday School at First Christian Church. But he prayed now, prayed for all he was worth. "Dear God, don't let my Mom worry too much, and let me get out of here somehow. Please. Amen."

But to be honest it didn't feel like any heavenly help would be on its way. How long would it take him to starve to death — or die of thirst — in here? Two or three days?

The other boys had just about reached the mouth of the cave when they heard the rumble. Almost falling over one another, crashing against the walls and stalagmites, they scrambled toward the light of day.

Once outside, breathing in deep ragged gulps, they could see small cuts on each other's arms and faces, some rips in their clothing. They also saw a wisp of dust floating from the cave they'd just escaped.

"Kenny's in trouble," Mikey uttered. "Richard, get on your bike and go to the Utica cops or firemen, whichever you find first, and tell them what happened. They gotta get here fast."

"But Mikey," Peewee protested, "we'll get in trouble. We weren't supposed to be in there."

"The heck with trouble. That's our friend in there."

Richard had already retrieved his bike from behind the buttonbush and was pedaling off.

"I'm gonna go find a store," Mikey went on, "where I can buy some flashlight batteries. I've got fifty-five cents on me; that oughta be enough. You stay here, Peewee, and wait for the cops and for Richard and me to get back."

Mikey pulled his bike from its hiding place and sped off. Peewee sat down on a rock and cupped his head in his hands.

* * *

Kenny's eyes opened. Gosh, he'd been asleep. Or knocked cold by those falling rocks more likely. Whatever. He knew he'd been in cuckoo land for awhile, had a whopper of a headache. But he wasn't dead. *Yet.*

He thought again about his mother. God, how he loved that good woman, Sarah Nielsen. His dad was okay too but he wasn't in Mom's league. Mean thought, but there it was. It would be horrible if he couldn't get back to his mother, the anguish it would cause her.

And with that thought in mind, he squirmed and found he could actually move a little, but not much, and not forward, just sideways a bit. Then he detected air movement. A slight draft of air washed over his face. Why was that? How could there be some ventilation in here? It was coming from ahead of him.

He attempted to crawl. Twisted and shook but no luck. Then, with all the strength he could muster, tried to raise his back. Found he could move his shoulders an inch or two to the left, then right, and left again — kind of a small rocking motion. As he did this, he felt a few rocks actually slide off his back. Well, that was something. A small victory.

Now he reached ahead with arms and hands and tried to tug himself forward. He actually gained a few inches. Wasn't totally pinned anymore. Keep going, he told himself. He shook himself more intensely. More rocks fell away. He could actually move a little now, much less weight on his back. A bigger victory.

He reached up and felt the cave top less than six inches above his head. *Man, this is low but at least I've got some room to crawl.* On he went, fingers clawing desperately, at first advancing inches at a time. Then, a foot at a time. He wished he could see something, anything at all. He was on a mission, a mission to live. To see his mother again.

That slight air flow was now a little stronger, not quite a breeze.

Then his hands bumped against something hard. He probed with his fingers, probably bloody fingers now. It was a solid wall of limestone. He'd reached a dead end. The word "dead" thudded into his mind, numbed his heart. He could hear his pulse thumping in his ears. In that tight space, there was absolutely no way to turn around. The brief hope he'd had faded. This was the end of the line for sure.

CHAPTER ELEVEN

What a difference five blocks can make, Jake thought as he hiked back down Trenton Street to the *Herald-Express*. The area had been on the shabby side since before the war, but it was growing worse. Hobos in ragged clothes sat empty-eyed and hopeless on doorsteps, and the all-night juke joints and taverns looked seedier than ever. The trolley car barns a block away on Georgia Street added their own brand of noise and grime to the neighborhood.

Still, Jake liked it. He'd worked here for years. Others found it depressing but he called it colorful. A bit of real life.

He paused at the newspaper's front door for a moment taking in the scene, then turned and entered the three-story stone edifice which had been here since 1925 when the neighborhood was more elegant.

Back in his office, Jake thought it was sure nice of Amy Noonan to help him out on this, but he had no idea whether she could cover the courts for them. They barely knew each other. He'd need to see some samples of her writing. He hoped that pretty lady wouldn't get in trouble with Ed Franklin. The man might have put two and two together after they'd met in the upper hallway that second time.

Jake laid out his notes on the desk and began to organize them. It had been W.R.'s own wish that Franklin draw up the trust agreement. And this had been done the previous November. Maybe the old man had known even then that his sons and his obstinate wife Millicent would throw his loyal Marion right off the bus.

Marion was now 55 and puffy looking from years of boozing and partying, no longer the charming youngster of her acting days.

The agreement, as Jake had noted minutes before in Amy's office, gave Miss Davies 30,000 shares of Hearst preferred stock and full voting rights over that stock. His five sons got the same. This arrangement gave Marion a huge say in the Hearst empire's future operations — *if* it held up. That was a big if.

He knew the agreement would be contested by Bill Junior and his mother. They'd bring in their own high-powered Eastern lawyers. And Jake thought that Ed Franklin, fond of his job, wasn't likely to give them much of a fight, if any. No, Marion Davies would need her own attorney, not the company's.

Hearings had been scheduled. Hearst's mental competency at the time he'd signed that agreement was sure to be questioned. They would seek testimony from editors, doctors and caregivers indicating that W.R. was acting pretty cloudy and ambiguous in those days. I have to admit, Jake told himself, that the chief had often been loopy but that on other days was as clear-headed as ever.

Okay, the hearings would be tough. Jake didn't know how he could help Miss Davies with those, but he'd try to come up with something.

Meanwhile, he still wanted to see Hearst's will. That was an entirely different thing than the trust.

Hearst had inherited his fortune long before his 1903 marriage to Millicent Willson, a teenage showgirl at the time, so California's community property law wouldn't pertain.

Or would it?

W.R. had gone bust in the 1930s, mostly because of lavish spending on his castle at San Simeon and loads of European art objects to stash in the place. Then he'd made millions again with his papers' huge recovery during the war. If it could be proved in court that he was broke in 1937, then everything he had when he died would have been earned since then. Under the community property law, Millicent would get 50 percent of his estate. *If* it could be proved in court.

Jake stared at his notes and scratched his head wondering what he could do.

CHAPTER TWELVE

Blocked in the cave though he was, Kenny now felt that slight flow of air brushing the right side of his face. He ran his hand over the wall toward where the air seemed to come from. And touched *nothing*. No rocks, no dirt, nothing. If he couldn't feel anything, there must be a gap there, an opening in the wall. He still saw nothing but total blackness. Realizing he could still move, he squirmed in the direction of that air flow.

When he crept into that opening the breeze felt a little stronger. He crawled as fast as he could, which wasn't fast at all. Then, a sound. He hadn't heard any kind of a sound since those rocks had fallen on him, however long ago that was. This was a faint bubbling noise. It scared the heck out of him.

He crawled on cautiously, the ground beneath him wet and spongy in that cramped space. His fingers raw and aching. That sound frightened him even more. Was he about to crawl into a stream filling this space he was in? He would drown for sure. In this tight squeeze he couldn't possibly turn around. There was no choice but to go on. Which he did.

Suddenly: light! Kenny saw some faint light ahead. As he struggled on and on, the gurgling sound grew louder, the light stronger. After being able to see nothing at all for a long while the glow hurt his eyes. He didn't mind. Light was good. Maybe his prayer was being answered after all.

At last he saw daylight — real, actual daylight. An opening lay up ahead. In a round aperture encircled by blackness, as if

41

through a telescope, he caught sight of green trees on a distant ridge. Marvelous sight. Adrenaline surged.

He slithered on, his heart beating faster. That beautiful disk of outside world grew larger. He just had to reach it. On and on he tugged himself.

At last he did reach it.

He crawled out through that gap and found himself on a bluff above the Illinois River. So the cave had an opening over here on its north side, an opening he and his pals hadn't known anything about. Thank God for that. The sound he'd heard was the flow of the river.

He just lay there a long time, resting his mind and body, filling his lungs with fresh air. He saw some power lines with birds perched on them, a few puffy cumulus clouds overhead. Watched the river flowing by. He'd never seen a more glorious sight.

Reflecting on that Indian talisman Peewee had found, with its piercing eye, Kenny forgot for a moment the bruises and the cuts and scratches on his hands and arms or the knifing pain in his back. The recollection of that strange Indian eye made him shiver.

He didn't know how much time had passed when he saw a boat approach. An outboard, its motor idling. Two men in slouch hats had lines in the water, trolling for fish.

"Hey," he tried to call out. His voice was weak. He swallowed, cleared his throat and yelled louder. "Hey! Help me."

The men looked up. Soon their boat was pulling up to the riverbank below him.

CHAPTER THIRTEEN

Jake knew if he openly helped Marion Davies on this, Bill Junior would hate his guts, would probably fire him. Once he officially took charge, that is. His wife Valerie would be sore as hell at him if he lost his job. He didn't want to work for the rival *Times*, but knew he could if it came to that. Knowing his reputation, *Times* owner Norman Chandler had actually made some overtures to him the last couple of years.

Jake's daughter Ilse had said she'd like to help. A UCLA senior and editor of its paper, the *Daily Bruin*, she was an excellent reporter with good instincts and ideas. They'd collaborated before and maybe could again. After their big exposé about Standard Oil's profiteering from Nazi Germany during the war, W.R. had said a job was waiting for her when she graduated. Would Bill Junior honor that now? Doubtful. And for sure not if Jake pursued this Marion Davies thing.

That line of thought broke when managing editor John Campbell, whose office was next door, stepped in. He saw the notes lying on the desk and asked, "Whatcha doing there, Jakey boy?"

Should he tell Campbell what he was up to? Might as well, Jake thought with a shrug. "Call me crazy, Johnny, but I'm thinking I might help Marion Davies on these hearings that are coming up."

"Aw, Jake, helping that old lush would land you in deep grease. You should get that idea right out of your head. Let the chips fall where they may."

"I know, Johnny, you're right, I should just forget this stuff, but I do like Miss Davies. She's got a good heart, was just swell to W.R. all these years. I'd hate to see her get stiffed on this."

Campbell shook his head. "You're a reckless fool, Jake."

"Johnny, you sound just like my wife. But how do you s'pose I could get to see the old man's will? You have any idea how I could find a copy of that?"

"Ed Franklin's got it, but he'd never let you see it. Give it up, Jake." Campbell turned to leave. "Give it up," he repeated over his shoulder.

Jake sat there thinking, *Wonder if I could sneak into Franklin's office some night?*

CHAPTER FOURTEEN

The rest of the Fearless Foursome were ecstatic with relief when Kenny reunited with them at the Utica police station.

"We were worried sick," Mikey said. "We thought you were a goner. Thank God you got yourself out." He slapped Kenny's tender shoulder. Kenny winced and said, "Ouch!"

"Yeah, no kidding," Richard said. "It's a miracle."

"Still don't know how I managed to do it," Kenny said. "I was really trapped. Passed out for awhile." He had bandages on his arms and hands, courtesy of the police. The second finger on his right hand hurt like the devil. He hoped it wasn't broken.

"Man, I hate caves," he said. "Won't ever go into another one long as I live."

"That's good thinking, son," one of the cops said. "Don't you scalawags ever try anything like this again."

"We sure won't," Peewee answered.

"I oughta send you all to our juvenile court," the officer scolded, "but I figure you've had enough trouble for one day. Just get your young asses back to Galesburg and watch your steps from now on."

"Are you gonna tell our folks or the Galesburg cops about this?" Mikey asked.

"I guess not. I did some foolish things myself when I was your age. Just stay out of Utica from now on, boys, and out of caves anywhere."

In his hospital bed, 31-year-old Kenny Nielsen remembered it all. The lieutenant colonel recalled that the Fearless Foursome were pretty quiet and sullen as they mounted their bikes and pedaled toward home.

CHAPTER FIFTEEN

Jake drove out to Beverly Drive to see Marion Davies. She still lived in the mansion there, and why not? She and W.R. had jointly owned it. As Jake turned from Santa Monica Boulevard onto Beverly, he thought she might still lose the place, though, depending on how the financial wrangling turned out.

Here was a supreme irony: If Millicent Hearst won on the community property issue, the widow and the lover would end up as co-owners of the place. Wouldn't that be something to see?

Jake was driving the four-door 1950 Chevrolet Deluxe he'd bought in January. Instead of retiring his aging Chevy Ridemaster coupe, he'd had the engine overhauled and given the car to Ilse, who was happy to have wheels of her own.

As he turned onto the long, curving driveway he recalled he many festive occasions that had occurred in this place. One soiree attracted scores of W.R.'s old motion picture cronies and that was the night he'd met young Congressman John F. Kennedy. He'd find a much different mood here today. Gloom would hang heavy over the rooms.

As he pulled the Chevy to a stop he saw another car parked just ahead, a late-model Lincoln. He knew with a sense of relief that it didn't belong to Bill Junior or Richard Berlin. Their death watch over, they had departed from the guest house and moved into the Beverly Hills Hotel. He also knew the car wasn't Marion Davies'. Her Chrysler convertible would be in the garage.

Jake had called so Miss Davies would be expecting him.

He got out, strode up to the tall oaken door and pushed the buzzer. Most of the staff had been let go but he knew that Charles, the faithful old butler, had been retained along with a maid and a cook.

The door opened a moment later and Jake said, "Good morning, Charles."

Standing about six-one, though slightly stooped and with wispy white hair and thick glasses making his eyes look huge, Charles took Jake's hat and said, "It's always nice to see you, Mr. Weaver. Come in, please."

As he was led toward the library, Jake asked, "How is she, Charles?"

"Very sad, I'm sorry to say. Rather depressed." No surprise there.

Reaching the library, Jake saw with a bit of shock a man who looked a lot like a younger version of W.R. standing there with Miss Davies. He was tall with brownish-gray hair and an aristocratic nose much like Hearst's. It was like seeing a ghost. Could this be one of the sons?

"Jake, so glad you could come," Miss Davies said. "Meet my friend Horace Brown."

Okay, not one of the Hearst sons.

The man offered his hand and Jake shook it. "Very nice to meet you, Mr. Weaver."

"Same here, Mr. Brown," Jake replied.

"I was just leaving," Brown said. He turned, gave Miss Davies a chaste little hug and said, "Don't bother Charles. I'll see my way out."

When he was gone, Miss Davies said, "I saw the look on

your face just now. Horace does look a bit like W.R., doesn't he? He used to be an honest-to-goodness sea captain, but now he's high and dry in real estate. He and I have bought some property together. So good of you to come, Jake. Please have a seat."

Miss Davies retained a shade of the sprightly looks she'd had as a young actress, though she'd gone a little portly. Her face was a bit puffy and her blond hair showed some gray.

The two sat in facing plush velvet chairs next to an end table that held a decanter of something that might be cognac. Jake hoped she hadn't been drinking already. It was about 10 a.m. Two glasses sat there, one empty, one about a third full.

Jake said, "I know this has been a tough time for you, Miss Davies. You certainly have my condolences."

"So kind of you, Jake, but it's Marion, please. After all, we're old friends." She reached over and touched his arm. "I haven't heard many kind words lately."

"You're welcome, Miss Da—, Marion. Since your call, I've been thinking about what I might do to help. Could you tell me about the funeral arrangements?"

Marion's face went dark. She looked about to cry.

"They've completely cut me out of that."

Now a tear did begin to trickle.

"They'll bury him in San Francisco, the old ancestral home. That's where his father, old George Hearst, got his start. I'm not even invited."

"Aw, man, that's cruel."

"Yes, isn't it? He'll lie in state at Grace Episcopal Cathedral for a couple of days so some phony bigwigs who only pretended to like him can come and cry their crocodile tears. Millicent is arranging it all."

"And she won't even let you attend? That's nasty."

"It's all right, Jake, I don't need the dramatics. He knew how he felt about me and how I felt about him. I would just be an embarrassment to the family. She's having former President Hoover and Governor Warren as two of the pallbearers. Can you imagine that?"

"Really putting on a show, isn't she?" Jake said. "Sounds pretty hypocritical."

She wiped at her eye. "Yeah, isn't it?"

"And I suppose all the sons will be pallbearers too?"

"Oh sure, of course."

"I managed to see the trust W.R. set up," Jake said.

"How on earth did you do that?"

Jake had no idea if she knew Amy Noonan but he didn't want to get the young attorney in trouble. "Reporter's secret," he said.

"My, my, even from the grave Willie would say you're still his favorite bloodhound."

Jake briefly grinned at that. "I learned about the Hearst preferred stock and the voting rights you'll receive, equal to what the sons get. The chief was very generous. But you know they'll fight you for that, contest it with some big legal artillery."

"I suppose they will," Marion said, frowning.

"Do you have a good attorney, someone other than Ed Franklin? Franklin won't fight Millicent and the boys on that."

Marion reached for the glass that might hold some cognac but stopped herself and cupped her hands in her lap like a good little girl. "I have two great lawyers but they're in real estate law. They might not be good at something like this. I'll ask them for some recommendations, though."

"Good, and I'll do some checking around too."

"Come to think of it" Marion said, "maybe Bing could

help."

Jake knew she and Bing Crosby were friends.

"Bing has all kinds of legal things going," she said.

"That's good, too. Now about the chief's will. Have you seen that?"

"Nope, Ed Franklin never let me even witness that. He's got it under lock and key. I have no idea what's in it."

"I'll give some thought to how I might sneak a look at that," Jake said.

"Still the bloodhound, aren't you?"

Jake left soon after that, Marion thanking him profusely for his help. Driving away, he again wondered if he could sneak into Franklin's office some night.

Jake's daughter Ilse would be twenty-one in a month. Although the UCLA senior now lived in a Westwood apartment three blocks from the campus, she kept in close touch with her father, calling him two or three times a week. She shared the apartment with Claudia Nielsen, a family friend who was in her last year of pre-med studies there en route to becoming a doctor.

After classes that afternoon, Ilse called her father at the *Herald-Express*. "Guess what, Vati. I'm going to interview Bela Lugosi tomorrow."

"Bela Lugosi, the old Dracula actor?"

"Right. I saw the Dracula film in one of those arts theaters the other day. Creepy. I hear that now Lugosi's in pretty bad shape and has a drug habit. Claudia says they've treated him a couple of times but he doesn't stay off the stuff for long. That's the UCLA connection, why it would make an interesting story for the *Bruin*."

"UCLA Tries to Resurrect Vampire," Jake said.

"I wouldn't quite put it that way, *Vati*."

"Just pulling your leg with a mock headline, *Liebchen*. But how would you like to have an old newspaper hack tag along with you?"

"You're not an old hack but sure, I'd like for you to go with me. That'd be swell. He has a room in some little house in the valley, Van Nuys I think. I've got his address."

As Ilse drove there the next day in the aging Chevy coupe she'd inherited from her dad, Jake said, "You handle the old buggy real well, kiddo, and it looks like you take good care of it."

"You bet. I get the oil changed regularly and I had her tuned up last month. I've got to take good care of *Schnucki* and make her last."

"*Schnucki?*" Jake said. You gave this old crate the German name for Sweetie Pie?"

"Yes, corny I know, but she's a good friend."

Jake laughed.

Turning from Sepulveda onto Saticoy Street, Ilse scanned house numbers and said, "It must be that one up there, third from the corner." She pulled to the curb, killed the engine, and tugged on the hand brake.

They piled out and walked to the front door of the little tan bungalow. The lawn was a sad-looking tangle of Bermuda grass. A potted geranium sat on the porch.

Ilse pushed the bell and soon a middle-aged woman opened the door, saying, "You're the people from UCLA? This way, please." As she ushered them down a hall, she leaned close to Jake's ear and said, "He's a month behind in his rent."

They reached a bedroom where they found Bela Lugosi

looking old and withered, sitting on a small single bed.

"Your visitors," the woman said, and left.

Lugosi got up unsteadily and said, "Welcome. I bid you welcome." Thick Hungarian accent just like Jake remembered from the movies. "To Castle Dracula," he half expected the man to add.

Lugosi wore a faded blue shirt and rumpled gray trousers, had thin silvery hair and a couple of days' worth of whiskers on a broad face etched with lines of age. He bobbed his head respectfully.

Jake noted that he stood about six-two, tall for a man born in the previous century. "I am afraid there is only one chair to offer you in my humble room," he said, gesturing with long and bony fingers.

Jake motioned for Ilse to take it, and leaned against a wall himself. A night stand held a small table lamp, a half-full glass ash tray, and a plastic Philco radio. An old *Dracula* movie poster hung on a wall, showing a much younger, menacing Lugosi and the words, "Screamy! Terrifying!" Another poster was from a more recent film, *Mother Riley Meets the Vampire*. Jake knew Lugosi had been reduced lately to taking penny-ante roles in some dreadful films.

The old man sat on the bed again as Ilse got out a notebook, saying, "Thank you for seeing us, Mr. Lugosi. I may write a story for the college newspaper. This is my father, Jake Weaver of the *Herald-Express*."

"Excellent," the old man said. "I am delighted to see you. I so seldom have visitors these days."

Holding a pen, Ilse said, "Things haven't been so easy for you lately, have they, sir?"

"That is a kind way of putting it, young lady. No, as you can see" — extending his arms and gesturing around the shabby little room — "I do not live in the lap of luxury.

I am afraid that my career in America has turned out less successful or lucrative than it might have."

"It all began with the vampire film, didn't it?" Ilse asked.

"I'd had several movie roles prior to that, but yes, *Dracula* was the best known for me. I received only thirty-five hundred dollars for that role. I should have asked for much more, but I needed that job. I was insecure, frightened that Carl Laemmle would hire someone else. Laemmle produced all those first horror films at Universal and was a notorious cheapskate. Although I became well known for that role, I did not retain an agent, a regrettable mistake, and I proceeded to choose roles unwisely."

Ilse scribbled in her notebook.

Lugosi fumbled at his pockets as if searching for something. "Do either of you smoke?" he asked. "I could use a cigarette."

"Sorry," Jake said. "We never took up the habit."

"Oh, too bad. Or perhaps I should say 'good for you.' Did you know," he went on, "that I portrayed Count Dracula only once more in this country, and that was for an absurd comedy called *Abbott and Costello meet Frankenstein?*"

"No I didn't," Ilse said. "I assumed you played Dracula several times."

"Not here. I did play Dracula in one forgettable British film but no, it was John Carradine who had the role in the next U.S. film, and then other actors in more recent years. Laemmle was a hard man and Hollywood is a cruel place." He shook his head sadly. "Here they forget one so easily."

"The things I did to scratch out a living," he went on. "I actually portrayed the Frankenstein monster himself in *Frankenstein Meets the Wolf Man*. The makeup was an ordeal." Lugosi's face grew wistful. He was seeing it all again. "I must admit I was not good in that role. In two films I even played Ygor, Dr. Frankenstein's strange little assistant. Pathetic, so pathetic was I."

"I hesitate to bring up the drugs," Ilse put in, "but I know you've had treatment. If you'd rather not—"

"No, my dear, I do not mind. That is just another unfortunate part of my life. One of my wives — I've had four wives, you know. Sorry creatures who devoured the movie magazines, excited to connect with someone who had a little fame. Bad mistakes on my part, they were. Terrible mistakes, every one of them. One insisted that I wear my Dracula cape around the house, can you imagine?"

Lugosi stopped and shook his head. "I am sorry, where was I? Oh yes, the drugs. One of my wives introduced me to cocaine. At first, it gave me relief, even some euphoria. I could forget about Carl Laemmle or having to play that silly hunchback Ygor. Sadly, though, I grew dependent on it, could not give it up. It proved easier to rid myself of wives than the addiction." Said with a little chuckle.

"I hope the UCLA treatments help," Ilse said.

"They do, yes, for awhile, but they are not long-lasting. I suppose I am weak willed. I am thinking of committing myself to the state hospital."

Ilse half stifled a gasp. "Really? The state hospital."

"I am considering it, yes. It might be the best course for me." Jake noticed a slight palsy in Lugosi's left hand, an unconscious trembling.

"Say, here's an idea," Ilse said. "Would you like to speak to the acting students at our school of drama? I think I could arrange that. There would be a small honorarium."

Lugosi's face brightened. "I should like that very much. Thank you."

Still leaning against a wall, Jake shifted his weight from one foot to the other. "How did you get your start in all this?"

he asked. "You were born in Hungary, weren't you?"

Lugosi said no, he was actually born in Lugoj, Romania, but that his father was a Hungarian banker. Lugosi had trained at the Budapest Academy of Theatrical Arts, then got a few stage roles. "There too it was difficult to earn a living as an actor," he said. "For a couple of years, before I turned twenty, to make ends meet I actually became a thief, a burglar."

Jake's eyes widened.

"What Americans would call a second-story man. Can you imagine that? I am not proud of it, but for a time I was quite a disreputable young man."

"A cat burglar?" Jake asked. "You broke into people's homes and stole things?"

"Not homes, sir, but places of business. Jewelry stores, you see. Oh, the thrill of it, the rush of adrenaline. After four such ventures without being apprehended, I ceased. Being caught would have disgraced my family. My father would have disowned me."

He went on to tell how after a few parts on the Hungarian stage he got into films and plays in Germany and eventually the U.S. He'd played Count Dracula on the New York stage before doing the film.

Jake had trouble concentrating on all that. Hmm, breaking into places of business, he thought. W.R. Hearst's will in Ed Franklin's office came to mind.

On their way out moments later, Jake asked the landlady how much Lugosi owed on his rent. She said one month, twenty dollars. Jake got out his wallet and handed her a twenty.

Was he really thinking Bela Lugosi might help him get

into Ed Franklin's office, Jake asked himself as Ilse drove away. An elderly drug addict? No, probably a bad idea, he told himself.

As if reading his mind, Ilse said, "The most interesting part of that was Lugosi being a burglar in his younger days."

"I've known hungry actors who did some pretty crazy things when they couldn't find work," Jake said.

"I won't include that in my story. His drug treatment at UCLA is the hook, and then I'll put in some details about his career. No need to besmirch the old man's reputation any more than that."

"Exactly right, *Liebchen*. You've got a good handle on this reporting business."

"That was nice of you to pay Lugosi's rent," Ilse said as she made a left turn onto Victory Boulevard.

"Couldn't help feeling sorry for him."

"Same with me, Vati. The fact that he portrayed Dracula only twice will surprise readers. I'll include that for sure."

"Good," Jake said. "Getting him to talk to the theater students was a fine idea. Can you really arrange that?"

"I think so. They like having actors and directors come in. They had Joseph Cotten a few weeks ago."

Ilse would come back and tell Lugosi when it was all set up, Jake thought. He would go along too. He wanted to talk a little more with the old man.

CHAPTER SIXTEEN

Kenny and Mikey insisted that they take the Indian talisman Peewee had found in St. Louis Cavern to the historical society.

When the Fearless Foursome arrived at the old brick building, they showed it to the elderly curator and explained where they found it. The man, who had wispy gray hair, examined it through thick eyeglasses and said, "This is most interesting, boys, definitely an Indian piece. That eye looks dark and ominous, doesn't it? We have a book here somewhere by an anthropologist at the University of Illinois that tells of Indian artifacts of this kind. Let me go and find it."

A few minutes later he was back with the book. He placed it on a table and began thumbing through it. The book had sections on the Blackhawk, Potawatomi, Shawnee, and other Illinois tribes. There were photos and drawings of various curiosities, arrowheads, feathered headdresses and so forth. It took him awhile to find what he was looking for.

Finally, in the Potawatomi section, there it was, a photo of Peewee's talisman. The curator read aloud: "This specimen is thought to have been created by a so-called medicine man. Members of the tribe believed that it had certain supernatural qualities. Whoever looked upon this eye would someday get the better of a fellow brave in some kind of contest."

Kenny glanced at Richard and got a strange feeling. Why he looked at Richard and not Peewee or Mikey he didn't know, but he had the spooky sense that there could be something going on that involved just him and Richard.

The old curator broke that thought, saying, "Why don't we keep this here and display it with our collection of Indian artifacts?"

"No," Peewee protested. "It's mine. I found it."

"Please, young fellow, it's your civic duty. That way others can enjoy it also. We'll place a message below it giving your name and expressing our gratitude. We'll say where you found this and that you are a fine citizen."

"Well . . ." Peewee muttered.

"People will see your name over the years and will honor you for your generosity."

"For years and years. Gee whiz," Peewee said.

Six years later.

Kenny Nielsen found himself hoping it would rain — hard — and wash out the ballgame. Galesburg High was going to play its crosstown rival Corpus Christi this afternoon and he dreaded the thought of it. His old friend Richard Lundquist, who was one of the Fearless Foursome a few years ago, would pitch against him.

Richard, now a tall righthander with a decent fastball and a nasty curve, was their ace. He'd struck out a ton of guys and won a lot of games this season. But he'd lost to Galesburg High 2 to 1 in their first meeting. Kenny had homered and doubled, driving in both runs.

Kenny "owned" Richard. They'd been playing with and against each other for years in youth league and junior-high ball. Kenny knew all his tricks, especially the way he telegraphed his curveball, raising his right shoulder a bit before starting his windup.

Kenny was a guy with powerful loyalties to his friends. He wasn't proud of showing up a kid he grew up with and shared many adventures with. He'd done it to Richard once already and hated the thought of doing it again.

Besides that, he had a crush on Richard's sister, Jacqueline, another reason he hadn't relished the victory. He didn't need Jacqueline's disdain.

He'd heard from their mutual friend Peewee that Richard was so upset by that defeat that he'd stayed home from school the next day.

The Fearless Foursome was no more. Mikey and his parents had moved to Peoria. Richard, a Catholic, had enrolled at Corpus Christi while Kenny and Peewee went to Galesburg High. Those three occasionally saw each other, though. Galesburg was not a big town.

A week after Kenny and the Silver Streaks beat the Friars in that 2 to 1 game, he caught sight of Richard on Main Street, half a block away. Richard had pretended he hadn't seen him, had ducked into the Walgreens. Saddened at his old friend's embarrassment, Kenny didn't follow. Let the guy be. He turned and walked the other way.

There'd be no ducking him today. Richard would be out there on that hill, sixty feet six inches away, facing his old pal — and now his nemesis. Jacqueline would be there too, in the bleachers behind the Friars' bench.

Gosh, Kenny again wished it would rain. But the sky was a clear blue that day, the spring air warm and dry. Maybe he should say he was sick and just skip the game. But no, that wasn't his style. He was no quitter. Besides, Coach Carson would have his ass if he ducked out on the game.

Richard, old friend, I'll be seeing you this afternoon and sitting on that curveball when I know it's coming. Darn it.

CHAPTER SEVENTEEN

The next day being their ninth wedding anniversary, Jake and Valerie went to dinner that night at Perino's, one of their favorite places. This dignified old restaurant on Wilshire Boulevard was popular with longtime Los Angeles residents who favored it over the Brown Derby and others of that ilk that had more Hollywood glitz.

The place featured waiters who'd been there so long Jake figured they might have served Calvin Coolidge or Rudolph Valentino. These venerable waiters brought meals to the tables on wheeled silver-plated serving dishes and carved the meat before diners' eyes.

Valerie wore a sleeveless green evening dress and Jake his best gray suit with a striped navy blue tie. A single rose decorated their banquette.

After taking their seats, the headwaiter made a show of unfurling Valerie's linen napkin and with a flourish placing it on her lap.

Valerie gazed at the peach- and pink-accented walls and said, "I wonder if it's true that Cole Porter once wrote a song here on the back of a menu."

"Oh, it's true, madam," said a wine steward who appeared at that moment. He said, pointing, "It took place in that far corner, his favorite spot, back in 1943."

"Which song?" Valerie asked, turning her gaze to that

corner, where a small table lamp illuminated an elderly couple.

" 'You'd Be So Nice to Come Home To,' I've been told."

Jake, who'd been scanning the wine list, ordered a bottle of Napa cabernet, 1945, and the sommelier scurried off.

Valerie readjusted her napkin and said, "You've always been nice to come home to, Sailor. Well, happy anniversary. It's been quite a ride, hasn't it?" She often called Jake sailor, knowing he'd had a hitch in the Navy before they'd met. "I wasn't sure if I could ever be happy again after Jim died, but then along came you, reckless, impetuous old you."

"There's never been a dull moment," she went on, "not since that first day we met at the Inglewood hospital. My lord, Jake, you sneaking in and out of Nazi Germany during the war spying for FDR and the British; battling L.A.'s crime lords; getting kidnapped in Detroit by the Purple Gang; your ankle broken by those thugs in D.C. No, never a dull moment."

"Yeah, afraid I've handed you a lot of worries over the years," Jake said. "Any regrets?"

"None at all . . . well, not many."

Jake reached over and touched her hand. "It's been fun watching your career too, Sweets. One of the first female tool designers in the aircraft industry and now one of the first in rocket design. Being married to me, though, hasn't been a garden party, like when your car damn near got forced down a canyon by one of Bugsy's thugs."

"Okay, that one I regret," Valerie admitted.

The wine arrived, was opened by the sommelier, and a small amount poured into Jake's goblet. He sniffed it for a moment testing the bouquet, took a sip, and pronounced it satisfactory.

When the glasses were filled and the wine steward was gone, Jake raised his and clinked it against Valerie's. "Here's to many more terrific years together."

"Absolutely," she agreed. They each took a drink.

"You know," Jake said, "life is full of what-if moments. For instance, if you hadn't moved out here after your hubby died and taken that job at North American we'd have never met. We wouldn't be sitting here right now. You might be married to some banker in Chicago."

"I doubt that. Bankers aren't my style. Or, though, if you hadn't gone to Germany in 1930, you randy rascal, for your Aunt Marta's memorial service, you wouldn't have met the woman — Winifrid, wasn't it? — who became Ilse's mother. There'd be no Ilse."

The waiter came by and Valerie ordered veal marsala, Jake the prime rib.

Not wanting to talk about Winifrid, Jake decided to change the subject. He was about to say that UCLA's school of drama had agreed to have Bela Lugosi come and speak, and that he and Ilse would go out to see the old actor again. But Valerie spoke first.

"Now that Ilse has that place of her own out near the college, it feels strange around the house. It's so quiet. We have an empty nest." She sipped some wine and gazed into Jake's eyes with a look he couldn't decipher. "I'm thirty-seven. I wonder if I'm too old to . . ." She stopped and let the sentence hang.

Have a baby? Jake thought in panic.

CHAPTER EIGHTEEN

May 1936.

The day remained dry and bright as a new penny. No rain. The ballgame between Galesburg High and Corpus Christi was on.

The grass had been mowed, batting practice taken, and the infield dirt dragged smooth.

As usual, Kenny was at first base during infield practice. When that was over, he caught Richard eyeing him from across the diamond, sitting on the visitors' bench behind third base. Kenny flashed a grin and waved. Richard hesitated, then gave a small, timorous wave-back.

When the starting pitchers began warming up, it wasn't Richard who was throwing on the sidelines. It was a little lefthander Kenny had never faced before.

"What the heck?" Kenny said. "Coach, can I see that lineup card?"

Coach Carson handed it over and said, "Yeah, Richard Lundquist's not pitching. I don't figure that." Sure enough, Gabe Lancellotti was penciled in as the Friars' pitcher, batting seventh in the lineup. If Kenny remembered right, Lancellotti played leftfield last time they'd met.

Had Richard chickened out?

The game began and neither team scored in the first two innings. Gabe Lancellotti was doing better than anyone expected. He didn't throw hard but his control was sharp, especially on his slow, teasing curveballs. Some of the Silver Streaks, over-anxious at his slow stuff, managed only harmless popups.

Batting third in the lineup, Kenny flied out to center in the first inning. In the bottom of the fourth, with a runner on second, he took the first two pitches, a ball inside and another one outside. Now with a 2 and 0 count, he measured the next pitch perfectly, strode into the ball, snapped his wrists, and laced a drive to left-center. The runner scored and the Streaks took a 1 to 0 lead. But another popup ended the inning, leaving Kenny stranded at second.

Richard, who was playing rightfield instead of pitching, singled in two runs in the top of the sixth and Galesburg fell behind.

When Richard took his lead off first, Kenny, positioned behind him, said, "Hey, Rich, nice hit. How come you're not pitching?"

"Search me," his friend said.

The next batter doubled and Richard, who always ran well, scampered around third and scored. Now the Friars were up 3 to 1.

In the bottom of the inning, Kenny got hold of a Lancellotti forkball and drove it to deep left. He was racing to first when he saw the leftfielder reach up and snag the ball just in front of the fence. *Damn.* Kenny scuffed at the dirt with his foot and shambled back to the bench.

Gabe Lancellotti eventually began to tire. The Streaks scored a run in the eighth on a single, an error, and two walks, one of them to Kenny. But they stranded two runners and so it was Corpus Christi 3 to 2 heading into the ninth.

After the Friars went down in order in the top of the inning, Coach Carson gathered his players around and urged, "Come on now, fellas. This is it. Let's go out and pound this little guy."

But it wasn't the little guy who took the mound. It was Richard. They'd brought in their ace to close it out.

Kenny was scheduled to be up fourth. He had dreaded this

game, hadn't wanted to show up his old friend again, but now with the game on the line his competitive instinct took over. His Silver Streaks needed to win. This was his team, his school. He hoped like heck he'd get a chance to bat.

Sitting on the bench, he grabbed his bat and held it tightly. He waggled it back and forth. "Come on guys, get on base," he pleaded.

The first batter was Galesburg's weak-hitting second baseman, ninth in the batting order. "Try to work him for a walk," Coach advised.

He couldn't. With the count 2 and 2 he took a fastball down the middle for a called strike three. Kenny groaned and slapped his bat.

The leadoff man came to the plate. With the count 1 and 1, Kenny saw Richard raise his shoulder a bit during his windup. He wanted to shout "curveball," but choked it back. Didn't want to tip Richard that he was telegraphing the curve.

The batter got a piece of that pitch and hit a grounder to first. The ball hit a pebble, took a funny bounce, and the first baseman couldn't handle it.

"Okay," Kenny thought. "Man on first, one out. Barring a double play, I'll get to bat." He hopped off the bench and stalked out to the on-deck circle.

Coach Carson was coaching third base. Before stepping into the batter's box, the next hitter looked over at him for the sign. Coach touched his hat brim, his cheek, and then the belt buckle. The "take" signal.

The pitch was low, the catcher bobbled it for just a second, and the runner took off. He slid safely into second by the time the catcher got off his throw. One out and a man in scoring position, Kenny thought, swinging two bats in the on-deck circle.

Now Coach touched his hat brim, his left wrist, left thigh, and finally his nose. *Hit away.*

The second pitch, a fastball, was lined toward short. The shortstop leaped as high as he could and managed to snag the ball in the webbing of his glove. The runner scrambled safely back to the base.

Two out and the tying run at second as Kenny stepped to the plate. *Okay, Richard, let's see you raise that right shoulder.* Then, an awful thought. What if they walk me? A walk here would put the winning run on base but it would also set up a force at every base but home.

Richard looked over to the Friars' coach. Would he hold up four fingers, signaling an intentional walk? His coach didn't. Kenny breathed a sigh of relief when the rival coach gave no signal of any kind.

Richard went into his stretch for a moment, and fired a fastball high and outside. Ball one. Again Richard went into his routine and again, no raising of the shoulder. Another fastball — this time heading right at Kenny. Man, that was coming in hot. Kenny tried to twist away from it, but wasn't quick enough. The ball caught him square on the fanny. *Damn, that hurt.*

If anyone else had been pitching, Kenny would have been tempted to rush the mound and slug the guy, but he couldn't do that to his old friend. The umpire jumped in front of him as a warning.

Kenny gave Richard a quizzical "what-the-heck" look as he jogged to first base. Richard offered a slight grin. He'd been smart to hit him, Kenny admitted to himself. Same as a walk.

Two men on, two out, the Streaks still down by a run. Before the cleanup hitter stepped in, Corpus Christi's coach called time and hiked out to the mound. The infielders gathered around for a conference. The coach gestured with his arms. Finally the ump strode toward them and said, "Break it up. Let's go."

The coach jogged off and everyone went back to their positions. Standing tall on the mound, Richard looked poised and confident. He reached down, scooped up some dirt and rubbed it on the fingers of his pitching hand. He glanced over his shoulder at the runner on second. Kenny wondered if they had cooked up a pickoff play. Then Richard looked at Kenny to see how much of a leadoff he was taking. Richard hadn't stepped on the rubber yet as he turned and looked in toward his catcher.

Kenny took his lead off first, six or seven feet. He studied Richard on the mound. *Why the heck is he taking so long?*

Suddenly he felt a nudge on his back. "You're out!" the base umpire barked.

What the heck. Kenny turned and saw the first baseman with a devilish grin on his face and the ball snuggled in his glove.

The hidden-ball trick! Kenny had fallen for the old hidden-ball trick. Game over, Corpus Christi the winner, 3 to 2.

Kenny stared at Richard and his friend stared back. "Gotcha," Richard said. "The Fearless Foursome strikes again."

Reluctantly, Kenny walked over and put a hand on his shoulder. "You old son of a gun." As Richard's teammates swarmed him, shouting their congratulations, Kenny walked off dejectedly.

"I should have seen that coming," Lieutenant Colonel Nielsen told himself fourteen years later. "Caught me napping. But at least I'd gotten a warm hug from Jacqueline afterward." He reached for a glass of water beside his hospital bed and suddenly remembered that old Indian talisman with the frightening eye. And the foreboding legend that whoever looked on it would someday get the better of a fellow brave in some kind of clash. A shiver chilled his spine. That was one of the last times he'd ever seen Richard Lundquist who, like Kenny, had stared at the thing.

CHAPTER NINETEEN

Jake and John Campbell were having after-work drinks at the Continental, the tavern across the street from the paper. Scotch and water for Jake, an old fashioned for his managing editor. They perched on stools at the bar where Shaker the bartender was wiping glasses with a towel.

Campbell brought up President Truman's firing of General MacArthur. This was big international news. "The general deserved it," Jake said. "Was getting too big for his britches, making speeches about blockading the China coast and all that. Dangerous stuff."

Campbell agreed, set down his glass and said, "You know Truman, don't you?"

"Not exactly but we've talked on the phone. He thanked me for corralling Wernher von Braun for us back in '45."

Campbell then brought up a story Marko Janicek had written that day on corruption in the city manager's office: selling two city-owned parcels of land to a developer at prices far below market value. "That was some great digging Marko did. He's becoming a real kick-ass investigative reporter. You taught him well, Jake."

A loud argument broke out between two guys at the pool table in the rear. A fight was brewing. Jake swung around and recognized them as workers from the L.A. trolley barns a block away on Georgia Street. One of them raised a beer bottle, threatening to bash it over the other guy's head.

Shaker rushed over. "Need any help?" Jake called.

"Naw, I got it, Jake."

Shaker grabbed the bottle, set it down, took the guy by the back of his collar, marched him to the door and threw him out. "You're blackballed, Rufe. Don't ever come in here again."

Shaker came over, wiping his hands on his apron and saying with a shake of his head, "The riff-raff I gotta put up with in here."

"Nice work, Shakes," Jake said.

The bartender refilled the little bowl of peanuts on the bar and said, "Well, fellas, what's gonna happen with the paper now that old man Hearst has gone to the Pearly Gates?"

"Status quo for now," Campbell said. "I'm still the m.e., Jake here is my assistant, and Aggie Underwood remains city editor. Bill Junior will take over but he hasn't yet, not officially. Who knows what'll happen down the road. Hard to say at this point."

Jake took a drink, set his glass down and said, "Circulation numbers are good, we're in the black, so I don't see any need for a shakeup. But young Hearst is a big unknown. No way to tell what he might be thinking, Shakes."

He might fire my ass if I openly help Marion Davies, he thought. Jake was still wrestling with that. He didn't want to see Davies screwed by the Millicent Hearst clan, and he was still itching to see W.R.'s will, which was locked up in Ed Franklin's office.

The next day Jake rode along with his daughter when she drove to Bela Lugosi's. Ilse was going to inform the old actor that his talk to the UCLA drama students was approved.

There would be a fifty dollar honorarium.

Reaching the little house where Lugosi roomed, Ilse parked at the curb.

Once inside, the room looked just as it had before: the same old movie posters on the wall, glass ash tray and small plastic radio on an end table. Ilse took the one wooden chair and Jake leaned against a wall.

Lugosi greeted Ilse's news with a smile and a slight clap of his hands. She handed him a note giving the date, time, and location on campus.

"I'm curious about your burglary days," Jake then said. "What I'm going to ask is strictly off the record. I won't write anything you say and neither will Ilse here."

"It is good that you will not," Lugosi, seated on the bed, answered him. "I am not proud of what I did when I was young, foolish and hungry. What is it that you wish to know?"

"Hypothetically, if one wanted to get into a locked office without forcing the door or damaging it in any way, how would he do it?"

Ilse shot her father a quizzical look.

"A curious question," Lugosi said. "Why would that interest you?"

"It's for some fiction I'm writing," Jake dissembled.

Another questioning look from Ilse.

"I see," Lugosi said. "Well then, if it were me I would bring a skeleton key, hairpins of different sizes and two or three small lengths of wire in varying widths. I found — by trial and error, you see — that one of these would turn the cylinder and open the lock. I of course always wore gloves. Hungarian police even back then could detect fingerprints."

Lugosi offered a wicked little smile and added, "Whose office do you hope to enter?"

"Nobody's. As I said, this is hypothetical."

"Of course it is," Lugosi said with a knowing grin.

CHAPTER TWENTY

August 1939.

Parris Island was a shock. Kenny Nielsen thought he was in top physical condition from playing baseball and basketball. Especially basketball. There was a whole lot of running in basketball.

But when he enlisted in the Marine Corps and got to boot camp at Parris Island, he quickly learned there was being in shape and then there was being *in shape*. The close-order drill, the survival-in-water training, the five-and ten-mile marches with fully loaded packs — were sheer torture. The suffocating late-summer South Carolina heat and humidity only made it worse. A few guys had collapsed.

Kenny fell into his bunk every night worn to the bone, but his aching muscles were taut and hard as boards. Sleep was a drug he couldn't do without. Morning colors always came too darn soon.

He figured he'd been lucky to get accepted by the Marines because at that time the Corps was small. Many were turned down. There wasn't enough manpower to form a division, only regiments. The Corps had seen action in Haiti in 1915 and then Nicaragua in the late Twenties and early Thirties during the "Banana Wars," when they'd been called sarcastically but with some justification "the United Fruit Company's army."

All that was over by 1939 when Kenny signed up. Signed up because fifteen months after graduating from high school he considered himself too old to deliver newspapers on his bike and he couldn't find another job. President Roosevelt's New Deal programs like the WPA might have eased the Depression some, but not all that much. Times were still hard and he was a drag on the family's modest finances. So he'd become a Marine.

The nine weeks of boot camp hell finally came to an end and a graduation ceremony was held on the big parade ground. It was a spectacular event, with platoons marching in formation, flags fluttering in the breeze, the band playing, and spectators applauding from seats in the little bleachers.

Most of the audience consisted of friends and family but no one was there for Kenny. His father wrote that he couldn't afford the railroad trip from Illinois. Kenny's pride at surviving boot camp, receiving his globe and anchor, and becoming a bona fide United States Marine was dimmed by a biting loneliness as the ceremony ended and most of his platoon mates were surrounded by fathers, mothers and girlfriends hugging and kissing them. Kenny stood there watching, a painful ache of aloneness wrenching his gut despite being in the midst of hundreds of people.

His onetime girlfriend Jacqueline Lundquist had moved to Chicago with her parents and brother Richard. That had been the end of that.

Kenny's thoughts turned to his dad and younger brother, and to his Fearless Foursome pals from years back. But most of all to his mother, who'd lost her courageous battle with cancer a year ago. Maybe she was looking down on him from heaven with that tender smile of hers. He wanted to believe that she was.

Kenny suddenly felt a hand on his shoulder. "Got nobody here, Nielsen?" said Sergeant Hadley Plunkett, his platoon leader.

"Nope, not today, Sergeant."

Plunkett was a mountain of a man who'd been damn hard on him and whom Kenny had tried to hate, but he'd sensed that a streak of kindness lurked somewhere beneath that veneer of cold stone. He knew not to call him Hadley, which the sergeant detested. He was to be called Had or Plunk or Sergeant. One recruit who'd called him Hadley had been corrected by a lightning-fast punch to the jaw.

"Me neither," Plunkett said. "My wife's got the flu, couldn't get here. Come on, Nielsen, I'll buy you a beer."

"Thanks, Sergeant, but I'm not legal. I'm only nineteen."

"Bullshit, you're a Marine now, kid, and you'll have a beer with me. Ain't nobody on this island gonna object."

Thus began a friendship that would flourish up through Guadalcanal, three years later.

Next up for Kenny would be ten days of leave. He didn't have the money to take the train home to Illinois, so he went to Washington, D.C., a shorter and less expensive trip. He spent two days there walking all over the place, gawking at the stately buildings and monuments. Hiking for miles all over the nation's capital was a piece of cake after those ten-mile marches at Parris Island.

Kenny went to the Lincoln and Jefferson Memorials. Being from Illinois like Lincoln, and Jefferson being his favorite president, he spent a lot of time in each place. He had an ice cream cone outside the Lincoln Memorial. Then it was on to the top of the Washington Monument. Looking down on the Mall from up there he realized he was higher above the ground than he'd ever been. He'd never flown in an airplane. This was better than the top of the Ferris wheel at the Knox County Fair.

He spent the night in a youth hostel. Next day he admired the White House from outside the iron fence, wondering if FDR was in there. Then he hiked up to the Capitol Building. He went in and found the office of Illinois Senator Hamilton Lewis. He was hoping to introduce himself but Lewis wasn't in.

Kenny spent a second night at the hostel and then, his money running low, took a train to the Marine Corps camp at New River,

North Carolina, happy that he'd had a good look at Washington. His only regret was that he hadn't had someone with him to share the experiences.

He checked in early at New River and spent the rest of his leave looking over the place that would be his new home.

CHAPTER TWENTY-ONE

Jake deliberated for two days on whether to sneak into Ed Franklin's office and search for Hearst's will. Deliberated by himself because there was no way he would tell his wife or daughter what he was considering. If he were caught he'd be a burglar, a criminal. Valerie would be humiliated. Bill Hearst Junior would surely have him fired.

But Jake had taken risks before, huge ones, like going into Nazi Germany in the middle of the war. If he had a good plan he could pull this off.

The plan he came up with was this: The *Examiner*, being a morning paper, would have staffers on hand till around midnight so he and Bela Lugosi would enter the building at 2 a.m. through a back entrance at the loading dock. Lugosi was experienced at this kind of thing and Jake needed him to get Franklin's door opened.

He would tell Valerie that he'd be at a poker game with some of the boys and it could run into the wee hours.

He drove back to Lugosi's without Ilse, told the old actor what he planned to do, and offered him twenty dollars to go with him. Lugosi said, "I knew you had something like this in mind when you asked me about door locks. Yes, it will be quite the grand adventure and I could use the twenty dollars."

* * *

Late that night the two of them crept into the alley behind the building. The breathless night air was cool and damp. They entered through the rear door that Jake knew about, so as not to be seen by the night watchman at the main entrance. It would be a disaster if anybody saw them.

They tiptoed past the now quiet *Examiner* news room on the second floor and crept up the stairs to the third level where Franklin had his office. They both wore gloves. Damn, they found one light shining, a white globe hanging from the ceiling at the far end of the long hallway. Jake had expected none of the lights to be on along the corridor at this hour. His nerve endings tingled. He'd brought a flashlight but didn't need it to reach Franklin's office.

Reaching the office, Jake flipped on the flashlight, focusing it on the lock so Lugosi could go to work with his picklocks. First, though, the old actor tried the knob with his gloved hand. The door opened. *Jesus*, it hadn't been locked.

Jake prayed he could find Hearst's will quickly in one of the file cabinets. His stomach quivering, he stepped in first and Lugosi followed.

Holy shit! Jake couldn't believe his eyes. His light found Ed Franklin lying on the floor, face up. That face bore a bullet hole below the right eye. Lugosi gasped. Jake nearly dropped his flash. Franklin's wide-open eyes showed a look of shock and fear. Blood trailed down the man's face onto his neck and pooled on the carpeted floor beside his head.

Lugosi looked closely, started to reach down with a hand.

"No. Stop," Jake whispered. "Don't touch anything. We gotta get out of here."

"They backed out into the hall. Trembling, knees shaking, Jake quietly closed the door, took a couple of steps.

Franklin dead. Murdered! Why? Who could have . . . ?"

The two of them were suddenly caught in a beam of light.

The night watchman approached, wielding a flashlight. "What the hell are you doing here?"

CHAPTER TWENTY-TWO

Hey, it's Ferguson, isn't it?" Jake said to the sixtyish watchman he'd met a time or two. "It's me, Jake Weaver, remember? How are you, Fergie?" The man wore a green rent-a-cop kind of uniform and some gray stubble on his chin.

"Okay I guess, Mr. Weaver, but I sure didn't 'spect to see nobody up here, 'specially you. What's goin' on?"

"I got a tip that people were shooting craps up here after hours, Fergie. Thought I'd check it out and scoop my friends in the *Examiner* downstairs, but found the hallway empty. Maybe I got the wrong night."

"Never saw a craps game up here in my life, Mr. Weaver, and I make my rounds ever hour or two." Looking at Lugosi, Ferguson asked, "And who are you? You look kinda familiar."

Pulling himself up to his full six-foot-two, Lugosi said in his thick Hungarian accent, "I am Bela Lugosi, the actor."

Ferguson's look of suspicion softened to one of almost awe. "Oh sure, Count Dracula himself."

"Precisely. I accompanied Mr. Weaver tonight because I have always wanted to get in on a big newspaper story."

"Could I get your autograph, Mr. Lugosi?"

"Why not?"

Ferguson pulled a scrap of paper from his wallet and Jake handed Lugosi a pen. The actor scrawled his signature for the man.

"That's swell, Mr. Lugosi, thanks. Now, I didn't see you guys come in. How'd you get past me?"

"You were sleeping in your chair," Jake contrived, "and I didn't want to wake you."

"Well, I do doze off once in awhile late at night. Please don't tell nobody."

"Sure won't, Fergie. Our secret," Jake said, laying a hand on the man's shoulder. "Well, some stories just turn out to be duds. We'll be on our way then."

The three of them padded down the stairs to the front entrance. As he and Lugosi left the building, Jake knew the body would be discovered later in the morning and the police would question Ferguson.

"I'm sure old Ferguson wondered why we wore gloves," Jake said as he drove Lugosi back to his room in the valley. "Hope he doesn't mention it when the cops question him. The gloves, I mean. For sure he'll say he saw us up there."

"For myself I do not fear misfortune with the law," Lugosi said. "I am old and sick. The notoriety might even do me some good, catch the eye of some producer, but I am sorry for you. We are sure to be suspects and you have family and a career."

"Listen, Lugosi, when we get questioned by the cops — and that's a certainty — tell them exactly why we were there. They won't buy that story I made up about a craps game, but don't say we went inside that office. Say Ferguson spotted us before we could try the door. Saying we found the body would dig us into a deep hole. You got it?"

"I understand. Yes, I will do as you say."

"Good."

Why in hell did I ever try to help Marion Davies with that will? Jake scolded himself.

* * *

It was almost 4 when he got home and slipped into bed, trying not to wake Valerie. The effort was in vain.

She rolled over, touched his arm and mumbled, "Hi, Sailor. I hope you won some big pots . . . Say, you don't smell smoky. You usually reek of cigar smoke after these games. Are you sure you were playing poker with the boys?"

"Go back to sleep, hon," Jake told his oh so perceptive wife. "I'll tell you about it in the morning."

And he would. He'd be grilled by the cops, probably become a murder suspect, and the *Times* and *Mirror* might get hold of it. That would be a personal and very public disaster. He'd level with Valerie over their morning coffee. The strength of their marriage would be tested like never before.

Jake closed his eyes and tried to sleep but he kept seeing Ed Franklin's face with a bullet hole in it.

CHAPTER TWENTY-THREE

Summer 1942.

When the 1st Marine Division went to war there weren't enough ships on the East Coast for the whole division so the 5th Regiment went to California by train to embark from there. Corporal Kenny Nielsen was among them.

The train passed through Galesburg, Illinois, a big rail center. It stopped there for ten minutes to take on coal and water. No one was allowed to get off. Kenny went to a window and caught sight of the depot and the big Congregational Church on the nearby town square, but not much else of his hometown. His home on North Prairie Street was blocks away. He hadn't seen it in a year and he couldn't see it now. Made him sad.

Two days later in San Diego, he and a pal, Skinny Wade, bowled some lines at the Tower Bowl on West Broadway, enjoyed a steak dinner at a place called Haynes' Streamliner, and rode the trolley to the zoo. Kenny had seen elephants and lions before, when the circus came to town, but never a giraffe or a zebra. "That guy with the weird neck must be twenty feet tall," he told Wade.

Nice little city, San Diego, but bursting at the seams. Aircraft workers and sailors in white caps seemed to be everywhere. "Sorry, No Rooms Available" signs hung on doors of the hotels. Most of the streetcars were packed with people. Little? Come to think of it, this was the third largest city Kenny had been in, after Chicago of course, and Washington, D.C., after graduating from boot camp.

He wondered if Wellington, New Zealand was bigger than San Diego. That's where he was headed next.

After the layover there, they sailed to New Zealand for what was supposed to be several months of additional training. The long, boring voyage took two weeks.

Only a few days after setting up camp near Wellington, naval intelligence discovered that the Japanese were building an airfield in the Solomon Islands, easy flying distance from Australia. That threat couldn't be tolerated so the division quickly piled onto transport ships to go and face the enemy and hopefully capture that airfield. It would be America's first counteroffensive against the Japanese, who'd overrun most of the South Pacific in the months since Pearl Harbor.

Only senior officers knew their target was an obscure island called Guadalcanal.

The third night at sea, Kenny sat talking with platoon sergeant Hadley Plunkett, the guy who'd bought him a beer after boot camp at Parris Island. They perched on bunks in a hot, crowded hold among hundreds of other Marines.

"Where do you think we're going, Plunk?" Kenny asked.

"Dunno, kid. They'll probly tell us the day before we land. For sure it'll be some Jap island somewhere. We'll have ourselves a big bloody scrap with them little yellow bastards, count on it."

"How many of us you figure will survive, Plunk?"

"Hard to say. More'n half of us, I reckon. You scared?"

Kenny hesitated before admitting, "Yeah, I guess so."

"Me too."

"Really, Plunk?"

"Sure, it's natural. Somebody who ain't scared going into battle's got a screw loose. Fear's an infantryman's birthright.

Makes you more alert."

"Hmm," Kenny muttered, pondering that. How would he do in battle? Could he be brave and do his duty or would he cringe and be a coward?

Plunkett wiped some sweat from his forehead and said, "Tell ya what though, kid, our platoon's gonna be okay. We're good Marines, well trained. I figure you'll be among them that makes it. You're smart an' clever, and a damn good shot. I think you got a lucky streak in you."

Kenny had never been told anything like that before. His father had seldom given his sons any praise. He appreciated Plunkett. The man felt like a big brother or a kindly uncle.

"Sure hope you're right about that, Plunk."

Kenny didn't sleep much that night. The ship's engines thrummed away, vibrating his bunk and most everything else in the old ship. *Barum, barum, barum.*

He kept thinking about Galesburg and wondering if he'd ever see his hometown again. But when he did doze off he had nightmares. He was trapped in a cave with little yellow men shooting at him from a side tunnel. He couldn't move, couldn't duck away from their bullets.

CHAPTER TWENTY-FOUR

Over breakfast Jake told Valerie everything. How he and Lugosi slipped into Franklin's office, found the man shot to death, and the lame story he'd given the night watchman about a possible craps game.

Dismay and anger darkened Valerie's face. She reached out a hand as if to hit him, but stopped short.

"Go ahead and slap my stupid face," Jake said. "I deserve it."

Valerie pulled her hand back. "The other night at dinner you asked if I had any regrets. I've got a hell of a big one right now, you darn fool. You've always been reckless but this goes way beyond that. I can't imagine why you ever tried to help Marion Davies in the first place, the old lush."

"That's true, Val, she's got a problem with booze, but she's a nice lady, gave old Hearst a ton of help. Still, I just didn't think this through. I'm stupid, stupid, stupid."

"If this gets out," Valerie said, "it could mean the end of your career, and think how it would humiliate Ilse and me. How could Ilse show her face at school, or me at the plant?" She leaned back in her chair and touched her coffee cup but didn't pick it up. Her face softened a little.

"Well," she said after a long moment, "I promised to stick by you through thick and thin, and this is as thin as it gets, but I won't break that vow. I'll stand by you. God knows why, but I love you, you loony stumble-bum."

Jake reached over and touched her hand. "You're the greatest. I don't deserve you."

"No, you don't. So what'll happen now?"

"Somebody will find the body, a cleaning woman or maybe his assistant, Amy Noonan. The night watchman will tell the cops I was up there and I'll get hauled in and grilled. Lugosi too. I'll tell 'em my only gun, that old German Luger of mine, hasn't been fired in years. Then I've gotta hope the bullet that killed Franklin is a different caliber than the Luger's."

Jake finished his coffee — he'd barely touched his eggs — and got up. "Time to go and face the music," he said. "I'm so lucky to have you."

"You can say that again."

When he was at the door, ready to leave, Valerie placed her hands on both sides of his face and gave him a warm kiss. "Good luck," she said. "I hope you won't have to call me from jail."

What a woman. I'm not worthy of her, Jake told himself as he drove off.

He had been at the office no more than an hour when he got a call from detective Owen Wannamaker at police headquarters. Jake knew Wannamaker, had dealt with him after Ilse had been attacked and stabbed by a fugitive Nazi "doctor" back in '47. Wannamaker had seemed like an okay guy.

"Come down to Central Division, Weaver," the detective demanded. "We've gotta talk."

"Sure thing, but what about?" Trying to sound surprised and innocent.

"I hope you don't know, but I think you do. Get here right away. If you don't, we'll send some uniforms to drag you in."

"Drag me in? Geez, pardner, I don't know what you're talking about but sure, I'll see you right away."

Jake parked in a visitors' spot at the station, entered, and asked for Detective Wannamaker. He stood there shifting his weight from foot to foot for a minute or two till Wannamaker came out.

"Hello there, Weaver." No offer of a handshake. About six-one, sandy hair, athletic looking. "Come with me." He led Jake through a swinging gate in a low wooden barrier.

"What's up?" Jake asked.

"You'll find out in about sixty seconds," the cop said, striding down a hall. "How's your daughter doing?" he asked, referring to the long-ago stabbing.

"Fine, thanks. She's a tough kid."

"Glad to hear it. I like the girl."

They reached an interrogation room. The door stood open. "In here," Wannamaker said, pointing.

Jake had seen rooms like this before. A small rectangular metal table with two chairs on each side, a large mirror covering one wall, sound-deadening wallboard covering the others. He knew the mirror was one-way glass so he could be observed from outside the room.

Another cop was there, already seated. Round face, deep-set brown eyes, lips turned downward in a scowl. Jake took a chair across from him, facing the mirror.

"This is Detective Sam Sixto," Wannamaker said.

"Pleased to meet you," Jake offered.

Looking at Wannamaker, Sixto said, "He's pleased to

meet me. Now isn't that sweet?" He turned his gaze back to Jake, a stern hostile gaze.

Jake wondered who might be staring at him from behind that glass.

Wannamaker took the chair beside Sixto who, still studying Jake's face, snarled, "Why'd you kill that lawyer last night?"

Trying to look surprised, Jake answered, "Kill what lawyer? What are you talking about? Is this some kind of joke?"

Now Wannamaker spoke. "An attorney named Ed Franklin was found shot in his office this morning, dead as a hockey puck."

Jake made himself gasp.

"Why'd you do it?" Sixto said, leaning forward, elbows on the table. "You were there last night. The night watchman caught you and another guy outside the stiff's office. We've got you dead to rights on this, pal."

"Here's the thing," Jake said. "Okay, yeah, I was there. I was hoping to go into his office and try to find old man Hearst's will. You see, I'm trying to help Marion Davies get her fair share of the Hearst fortune. It was stupid of me, I know."

"That's crazy," Wannamaker said. "Were you trying to steal the will or what?"

"Nope, just wanted to look at it, see if it left anything to Miss Davies. I'd asked Franklin to let me see it, but he refused. Attorney-client confidentiality. So what am I charged with? It's a public building. Never got a chance to try that office door when the watchman found us. Never saw Franklin."

Sixto: "So you say. How come you were there so late at night?"

Jake: "Had to wait till the *Examiner* news room was empty. How long had Franklin been dead?"

Wannamaker: "The medical examiner's working on that."

Jake: "Okay, I'm guilty of walking while stupid, but that's all. No trespassing since it's a public building, no breaking and entering since I never went into that office."

"Don't play coy, pal," Sixto said, leaning even closer across the table. "You're in deep grease here, a murder suspect."

"I never killed anybody in my life," Jake lied. He'd killed three Germans during the last year of the war, all in self defense.

"You have a firearm, Jake?" Wannamaker asked.

I'm Jake now? Oh, I get it. He's playing the nice guy while Sixto is the bastard.

"Yeah, a Luger I picked up during the war. It's boxed up at home, hasn't been fired in years."

"We'll want to see that pistol."

"Fine. I've got no problem with that. Check it out all you want, Owen." *I can play that game too. If I'm Jake to him, he can be Owen to me.* "What kind of a bullet, or bullets, killed Franklin?"

Wannamaker: "We don't know yet. Our m.e. is working on that."

Sixto: "Who was that guy with you up there?"

"Bela Lugosi, the actor. He'd done some burglary in his younger days in Hungary. He was gonna try and get that door open but we never got the chance."

"Yeah, we know it was Lugosi," Sixto said. "The watchman told us that. We'll be questioning him too." Sixto laughed mirthlessly. "A silly newspaper reporter and a washed-up old actor on the prowl at two a.m. Must of been one hell of a funny sight. Funny, except that one of ya committed a homicide."

"Yeah, real funny," Jake said. He hoped like hell Lugosi would keep his word and say they never entered that office. "Is there anything else you fellas want?"

"We'll come to your place and have a look at that Luger," Wannamaker said.

"With a search warrant if we have to," Sixto added with a scowl.

These guys are quite an act, got it all choreographed. "You won't need that. You can come into my house and look at anything you want."

"Thanks," Wannamaker said. "You can go now."

"You're letting this guy walk?" Sixto said, frowning.

"Yep, he's not gonna skip on us."

Sixto pointed a finger at Jake. "One hour! Be there."

CHAPTER TWENTY-FIVE

Only Wannamaker showed up at Jake's house on Saturn Avenue. That was a relief.

"Come on in," Jake said. "The Luger's in my bedroom."
As he led the way, Wannamaker looked around curiously, checking out the house he'd been in the day Ilse was attacked.

In the bedroom, Jake went to the closet, reached up to the crawl space and pulled down the shoebox holding his Luger. He handed it over, saying, "Here it is. My prints will be all over it."

Wannamaker opened the box, pulled out a handkerchief and used it as he examined the weapon. He held it up to his nose and sniffed, then checked the magazine and found it empty. No bullets. He replaced it in the box and put the handkerchief back in his pocket. "Okay, thanks. Hasn't been fired in quite awhile. Any other guns in the place?"

"My wife's .38, a police special." Jake went to the chest of drawers and pulled it out. Wannamaker did the handkerchief thing as he inspected the .38. Again, an empty magazine and no scent of gunsmoke. Wannamaker handed it back and Jake put it away.

"Look," Jake said, "I know I was dumb going there last night. Didn't think that one through. My wife's real sore at me about this."

"You told her about it?"

"Damn right. I never keep anything from her." *Except killing those Germans and a roll in the hay I had in '42 with a pretty British spy.*

"I wanta find out who killed Franklin as much as you do," Jake went on. "He was an okay guy, even if he wouldn't let me see that will. I'm a good investigative reporter. I'll look into this too, help you all I can."

"Better not, Jake. Let us handle this. Although I believe you, you're still a suspect. I have to tell you not to leave town."

"That's bullshit, Owen. You know you can't tell me that, not without a court order."

"Oh, I do apologize," Wannamaker said, dripping with sarcasm. "What I meant to say was I'd be obliged if you'd do me the courtesy of letting me know if you need to leave town."

"I'll do that," Jake said. "Look, I'm on your side here. I wanta help. Say, does this have to go on the blotter? I'd hate for the other papers to get this."

"Nope, you haven't been booked — not yet anyway — so your name's not on the blotter."

"Thanks. That's a relief."

As he left, the detective said, "Give my regards to your daughter. She's a brave young woman."

Jake thought, leave it to them? Nope, he was going to try to figure this one out, too.

He locked up and drove to the paper, Wilshire to Figueroa to Pico, somewhat relieved, though the words "you're still a suspect" rang in his ears.

It was almost noon when he arrived. Managing editor John Campbell came over and said, "Where've you been?

Haven't seen you around this morning. You look kind of upset."

"Upset? Naw, something came up I had to take care of right away. Nothing to worry about. Did you need me for something?"

"Wanted your opinion on a story Richie Millsap wrote on a wounded GI from Korea. Kid from El Monte. I know your friend Kenny Nielsen's pretty banged up too. Aggie and I approved it, though. It's on page one of the local section. Read it and see if it needs any fixes for the later editions."

"Will do, Johnny." Jake felt some guilt that he hadn't gone to the naval hospital in San Diego to see his old friend, or even called, in quite awhile. I'll go down there this weekend, he told himself. Wait! He'd been told not to leave town, but that was bogus. Since he hadn't been booked, the cops had no legal right to tie him down.

He picked up a copy of the first edition and read Millsap's story. He didn't have any problem with it.

After grabbing a bite of lunch across the street at the Continental — ham sandwich and a beer — Jake got a call from Valerie at Lockheed about 1:30. "Well, Sailor, how are you? Have you seen the police?"

"Yeah, hon, they called me in for questioning, then came out to the house to check my Luger. They're satisfied it hasn't been fired in like, forever. I think it's gonna be okay, but—"

"But what?"

"They're still going to suspect me till they find the real killer."

"I hope they do that real soon. I'm sorry I lost my temper this morning. It was just—"

"That's okay, Sweets. I deserved it. Like I said, that was a real dumb stunt I pulled. Won't ever do anything like that again."

"Ha, not till you do something even stupider. Well, I'll see you tonight and we'll cook us up a nice dinner."

Jake leaned back in his chair and scratched his head. Who could have killed Franklin? he wondered. One of Hearst's sons? But what motive would they have had? Had Franklin crossed them? Not likely; he wouldn't want to lose his big client, the Hearst papers.

Jake was scribbling names on a notepad.

Millicent Hearst? Richard Berlin, the president of the corporation? Same answer: what motive?

He snapped his fingers. Franklin's wife? He knew nothing about the woman, had never met her, didn't even know her name. But he knew that in homicides the spouse was always one of the prime suspects. He had no way of knowing if it was a happy marriage or one gone bad. Yeah, it could have been the wife.

Did Franklin have kids? Jake didn't know, couldn't remember if he'd seen any family photos in Franklin's office.

Some angry client, where Franklin lost a big case that created a financial disaster for the man? Maybe.

If I'm going to look into this, Jake asked himself, where the devil would I start?

His phone rang. He picked up the receiver. "Weaver."

"It's Wannamaker. The m.e. says Franklin was killed by a .22 short. One shot to the head at close range. Your Luger fires 9-millimeters so I'm buying your story. But before you get all excited, you're not completely off the hook. Sixto thinks you coulda used a .22 and ditched it afterwards."

"Aw, that's crazy. I don't have a .22, wouldn't even know where to get one."

"Come on, Jake, you know it's easy to get a gun in L.A., they're all over the place. I still buy your story, though, but Sixto's a good detective, has good instincts. So you're still a suspect, though not a hot one, not till we get deeper into our investigation."

"Well, shit," Jake said. "Have you thought about the wife?"

"Course we have. That's often the case in killings like this. That's where we're gonna start. Remember, keep out of this."

"I will," Jake fibbed. "Thanks for telling me about the bullet. So long for now."

CHAPTER TWENTY-SIX

October 1943. Melbourne, Australia.

After more than four months of brutal fighting on Guadalcanal the battered but victorious 1st Marine Division had been pulled out, leaving the Army to mop up against the decimated, starving Japanese. Kenny Nielsen could hardly believe he'd survived when so many of his buddies had lost their lives defending the airfield in savage fighting, eventually driving the enemy to the southwest end of the island.

The hardest to take of the deaths was that of Platoon Sergeant Had Plunkett, who'd become his best friend. Even now, all these months later, it was painful to recall the good times they'd had, the fatherly advice Plunk had given him. That loss left an empty hole in Kenny's heart.

But I'm an officer, he marveled. A small-town Midwestern boy like me with a high school education. He'd received a field commission on that vile island, becoming a mustang second lieutenant.

The worn-down Marines had been sent to Australia to recuperate and reorganize, first in Brisbane and now Melbourne. There, Kenny had been bumped up to first lieutenant and given command of a company.

He didn't know where the division would go next but it was sure to be some island hell where they'd face those fanatical Japs again.

Jake hoped they wouldn't have mutton again at evening chow. He was getting sick of that sheep stuff. Didn't this country have any beef cattle?

Kenny thought every day about nurse Claudia Chase. Wounded with a piece of shrapnel in his chest, he'd been treated at the fleet hospital on Espiritu Santo Island in the New Hebrides, where Claudia had nursed him. He fell head over heels for the kind, beautiful woman, he reminisced, and luckily she felt the same.

During his first leave in Brisbane he'd hitched a ride on an Army plane to Espiritu Santo and reunited with her. During five happy days together they'd begun to speak of marriage.

Now, in his little room in the camp outside Melbourne, he was answering one of her letters. They wrote to each other often. Wartime mail could be slow and inconsistent but occasionally fairly efficient.

Kenny thought the world of Claudia and hoped they could spend the rest of their lives together — *if* he survived the war. He'd had a little thing for Jacqueline Lundquist back in his hometown but that was nothing compared with this. He finished his letter, signed it "Love, Kenny" and dropped onto his bunk. He laced his hands behind his head and envisioned Claudia's auburn hair, hazel-green eyes, and that puckish little mouth he loved to kiss. He wished he could be kissing it right now. A warm ache settled in his chest.

Kenny had a weekend pass and on Sunday he decided to go to services at the pretty little Church of Christ he'd seen a few blocks from the base. He'd often attended church as a kid in Galesburg, but that habit faded away after his mother died of cancer.

He didn't consider himself particularly religious anymore, but God — or *something* up there — had seemed to watch over him at Guadalcanal and help him survive.

A lonely Yank in a strange land, Kenny hiked over to the dove-gray wooden building and stood outside for a moment gazing up at the bell tower and high white cross. The place reminded him of village churches in New England he'd seen pictures of.

Climbing the steps, he entered the nave and took a seat in one of the rear pews. Soft, warm light seeped through stained-glass windows on the side walls. The front of the hall contained a crucifix, a choir stall, and the pastor's pulpit. Kenny felt comforted by these familiar sights, was glad he'd come.

He noticed the sanctuary was about half full, mostly women and elderly men. Australia's young men were at war.

The service proceeded with hymns, prayers, the passing of collection plates, and finally the sermon. Kenny tossed two Australian pounds on the collection plate when it came his way.

A time or two during the service, a young woman seated to his left glanced over and offered a smile. He responded each time with a small nod. She had a pale, heart-shaped face, vivid blue eyes, and wore a simple yellow and white dress. Looked to be in her early twenties.

When the service ended and the benediction was read, the pastor urged parishioners to attend the social hour in the fellowship hall. As Kenny stood, the young woman lightly touched his arm and said, "My name is Sophie. I hope you'll come to the social. We have coffee and biscuits."

CHAPTER TWENTY-SEVEN

Not for a second did Jake suspect Marion Davies of being the killer. He just wanted to know if she had any notions about who might have shot Ed Franklin. He called that afternoon and asked if she'd heard about the man's demise.

"No, Jake, what about Ed Franklin?"

"I'm sorry to say he's been murdered, Miss Davies."

"Murdered?" Her voice rising. "Ed Franklin? Really?"

Her surprise felt genuine to Jake. "I'm afraid so. He was found shot to death in his office this morning."

"That's terrible. He was always good to me."

Jake heard a clinking sound and a gulp, figuring Davies was taking a drink. "Do you have any idea who might have done this?" he asked. "Know of any enemies he might have had?"

"No, I sure don't."

"Was he happily married?"

"I have no idea. I wasn't all that close to him. You think his wife might've killed him?"

"I don't really think anything, Miss Davies. The police are investigating. They might contact you and ask some of these same questions."

"If they do, I'll tell them whatever I can, which is basically nothing."

"Thanks, Miss Davies. Sorry to upset you with this sad news, but I wanted to give you a heads-up. I'll let you know if I learn anything else."

Jake was getting nowhere and wondered if the cops were doing any better. Could it have been Millicent Hearst or one of the sons? he asked himself again. As before, the answer was "Whatever for?"

He thought about calling Franklin's assistant, Amy Noonan, but decided not to, not yet at least. He doubted that she'd have done it.

Before he could think further about Noonan, his phone rang. It was Detective Wannamaker. He said they'd questioned Bela Lugosi. "That guy's a strange duck but his story matches yours right down the line, Jake, so we're looking elsewhere."

"Like where, Owen?"

"You know I can't tell you that. How come you know Lugosi anyway?"

Jake told him that his daughter Ilse was doing a story on the actor for the UCLA paper, had invited him to speak at the school, and that's how they'd met.

"I see. Okay then, but you keep out of this now."

"I will," Jake white-lied.

October 1943. Melbourne, Australia.

Kenny followed the woman who'd introduced herself as Sophie into the church's fellowship hall, a long rectangular room with cinder-block walls and fluorescent light tubes hanging from the ceiling. "Nice to meet you," he'd said. "My name is Kenny."

To his surprise, Sophie took his arm as if they were old friends. "Lieutenant Kenny, I'd say," taking note of the bars on his shoulder. "We don't see many Yanks at our services. I'm pleased to meet you. Fazzy that you came."

Fazzy? Did that mean fabulous? Kenny was still learning Aussie-speak.

The room held about thirty people. Some of them gave this unfamiliar Yank a good looking-over.

"Coffee then?" Sophie asked.

"Sure."

She led him to a table set up with coffee urns, pitchers of tea, cups, saucers, and plates of "biscuits," which turned out to be cookies.

Sophie filled a coffee cup and handed it to him, asking, "Cream and sugar, Lieutenant Kenny?" Her blue eyes were really very striking.

"Nope, I take it black, and please forget that lieutenant business. Just call me Kenny." He put his cup down for a moment and, returning the gesture, filled one for her.

"Well thank you, kind sir." As she spooned some sugar into her cup, the pastor approached. Medium height, eyeglasses, black suit with a white collar, about forty.

"Reverend Clifford," Sophie said, "meet Lieutenant Kenny, an American visitor with us today."

Clifford extended a hand, which Kenny shook, and said, "Delighted, Lieutenant, and welcome. So glad you came."

"Thanks, sir. That was a fine sermon."

"Pleased that you thought so. Saint Paul is always a good subject." The pastor pulled Sophie several feet aside and whispered in her ear. Kenny wondered what that was about. He managed to hear her response: "There's nothing to fret about, Reverend."

The man gave Kenny a smile, then moved off to talk with some of the other parishioners.

"He worries about me so," Sophie said, back at Kenny's side.

He noticed that some of the women were sneaking curious looks at the two of them. "Please tell me about yourself, Kenny."

"Not much to tell, ma'am, I mean Sophie. I'm just a guy in the 1st Marine Division, enjoying your Australian hospitality while we train and reorganize. How about you?"

"I am a school teacher, lower forms." Her face darkened. "I also fear that I may be a war widow," she said quietly. "My husband is missing in action in New Guinea. I am afraid that one of these days I'll be told that he's come a gutser."

"How awful for you. I'll pray that he's alive and will come back to you."

"Most kind of you." Sophie picked up a chocolate-chip cookie and raised it to Kenny's mouth like a mother bird feeding her young. Her act caught the attention of several nearby women. Kenny took a bite and pulled the remainder from her hand. "That's good," he said.

"Thank you. I baked those. All of these biscuits were made by our church women. Now please tell me more about yourself, Kenny. What part of the States are you from?"

He told her that he was from a small town in the middle part of the U.S. and that he'd been a Marine for more than four years.

"Are you married?" *Man, this woman gets right to it.*

"No, but I'm spoken for. You see, there's this Navy nurse. She and I—"

"She's a lucky woman then. You strike me as a wonderful fellow, Kenny."

Flustered, Kenny said, "I think I'm the one who's lucky."

They each drank coffee, ate another cookie, and continued to chat. Sophie said she originally was from the nearby town of Werribee but now had a place close by. She had been married only eight months before her husband went into action. She enjoyed cooking and reading English novels. Kenny told about his high school days in Illinois.

As the crowd began to thin out, Sophie said, "How would you like to have a nice home-cooked meal, Kenny? Please come over to my flat. I have some nice corned beef."

If she'd said mutton Kenny would have declined. But something told him, Why not?

CHAPTER TWENTY-EIGHT

Jake got to the *Herald-Express* about 8 the next morning. This being an afternoon paper, many staffers had been there for an hour or more. Instead of the usual warm hellos he got some strange looks from most of them. He had no idea why, but it was unsettling. Was his fly open or something?

He reached his office, parked his jacket and hat on the coat rack and settled into his chair. A copy of the morning *Times* lay open on his desk. A front-page headline stared him in the face. **Dracula Actor and Herald-Express Editor Implicated in Mystery Slaying.**

What the hell!

Hands shaking, Jake began to read the story. It bore the byline of police reporter Al Baxter. Jake had met Baxter a time or two at the Press Club, hadn't particularly cared for him. Seemed too full of himself.

Jake read: "Actor Bela Lugosi and *Herald-Express* assistant managing editor Jake Weaver were seen at the office door of a local attorney the very night that man was shot to death, the *Times* has learned. Hours after that sighting, the body of attorney Edwin Franklin was discovered inside his office in a building on Broadway, south of downtown. The victim, who was killed by a single gunshot to the face, was found Tuesday morning by Franklin's secretary, Edith Harris, when she arrived for work.

"When questioned by this reporter, the building's night watchman, Horace Ferguson, said he'd found Lugosi and

Weaver together outside Franklin's office door at about two a.m. when making his rounds. It has been confirmed that the pair has since been questioned by police but not yet charged.

"Lead investigator Owen Wannamaker said he had nothing to say at this point except that the homicide investigation was ongoing. He wouldn't indicate whether Lugosi or Weaver were suspects. Sam Sixto, another detective working the case, said, however, that their appearance at a murder scene was highly suspicious.

"Lugosi, a native of Hungary, came to fame in the 1931 film 'Dracula,' in which he played a cunning vampire. Lately his career has—"

That's as far as Jake got in the story when he saw managing editor John Campbell and city editor Aggie Underwood standing in his doorway.

"You have something to tell us?" Campbell asked.

At her apartment near UCLA, Jake's daughter Ilse had cleared away the breakfast dishes and was about ready to leave for school when her roommate, pre-med student Claudia Nielsen, looked up from their little kitchenette table. "Have you seen this?" she asked, holding up the front page of the *Times*.

Ilse had a tall glass of orange juice in her hand. She put it down and saw the headline, sank onto a chair and began to read, dark lines furrowing her brow. "*Vati, Vati,* whatever have you done?" Jake had told her nothing about this.

"He has always done some risky things, but this—"

"What could he have been doing there?" Claudia asked.

"I don't know. He's been trying to help Marion Davies get her rightful share of Hearst's fortune, but I don't know of any reason for this."

"What will people say to you at school?" Claudia asked. "This could be a rough day for you."

"I'm not worried about that; let them say whatever they want. I am concerned for my *Vater*."

Could he go to prison?

"I know this is embarrassing for you guys," Jake told Campbell and Underwood.

"I'm sure sorry about that. Goddamn that Al Baxter, but once he heard about the killing he was smart to go and interview that night watchman, I'll give him that. Sure, Bela Lugosi and I were there and here's why."

Jake told them everything, how he'd wanted to see Hearst's will and maybe help out Marion Davies. Repeating the lie he'd told the police, he said he hadn't entered the office and had no idea Franklin was dead in there.

"Jesus, Jake," Campbell said, "that was stupid of you."

"Yeah, my wife says the same thing. She's pretty sore at me. So what do we do now?"

"The Hearst boys haven't taken over the paper yet," Campbell said, "so just go about your business for now. Later, well, who knows?"

"I'll dictate a story to rewrite," Aggie Underwood put in, "saying you're innocent and that your appearance there was totally unrelated to the killing, that you're not a suspect. This won't exactly refute what the *Times* had, but it's the best we can do right now."

Campbell: "It'll be vague as hell but we've gotta stand up for our own, even if it's standing on shaky legs. So back off now, Jake. Forget about Marion Davies. You hearing me?"

Jake pursed his lips. "Yep, I am."

The two editors turned and left. Jake sank onto his chair and buried his head in his hands.

Minutes later, gangster Mickey Cohen called. He and Jake had known each other for several years, doing each other a favor once in a while.

"I saw that story in the *Times*, Jakester. Damn dirty trick if you ask me. I know you wouldn't kill nobody, not that you don't have the guts. You just ain't the type. I'm gonna look into this for you."

"Aw, Mick, you don't hafta do that."

"Maybe I don't have to, but I will. Been kinda bored lately."

What a character, Jake thought after hanging up.

CHAPTER TWENTY-NINE

October 1943. Melbourne, Australia.

Sophie linked her right arm through Kenny's left as they strolled the four blocks to her flat. The uninvited gesture surprised him, but he thought it would be rude to resist. A chill wind whistled over them. It was springtime down here, a rather cool one, and the closeness probably made her a bit warmer.

A black flivver with running boards and a spare tire lashed to its backside coughed and wheezed up the street. To Kenny it somewhat resembled a Model T Ford. "That's an old Tarrant," Sophie said, "running on kerosene. With our rationing and shortages, some of those old buggies are resurfacing."

Moments later, Kenny asked, "Here?" when she stopped in front of a three-story building of yellow brick fronted by a neat lawn and a scattering of flower beds.

"None other," she said, and led him up the concrete steps to the front door. Before Sophie could open it, a middle-aged woman in a brown coat came out, looked Kenny over and said rather icily, "G'dye, Sophie." The woman walked out toward the street, looking back at Kenny once again. Embarrassment for Sophie gnawed at him.

They encountered no others while climbing a flight of stairs to Sophie's rooms on the second floor. She unlocked the door and ushered Kenny in. "This is it, my little crib," she said. The front room had a fabric sofa, two chairs, a couple of lamps, and a cherrywood sideboard. A copy of an Impressionist painting hung on a wall. Monet, maybe. Beyond an arched opening he saw a tidy little kitchen.

"Nice place," Kenny said.

Sophie took off her jacket, opened a door to her bedroom and tossed it on the bed, a double bed topped with a rose-colored comforter. Kenny caught a glimpse of a small desk with books and papers scattered on top. Some of her teaching materials, no doubt.

Returning, Sophie gave Kenny a hug, which he felt like resisting but didn't. She said, "More coffee? Or maybe a drink?"

Pulling away, Kenny said, "No thanks. I'm fine." Looking around, he expected to see a picture of her husband, but no. He saw no photos at all.

"Come into the kitchen then and keep me company while I budge us up a meal."

Kenny sat in a chair at a small enameled kitchen table while Sophie pulled things from the icebox and set to work. She lit the gas cookstove with a wooden match — it flared up with a whoosh — placed corned beef in a pan and slid it in the oven. Then, while she chopped vegetables, Kenny asked, "What about your family? Do you have brothers and sisters?"

"I have a younger sister, Millie, who's still in school in Werribee. Hopes to be a teacher like me one day. Pops is a railroad worker, a signal engineer on the Canberra line. My mum's a housewife, a washing and ironing slave."

"I hope you're close to her," Kenny said. "My mom passed away. Cancer. Can't tell you how much I miss her."

Sophie put down her knife and touched his hand sympathetically.

A tasty aroma began to seep from the oven. Kenny told her he was glad it wasn't mutton, that mutton seemed to be the main meal every day at the base.

"Yeah, we have scads of sheep here in Victoria state. I think our station people are getting rich selling mutton to you Yanks."

"Station?" Kenny asked.

"Right, we have sheep stations all over the outback. What do you call them? Ranches? Farms?"

Kenny grinned and said he was still learning some of the local idioms.

Setting some sliced cabbage on a plate, Sophie asked, "How do you find Australia?"

"Get a boat in New Caledonia and sail southwest."

Sophie touched his hand and said, "Silly. You know what I meant."

"Sorry. I like Australia fine."

Later, after the meal, Kenny said, "Thanks a lot, Sophie. Best feast I've had in quite awhile. I think I should be getting back now."

"Nonsense. What's the rush? Let's have tea in the front room and chat a bit more."

Well, okay, Kenny thought. He was enjoying himself.

Soon seated on the sofa a discreet distance from her, he took a sip of tea from a china cup and said, "I sure hope your hubby will get back to you. Tell me about him."

"We met at a pub in Melbourne. He was tall and good looking like you."

Like me? Kenny didn't appreciate being compared like that.

"We hit it off at first, and got married about six weeks later. Had a cozy honeymoon by the sea out at Perth. After a bit, though, he grew restless and would leave for days at a time. I think maybe he had a little something going on the side. He slapped me around once when I confronted him on it."

"Oh no. Sure sorry to hear that."

"Then his draft notice came. I saw him just a time or two during his basic training. Then his regiment was called into action in New Guinea. He took part in driving the Japs from Port Moresby over the Owen Stanleys and on to the north coast. He seldom wrote me. I began to think of divorce."

Uncomfortable at hearing all this, Kenny was sorry he'd asked about the man.

"He was in action in the battle at Buna," Sophie went on, "and that's the last I heard until the notification came that he was missing. I know he is dead. I can just feel it."

As Kenny was saying he sure hoped not, Sophie slid over next to him. She put her hands on his shoulders, her blue eyes moist.

"Kiss me," she said.

CHAPTER THIRTY

Jake's phone rang. "Weaver."

"It's Bill Hearst, Mr. Weaver," W.R.'s eldest son said. "We won't announce it till next week, but mother is appointing me publisher of our papers, both the *Herald-Express* and the *Examiner*."

Jake swallowed hard. Surely this guy had seen the *Times* story revealing he'd been at the Franklin murder scene.

"In the meantime I'm meeting with several of our editors and top reporters to get myself orientated."

Is that a word? Jake wondered.

"Could you have lunch with me at the Beverly Hills Hotel, say 12:30 in the Polo Lounge?"

Jake knew this was more command than request. "Sure, Mr. Hearst. I'll look forward to meeting you."

"Likewise, Mr. Weaver. Till then."

Jake felt his gut tighten as he put the receiver on its cradle.

A few minutes later, Valerie called. She'd seen the story in the *Times*.

"Oh Jake, this is terrible. I'm damn mad they went and wrote that. Are you okay?"

"You know me, Val, old Roll-with-the-Punches Jake. Yeah, I'm okay, but what about you? Are you getting some grief at the plant?"

"Not really, though I've caught a few people sneaking some pretty odd looks at me. One guy said if you go to prison would I go out with him. I told him to do something that's anatomically impossible."

Jake laughed and said, "Perfect. Good for you, Sweets. The paper is backing me on this. Aggie's running a story today saying I'm innocent and in no way a suspect."

"I guess that'll help some," Valerie said. "Well, keep your spirits up, Sailor. I'll see you tonight."

After hanging up, Jake thought, "What a trouper. She'd have every right to be mad as hell."

Apprehension ate at Jake while driving to the Beverly Hills Hotel. Was he going to be fired?

He arrived and turned his car over to a valet. The maître d' at the Polo Lounge told him that Mr. Hearst was in the outdoor dining area, and led him to a booth out there, passing under arched arcades with tiled roofs and tons of flowering plants. Jake had been here once before. He took in the umbrella-shaded tables, bouquets of bright flowers on each one, and booths that were screened from one another by walls of short, cream-colored lattice-work. It was all very California chic.

Bill Hearst got up and took Jake's hand. A martini glass stood next to his plate.

"Thank you for coming, Mr. Weaver," the man said. "Nice to meet you." The cordiality felt fake. He didn't much resemble his father. At least two inches shorter and with eyeglasses and neatly barbered black hair. About forty-five years old, Jake estimated. His dark, double-breasted blue suit and conservative gray tie screamed East Coast. No surprise. The man had lived almost all his life in New York.

"Have a seat, Mr. Weaver. What will you have? I just ordered a martini."

"As a rule I don't drink a lot at lunch, Mr. Hearst. Just

a beer I guess."

A waiter appeared like magic and Jake said, "I'll have a Falstaff."

"Very good, sir." He placed a bowl of breadsticks on the table and left.

"How do you like *El Pueblo de Nuestro la Señora de Los Angeles de Porciuncula?*" Jake asked Bill Hearst.

"Whatever is that? One of the Spanish missions?"

"No sir, that's this town's full name. Los Angeles is the short version."

"I see. I would write that down except I'm sure I'll never need it. How do I like it? I can't say yet. I'm still getting acclimated. Now then, I understand you were one of father's favorite reporters. Broke a lot of big stories during the war and afterward, but that now you're an editor."

"Right, sir, assistant managing editor, but I still chase down a story now and then. I like to keep my hand in."

"I see. And you coauthored a book about the war. You have quite a record with the *Herald.*"

The beer arrived. The waiter poured most of it into a glass, laid down two menus, and left.

Hearst raised his martini glass and said "Cheers." His glass was a delicate little thing so Jake didn't clink his against it, merely held it close.

Glancing off to his left, Hearst asked, "Is that Ava Gardner over there?" Looking impressed.

"Yeah, I believe so."

"She looks just as attractive as she does on screen. Who's that fellow with her?"

"Don't know, sir. Maybe her agent or a writer from a fan magazine."

Out-of-towners often got all googly-eyed when seeing a real live movie star. For locals it was old hat. *Don't go and ask for an autograph*, Jake urged silently.

Hearst took a cigarette from an elegant silver case and offered it to Jake. "Thanks, sir, I don't smoke."

Picking up a Polo Lounge matchbook, Hearst lit it for himself and slipped the matchbook in a pocket. Souvenir.

Hearst cleared his throat and said, "Now then, that was a very damning story today in the *Times*."

Jake knew that chicken would come home to roost.

"Is it true? Did this man get his facts straight? Were you really up there in the middle of the night where Mr. Franklin was murdered?"

Jake admitted that yes it was true, and trotted out his story about trying to uncover an illegal craps game but that it turned out he'd got a false tip.

"I see. You were after one of the stories you still occasionally try to chase down?"

"Right, sir. It was a bad idea. I'm sure sorry I embarrassed the paper the way I did."

Hearst drove plumes of smoke from his nostrils and with a steely look said, "As well you should be. I don't know who will take over Franklin's practice and what we will do now about legal representation here for our papers." He dropped his gaze and turned to the menu. "I'm staying here temporarily, as you may know, and I rather fancy the McCarthy salad."

Jake had never heard of the McCarthy salad. "What's in that, sir?" he asked, picking up his own menu. "I've only eaten here once before."

Hearst described it: "Grilled chicken, eggs, romaine lettuce, bacon, a few other things." The waiter reappeared and that's what he ordered. Jake, who didn't have much appetite, asked for the tuna salad.

"I don't know a great deal about running newspapers,"

Hearst said when the waiter was gone, "but I'm a fast learner. I will need advice, though. Jack Campbell strikes me as a worthy editor and I've heard good things about Miss Underwood." He took a last hit on his cigarette and snuffed it out in a crystal ashtray. Sipped some of his martini. "They could be helpful to me."

Hearst said he'd met with Jack Campbell and he'd had good things to say about Jake. "I've not met Miss Underwood yet, but we'll be having breakfast tomorrow. As to you, Mr. Weaver, you are obviously a splendid reporter, if a bit reckless, but I have no idea how you stack up as an editor."

"Pardon my candor, sir, but I'm a damn good editor, one of the best at tutoring young reporters."

"Are you?" Said with a chill squint. "I could do one of three things with you." He held up a finger. "Let you continue in your present role." A second finger went up. "Put you back to reporting, which you do so well." A third finger. "Or simply release you."

"Of course that's your call, sir. If you do number three, I could get a job with a rival paper within an hour, but I sure hope I won't have to. I've given thirteen years of my life to the good old *H-E*."

The meals arrived at that moment and Hearst picked up a fork. "As you can see, I have a lot to think about," he said.

And so do I, Jake thought.

CHAPTER THIRTY-ONE

October 1943. Melbourne, Australia.

Kenny did kiss Sophie, a chaste little tap on the lips. Then he pulled away from her arms, got to his feet and headed for the door. No way was he going to get sexually involved. "Thanks for a fine lunch," he said. "Now I really have to go. The best of luck to you."

Sophie sat there looking frustrated, her mouth open.

Kenny closed the door behind him and hustled down the stairs. Once outside, heading toward the street, he heard his name called. Glancing back, he saw Sophie standing on the front stoop looking sad and forlorn. Hands open, palms forward as if saying, "What?"

He gave a little wave, quickened his steps and soon was far down the street. It was about half a mile back to camp. It would give him time to think.

Sophie was a good woman. Good but sad, lost, and hungry for affection. She was in a bad marriage but could get out of it. Maybe she was already out of it. She was probably right that her husband was dead. He hoped she would find happiness some day.

Had he seen the last of her? He was pretty sure he had. She could come to the base but wouldn't get anywhere. He hadn't told her his last name or what outfit he was with. He'd be just one of a horde of lieutenants there.

A streetcar rattled past, soon followed by a kid on a bike.

If he wasn't engaged to the sweetest girl in the world, Kenny told himself, a little roll in the Aussie hay would have been swell. But he *was* engaged to the sweetest girl in the world and glad of it.

A happy memory surfaced. He and Claudia were holding hands in the sunny courtyard of the fleet hospital on Espiritu Santo Island under a spreading banyan tree. A breeze off the Coral Sea washed over them. He got down on a knee and asked if she'd do him the great honor of consenting to be his wife. In accepting, she said, "If there's a God I thank him for sending you to me."

Kenny hoped they could be married on his next leave. That would be on Guadalcanal, where Claudia now worked in the new fleet hospital there. They could find a Protestant chaplain to perform the ceremony.

Kenny visualized her hazel-green eyes and auburn hair. Her quiet smile, her slender figure. He always carried that snapshot in his mind. He wished this darn war would be over soon so he could be with her all the time.

A B-25 Mitchell bomber came into view with U.S. markings on its wings and fuselage, a stark reminder that he would see more war, probably a lot more.

CHAPTER THIRTY-TWO

That could have been worse, Jake thought as he turned his Chevy Deluxe onto Wilshire from Beverly Drive and began the slog through L.A. traffic back to the paper. At least Hearst Junior hadn't asked about Marion Davies, was I close to her and so forth. He surely detests the woman and I would've had to do a little tap dancing. The tuna salad was good, though.

Jake wasn't a big fan of the *Times* but liked it better than the *Mirror* and *Daily News*. If he got fired, maybe that's where he'd go. Its publisher, Norman Chandler, had made overtures a couple of times. But had Al Baxter's story queered that? A possibility.

Those thoughts were bouncing around in his head when he heard the whine of a siren. In his rear-view mirror he saw a red fire truck approaching fast, lights flashing. He pulled to the curb along with several other cars and let it scream past. His reporter instinct said follow it, see where the fire is. But no, he wasn't a reporter anymore. So, he took a right onto Vermont and headed south.

When he was at last back at the paper, Aggie Underwood ambled over and asked, "How did it go with Junior?"

"Not bad, though he said he might fire me."

"Fire you?"

Jake told about the three options Hearst had laid out. "He was pretty steamed about Al Baxter's story. I hear you're having breakfast with him tomorrow."

"Yeah, that'll be a thrill. I'll fight for you."

"Naw, don't do that, Aggie, I'll let my chips fall where they may. Just relax and enjoy it. He's an interesting guy.

Got all starry-eyed when he saw Ava Gardner sitting across from us."

"One of those, huh? I'll be candid as hell with him, that's for sure. Won't take any shit."

"You never do, Aggie. You're a tough . . . uh, lady."

"You were about to say old broad, weren't you?"

"Me? No way, Aggie."

"Liar. Well, okay then, Jake. See you later."

Jake picked up a copy of the day's second edition and there on the front page was the story Aggie had dictated. The head said: CLAIM THAT OUR MAN'S A MURDER SUSPECT IS FALSE.

Good for Aggie. Bless the old broad's heart.

His daughter Ilse came over for dinner that night full of questions. She'd seen the story in the *Times*. As he'd done with everyone else, Jake admitted that he'd been at Franklin's office and that had been stupid of him.

"Why on earth was Bela Lugosi with you, *Vati*?"

"Since he had that burglary experience, I was hoping he could get me into that office. I gave him a few bucks. I suppose the school will cancel his talk to the drama students now?"

"No, not at all. They're even more excited to have him come."

"No kidding? Notoriety trumps prudence. I'd love to go and sit in on that but no, I'd best keep a low profile on all of this."

"Darn right you should," said Valerie, who was arranging a green salad.

Jake had cooked up some spaghetti to go with French bread and the salad. When everything was ready, they sat around the table. Valerie poured some Sonoma cabernet into their glasses.

"I want to help you figure out who killed Mr. Franklin," Ilse said. "Where would we start?"

"We?" Jake asked, but then said, "Maybe that's not a bad idea; you're a darn good reporter. For starters, I'd like to find out about Franklin's family, his wife and kids, if he had any, and I think he did. I also want to look into his assistant, an attorney named Amy Noonan."

Valerie sipped some wine and said, "Exposing Standard Oil's profiteering in Nazi Germany was only the start? Now you intrepid reporters are going to solve a murder, is that it?"

"Absolutely, *Muti*, we've got to get *Vati* off the hook and stick it up that Al Baxter's ass."

"Ilse!" Valerie thumped her wineglass down hard. "Such language."

"Sorry, *Muti*, but that's how I feel. That's how reporters talk, right, *Vati*?"

"See there, Jake? You've corrupted the child."

Jake: "First off, she's not a child and—"

"With the things I've seen," Ilse interrupted, "especially in Germany, I was corrupted long ago. The Gestapo hauling terrified civilians out of their homes. Dead women and children, their bodies torn apart in shattered streets after the bombers came over. You have no idea."

"You're right," Valerie said softly. "You can swear all you like."

"I only swear selectively, *Muti*, like when *das Arschloch* reporter smeared *Vati*'s character."

"Das Ashcock?" Valerie asked, mispronouncing it.

"It's German. I'll tell you sometime."

Jake, twirling some spaghetti onto his fork, couldn't

hide a grin.

He and Ilse began talking about who would do what: look into Amy Noonan or Mrs. Franklin?

Valerie surprised them, saying, "I'll do Mrs. Franklin."

"You?" Jake and Ilse said almost in unison.

"Sure. I'm guessing we're close to the same age, though she might be a little older. You'd scare her to death, Jake, and she'd be unlikely to open up to a kid —pardon me, Ilse — to a young woman who swears in two languages."

"Three reporters in the family now?" Jake said. "I'm not sure I like that, Val."

"No, not reporters, detectives," Valerie insisted. "And bullshit — I guess coarse language is the thing today — if you don't like it. I really want to do this, for the same reason as Ilse. We've got to clear your name. First I'll need to find out if Franklin was married."

Jake laughed inwardly. Detective Wannamaker had told him to keep out of this but he hadn't mentioned Valerie. "I'm pretty sure he was married. I saw two pictures of a woman on his desk — must've been his wife."

"Okay Jake and next, where does he live? There can't be too many Edwin Franklin's in the phone book."

"I can ask Johnny Campbell, Val. He'll know if he was married and maybe also where he lived. Meanwhile, I'll talk with Amy Noonan."

"What about me?" Ilse declaimed. "You guys are hogging all this."

"Don't worry, kiddo," Jake said. "We'll come up with something. Maybe one of Franklin's kids. There were two boys along with the presumed wife in one of those pictures I saw on his desk. They were probably his sons."

"But do you really think his sons could be suspects?" Ilse asked with a quizzical squint. "Kill their own father?"

"It's been known to happen. There was a case last year in Downey, a twelve-year-old. Said his father was mean, used to beat him, so he shot him with his dad's own gun."

Talk gradually turned elsewhere as the three of them finished up their dinner. "How's your roommate Claudia doing?" Valerie asked Ilse.

"Fine, *Muti*. She's working real hard on her pre-med studies. Hopes to start her residency in a year or so."

"I wonder how her poor old hubby Kenny's doing in that Navy hospital," Valerie said.

"I don't know the latest. She hasn't said anything about that in awhile, been so busy with her anatomy studies and all. I know she's worried about him, though."

Jake finished off his wine and said, "I'm gonna go down there and see him one of these days."

After dinner, Ilse took Jake aside and said, "I'd like to know more about my real mother, *Vati*, what she was like. I've been thinking a lot about that lately."

Jake took her hand and led her into the front room. Ilse took a seat on the sofa and Jake plopped onto his favorite easy chair facing her.

"I was in Berlin in 1930 for the memorial service for my Aunt Marta," he began. "She was Uncle Dieter's wife, you know. Winifred was a friend of Marta and Dieter. I met her at the service. We hit it off right away. She was clever and smart, and oozed with personality."

"What did she look like, *Vati*?"

Valerie stuck her head around the corner at that moment. "Is this private talk?" she asked. "Would it bother you if I listened in?"

"You've heard some of this before, Sweets, but I don't mind. Do you, Ilse?"

"No, of course not, *Muti*." Valerie came over and sat on

the sofa close to Ilse.

"You asked what Winni looked like," Jake said. "She was very pretty. Green eyes and dark blond hair."

"Then I got more of your genes than hers," said Ilse, whose reddish hair and brown eyes were much like Jake's.

"We talked about the chaotic politics at that time in Germany, how the Weimar Republic was staggering and the ugly street brawls between the communists and this furious new Nazi party. Winni had become a communist because she thought they offered a better path, an answer to the powerful industrial barons who were holding the common people down. I didn't buy all her arguments but she articulated them well. She was an insightful conversationalist. I took her to dinner that night and afterward, well . . . are you sure you want to hear this, Val?"

"No problem, Sailor. We wouldn't meet for years yet. You were a free, healthy young man back then."

"Okay then. I guess you can tell what happened later that night, and then for the next two more. We had a three-day affair."

"I knew you'd made love, obviously," Ilse said, "or else I wouldn't be here. But I didn't know what she looked like or what kind of mind she had. Thank you for telling me this."

"Sure, *Liebchen*. When I left Berlin she said she would never forget me. I said I hoped I could see her again someday, but of course that never happened. I had no idea she was pregnant and she never wrote to tell me."

"And then the Nazis came to power," Ilse said, "and they murdered her in a concentration camp. Those evil *Schwein*." A tear began to dampen her cheek. "*Mutter* was intelligent then and had spunk. I am so glad to know this." She got up and gave her father a warm hug.

Ilse left soon after that but not before kissing Valerie

on the cheek and saying, "I have two mothers, and you are a most *wunderbar* one."

On his drive to work in the morning, Jake noticed that a black Ford, maybe 1948 or '49, had been behind him for quite awhile. Sometimes it was directly behind, other times a car or two back. He had no idea why somebody would be tailing him, but he didn't like it.

Nearing the paper, when he turned from Pico to Georgia Street to park, the car rolled on past. The driver tried to divert his head but Jake caught a glimpse of his profile. Sam Sixto! The detective who still thought he'd killed Franklin. Anger swept over Jake like a hot wind.

CHAPTER THIRTY-THREE

As he slipped into his office and hung up his hat and coat, Jake wondered why in hell Sixto would be tailing him. Did the guy think he might have been going to some suspicious place, a gun shop or something? Or to Mickey Cohen's? Sixto might know he was a friend of the mobster. That wasn't exactly a secret.

Well, Sixto could go screw himself. Let the fool suspect him all he wants. Jake had other things to do.

It was Friday and he'd decided to go to San Diego tomorrow and visit his friend Kenny Nielsen. He called Detective Wannamaker at Central Division. Wannamaker wasn't in so he left a message for him to call.

Which he did fifteen minutes later.

"Hi Owen, thanks for getting back to me. I promised to let you know if I was leaving town, so, I am. Going to San Diego tomorrow to see my friend Colonel Nielsen in the naval hospital down there. Poor guy was wounded in Korea. It'll be a quick trip. I'll be back that night." He decided not to tell Wannamaker that he was tailed by Sixto that morning. That might sound paranoid. Sixto might tell him anyway. Or not.

"Okay Jake, now don't be slipping into Mexico," Wannamaker said with a little laugh. "Thanks for letting me know. Say, the medical examiner is through with Franklin. We're releasing his body to the wife. There'll be a funeral service Monday at Holy Cross Cemetery."

"Thanks, Owen. Maybe the wife and I will go."

After Jake hung up, Aggie Underwood came in.

"Hi Aggie. How'd breakfast with Hearst Junior go?"

"Not bad, but the guy hasn't a clue what he's doing. I told him we were doing fine here and he didn't need to be making any quick changes."

"What'd he say to that?"

"Just that he'd take that under advisement. I put in a good word for you. He said he'd take that under advisement too."

"Thanks, Aggie. So it's business as usual for the time being till we see what Junior does?"

"Right. Did you see the *Times*' rebuttal of our rebuttal? Said maybe you and Dracula weren't officially suspects but it was still damn suspicious that you were up there near the man's door. No point in our answering that. Let's let this be the end of this little pissing match."

Reaching San Diego the next day, Jake turned off Pacific Highway at A Street, rolled up A to Park Boulevard, passed San Diego High, and parked at the big pink naval hospital. It perched on a hilltop overlooking downtown and the harbor.

Valerie, busy with the Viking rocket series at Lockheed, said she had to work overtime that Saturday, so Jake went by himself.

He'd been here before so he knew how to find Kenny's room. Reaching it, he stopped in the open doorway and saw a nurse standing at the bed with a thermometer in her left hand.

Kenny looked up and with a broad smile said, "Hey, Jake, great! Come on in." His head was propped up on two pillows, his face drawn and tired. A plaster cast encased his left leg, from the foot to three-quarters up the thigh.

"Say hello to Rosie," he said. "Wonderful nurse."

"Being an expert on nurses, you should know, being married to a great one yourself." Kenny didn't smile as much at his remark as Jake had expected.

"You must be Mr. Weaver, the coauthor," Rosie said. She extended her right hand and Jake took it. Rosie had red hair, similar to Jake's, a heart-shaped face, lively green eyes, cheeks like peaches.

"I've heard a lot about you and the book you two wrote," she said. "A pleasure to meet you." She tucked the thermometer in a pocket on her white smock. "Ninety-nine-one today," she said to Kenny. "Not bad, sweetie."

Sweetie? Jake wondered. Well, it probably didn't mean anything. Some women tossed the word out casually.

Rosie said, "He's a swell patient. I'll take off now and let you fellows do your man talk."

Jake peeked at her calves and ankles as she left. He always appreciated nice legs. He turned, pulled up a chair and sat beside the bed. "Sorry I haven't been down here enough lately, Kenny. Been damn busy. So how's it going?"

"Real frustrating. I'm so darn tired of this room. And this cast. Sometimes it itches like crazy under there. Once in awhile one of the nurses wheels me outside, though, so I can get some sun."

Jake lightly touched the cast. "How much longer will you be strapped up in this thing?"

"Don't know. The docs aren't very forthcoming about that. When it does come off, they say I'll have a long period of rehab. Now what have you been busy with, Jake?"

"For starters I'm a murder suspect."

Kenny chuckled. "Oh sure."

"It's not a joke, I really am." Jake proceeded to tell about it. How his efforts to help Marion Davies avoid getting shafted by the Hearst family had led him to Ed Franklin's office at night, where he'd found the man shot to death. That he'd tried to convince the police that he hadn't actually entered the room.

Kenny asked a lot of questions about all that and Jake filled him in.

"You need to find the real killer and get yourself cleared."

"Exactly. Ilse's going to help me with that."

"Good for her. How is that swell daughter of yours? And Valerie too?"

"They're fine. Valerie's busy on her rocket thing and Ilse is studying like mad."

"I'm glad she and Claudia are sharing an apartment," Kenny said. "Does Ilse say much about Claudia?"

"Not a whole lot, just that she's buried in her pre-med studies." Jake caught a slight grimace on Kenny's face.

"Yeah, I know she is. She's real eager to get through this and become a doctor. I wish she'd visit more, though, or at least call more often. It's no fun being away from her like this." *Like a knife in the heart.*

Jake felt his anguish, but didn't know what to say to that, so he turned the conversation elsewhere. He mentioned detective Sixto's annoying suspicions about him, and that even Bela Lugosi was involved in this.

"Bela Lugosi? Man, that you'll have to explain."

Kenny smiled a time or two as Jake did explain.

"Count Dracula used to be a cat burglar? Imagine that."

"Yep, he's an interesting old guy. His film career went down the crapper and he's got a drug problem. Hasn't got a pot to piss in or a window to throw it out of, but with all of that, still pretty likeable. Say, can I get you something? Some snacks or magazines, anything like that?"

"Naw, thanks. They're taking good care of me."

"I s'pose you don't want to talk about Korea?"

"Nope." Kenny's face became a hard mask. "I'm now a pacifist. Dyed in the wool. My God, the strategic mistakes MacArthur made out there."

Yeah, this poor guy's suffered too much. Way too much.

Jake changed the subject, told how Bela Lugosi was going to speak to UCLA's drama students.

When it came time for him to leave an hour later, he said, "That Rosie's a good-looking babe. Seems nice, too."

"She's terrific. I think a lot of her."

Hmm, Jake thought.

"Well, so long buddy. Keep your chin up. Next time I'll try and bring Val and Ilse with me. Maybe sneak in some booze, too."

Jake drove off, heading toward downtown. He planned to go to the Press Room, a joint across the street from the *Union-Tribune* building at 919 Second. It was a newspaper hangout, San Diego's version of L.A.'s Continental. He'd grab a sandwich and a brew and maybe he'd know some of the news people in there.

As he turned from Park onto Broadway, he had one of his wicked thoughts. Could Kenny do it, with his leg all cemented up like that? Yeah, probably, if the gal was on top.

CHAPTER THIRTY-FOUR

Valerie didn't have to work overtime at Lockheed that Saturday. That was a white lie she'd cooked up so Jake wouldn't know what she was up to. She thought he didn't really like the idea of her sleuthing, even though he'd agreed to it — she knew her hubby pretty well. She decided to act quickly, before he changed his mind.

She looked up Edwin Franklin in the phone book. There were three of them. One was down south in Watts, one in the valley, Van Nuys, and the third on Larchmont Street in West L.A., actually only eight or nine blocks from her own home. The first two were unlikely to be the dead lawyer's, so she drove her Plymouth Mayfair out to the one in West L.A.

Valerie found it to be a cream-colored craftsman with green trim, a manicured lawn and several bougainvillea plants. She parked, strode to the house, heels clattering on the sidewalk, and pushed the bell.

Moments later the woman answered. Paisley housedress, leather sandals, neatly cut brown hair showing some gray. "Yes?"

"Good morning, ma'am. I'm Valerie Weaver, wife of Jake Weaver, the reporter. I'm so sorry about your husband. You certainly have my condolences. I know this is a bad time for you, but could I ask you a few questions?"

"The police have already asked me a lot of questions." Looking irritated. "They act like I'm a suspect too. I'm really not in the mood—"

"Please, ma'am. I'll only take a few minutes of your time."

"Okay then, if you must." Reluctantly, Mrs. Franklin opened the door wider and stepped aside. "Come on in."

The front room contained a fabric sofa, two easy chairs, end table, lamps, and a large walnut TV-radio console. No family photos in sight.

Mrs. Franklin gestured toward the sofa. "Have a seat, Mrs. Weaver. Would you like some coffee?"

"No thanks, ma'am, and please call me Valerie."

"All right, and I'm Penny." She sat in a facing chair and crossed her legs. "Two detectives came to see me," she said. "One of them was pretty rude. Said the wife is often the guilty party when a man is murdered." Her right hand became a fist. "They wanted to know if I was the beneficiary of his life insurance. I said, 'Sure, that's normal, so what?' Oh how I wanted to throw them out."

"I'm sure it was rough for you, Penny."

"Now what is it I can tell you, Missus, er, Valerie?"

"Neither you nor my husband did this, Penny. So who do you think might have? Did he have any enemies?"

"The police asked the same thing. None that I know of, but as a lawyer he didn't win every case. Maybe some client who'd lost felt Ed had let him down, someone who harbored a grudge over that. Who knows?"

"Do you have children, Penny?"

"Two sons, Freddie, he's 17, and Tommy, 13. The cops asked if they got along with their father. Had he been mean to them? Those darn fools, suspecting my own sweet kids."

"I hate to ask this, Penny, but were you happily married?"

Penny grimaced. "You sure you're not a cop? Coming at me from a different direction? You sound just like they did."

Valerie tried a laugh. It didn't come off too well. "I'm certainly not a cop. I'm actually a novice rocket engineer at

Lockheed." She reached for her purse. "I can show you my factory ID."

"No, never mind. Sorry I even said that. I'm pretty touchy these days. You can probably understand that."

"Of course I can. So, was your marriage okay?"

"I'm happily married . . . for the most part. Ed is, was, very busy with his practice, though. Worked long hours, was occasionally gone overnight."

Gone overnight? Valerie pondered that.

"I'd hoped to have more togetherness than we did. I suppose a lot of marriages are like that in these busy times. Working like you do, maybe you don't see your hubby as much as you'd like?"

Jake was often away from home, had even gone overseas a lot, but Valerie wasn't going to bring that up. "Sometimes," she said, "but we make it a point to make our time together as special as we can."

"Good for you. Now if you were a cop you'd ask if there were any guns in the house. The answer is yes, an old .45 Ed picked up in the war. He was an officer in Europe. The thing hasn't been fired in years. They say Ed was killed with a .22, not a .45."

A sad look crept across Penny's face. "I think he cheated on me a few times over there. There are lots of pretty women in France, you know. But I forgive, or rather forgave him. Who doesn't give in to temptation once in a while?" Said with a slight drop of an eyelid, almost a wink.

Penny was rather pretty, Valerie thought, probably beautiful ten years ago. Was she saying she'd fooled around too?

Penny said, "I'm sure there are some good-looking fellows in your factory, Valerie."

"I've been hustled a few times, but I always turn them

down. I'm very happy with Jake."

After a few more moments of conversation, questions that didn't lead to much of anything, Valerie took her leave. "Goodbye then, Penny. Thanks for letting me talk with you."

Back in her car, Valerie thought: Her husband had cheated on her and she played around too. *She could have done it.*

Passing San Clemente on his way back to L.A., Jake dismissed that wicked thought he'd had. Sure, Kenny was attracted to that pretty nurse Rosie; who wouldn't be? But he wasn't the type to mess around. Although he was screwed up both physically and emotionally, needed affection, he was straight arrow, very devoted to his Claudia. *Sometimes you've just got a weird mind, Jake.*

He hadn't met any newsmen he knew in the Press Room, but he'd had an entertaining conversation with a muscular black fellow who'd introduced himself as Archie Moore. Moore was a contender for the world light-heavyweight boxing championship. Jake had mentioned his own boxing days in the Navy and they'd had a great chat.

Jake had a beer but Moore was drinking lemonade. He said he was in training for an upcoming fight against Chubby Wright. He'd just been interviewed across the street by a sportswriter, Phil Collier.

He asked about Jake's own career. "I was 22 and 6," Jake said. "Was briefly the middleweight champ of the 6th Naval District till the day I ran up against a Mexican kid with hands like lightning. That was the end of my so-called boxing career."

Highway 101 took Jake through every darn beach town. It was a long slog. He knew a San Diego-to-Los Angeles freeway was on the drawing boards but construction hadn't started.

In Laguna Beach, there was that raggedy old man with a long gray beard and shaggy hair, standing beside the road waving at every car. Jake waved back. The eccentric old coot was an institution in this town.

Jake thought about Bill Hearst Junior and wondered if he'd still have a job at the end of the month. That and Kenny's condition threw him into a gloomy mood. The guy faced a long hard road to recovery. That stupid war. A stupid war Jake had predicted in print. After the Chinese Reds had swarmed in by the thousands and driven U.N. forces out of North Korea, the fighting had turned into bloody stalemate. Good young kids losing their lives, and for what?

Since Valerie had done okay at Penny Franklin's, she decided to go ahead and tell Jake what she'd done.

It was 5 o'clock when she heard him pull into the driveway. She poured a couple glasses of Dewar's White Label, added some ice. Jake came in, looking drained.

"Long drive, huh, Sailor? You don't look happy." She handed him a glass. "Maybe this will help."

"Thanks, hon. Just what I needed." He took a drink and grinned. "Let's have a seat in the front room and I'll tell you all about it." They sat together on the sofa and set their glasses on the coffee table.

"Poor Kenny's got his leg cocooned in a huge cast," Jake said. "Only gets out of bed once in awhile in a wheelchair so he can get outside for some sun. He's pretty down, wishes Claudia would come see him more often."

"She's real busy with her studies, Jake, but I wish she would too."

"At least he's got a good nurse. Swell gal. Sorry you had to work today, Sweets. How'd it go?"

Valerie took a sip of Scotch and said, "I didn't have to work after all, so I went and saw Ed Franklin's wife."

"Really? How'd you manage to find the woman?"

"I looked it up in the phone book. The Franklins actually don't live very far from here. She wasn't happy to see me at first. Real sore at the cops for suspecting her. She finally warmed up a bit, though, and we had an interesting talk. She wasn't too happily married and thinks Ed had cheated on her."

"Really? Ed Franklin?"

"Yes, and she basically let on that she'd been unfaithful too."

"Yikes. A rocky marriage for sure. Maybe she killed him after all."

"That's what I thought too, Jake."

"Good work, Val, really good work." He leaned over and gave her his A number one kiss.

"Mmm, you've still got it, big boy. Say, I'll bet you're famished. I've got a couple of nice big steaks we can broil. And afterward . . ."

Jake felt better than he had in hours.

CHAPTER THIRTY-FIVE

In the morning Jake called Ed Franklin's erstwhile assistant and asked if he could stop by. Amy Noonan said she had to take a deposition but she'd be glad to see him at 2 o'clock.

Jake trudged over to the *Examiner* building a little before two and hiked up the stairs to the third floor. His spine tingled as he passed Ed Franklin's office on his way to Amy's. It was eerie being here for the first time since that fateful night, looking at the door Bela Lugosi had so easily opened. If there had been any crime-scene tape it was gone now.

After he knocked on Amy Noonan's door it was opened by a fiftyish woman he didn't know. Stern look on her face. "Mr. Weaver, I assume?"

"That's me, ma'am."

"I'm Edith Harris. I am, or was, Mr. Franklin's secretary." Jake hadn't seen this woman before — she hadn't been in Franklin's office when Jake met the man a week ago. She said, "I'm temporarily with Miss Noonan now, sorting through Mr. Franklin's files and so forth. I'm hoping to make the arrangement permanent."

She needs the job, Jake thought. He figured her distrustful look meant she thought he might be the killer. She'd probably seen the stories in the *Times*. "I hope you can make it permanent too, Miss Harris," he said.

"It's Mrs. Harris, sir," she corrected him. "Please have a seat. I expect Miss Noonan any minute now."

Jake took a chair facing Amy Noonan's desk and said,

"I'm sure it was a great shock finding the body as you did. Must've been terrible for you. Was Ed a good boss?"

"Heavens to Betsy, yes. Mr. Franklin was a fine man."

Jake heard heels clacking in the hallway. "That must be Miss Noonan now," the woman said. "Would you like some coffee?"

"Sure, black please." Jake saw a small desk off to the side, apparently Harris's, plus a water dispenser and a hotplate bearing a coffee pot.

Amy Noonan came in carrying a briefcase and said, "Hello there, Mr. Weaver. Hope I haven't kept you waiting long."

"Nope, just got here. The name is Jake, remember?"

"That's right, Jake it is." She tossed her case on the desk and took her seat behind it. Edith Harris brought Jake a cup. He said thanks.

He got out his notebook and said, "Appreciate you seeing me, Amy. We agreed I should call you Amy, didn't we?"

"We certainly did, Jake." Flashing a smile.

Speaking softly, head turned away from Mrs. Harris, Jake said, "I wonder if we could speak privately."

"Sure. Edith, would you run down to Ed's office for awhile? Look for those Flannery files we talked about this morning."

"Of course, Miss Noonan." Harris turned and left, looking reluctant before closing the door behind her.

"Thanks again for showing me that Hearst trust the other day," Jake began. "Real nice of you." He would bring up the killing and who might have done it later. "You mentioned that you'd like to get a newspaper job as a legal writer," he went on. "Our paper has a freeze on new hires till Bill Junior takes over, but I've got good contacts at the

Times. I'll see if I can get you an interview."

"That would be swell, Jake. Thanks a bunch. I could show you a piece I did awhile back for the local law journal on child-abuse issues."

"Sure, Amy. I'd like to see your writing style." Jake picked up his cup and drank some coffee. "Ed refused to show me Hearst's will, you know. If it's not asking too much, would you do that for me?"

"Since you're going to help me with the *Times*, sure, I'll be glad to. Tit for tat."

"That's swell, thanks. Now then, who do you suppose killed Ed?" Was it you? he wondered.

"I've been racking my brain on that, Jake. He was having some problems at home but I don't think his wife would have killed him, and certainly not in his office."

"Why not in his office? She'd have had lots more trouble if she shot him at home. Have a body to dispose of, a mess to clean up."

"Well yes, I hadn't thought of that."

"So he was having wife trouble. Did he mess around? Make a play for you, for instance?"

"He made a few suggestive remarks once in awhile, but kind of playfully. He never actually propositioned me."

"You're very attractive, Amy. If I wasn't married . . ."

"Why thank you, Jake." Said with a smile. "What a nice compliment. As to Ed's playing around, though, yes, I think he might have."

The murder possibilities seemed endless. A jilted girlfriend? An unhappy client? Franklin's wife?

"Can you think of any clients who might be sore at him?" Jake asked. "Maybe lost a fortune?"

"Not really. He did some case law but the Hearst papers were by far his biggest client."

"Will you be able to take over his practice?"

Amy gave a doleful laugh. "Probably not without letting half the Hearst boys ride me. No, I think the old woman will get someone with more pedigree. That's one of the reasons I'd like to make a change."

Edith Harris returned just then, carrying a couple of files. "Is it all right if I come in now?"

"Sure," Amy said. "Take care of the place for a minute. Mr. Weaver and I are going down to Ed's office for a bit."

"Thanks for the coffee," Jake said. "It was good."

He and Amy walked down to Franklin's office. That quiver chilled his spine again when he saw a dark spot on the carpet, the blood stain not completely wiped away.

Amy opened a cabinet and leafed through some files. "Ah, here we are," she said and handed Jake Hearst's will.

He sat in a chair and began to read. "Being of sound mind and body, et cetera," he said. "Hmm, the great majority goes to Millicent Hearst and the sons, with small bequests to the March of Dimes, the Huntington Library, and Julia Morgan. If I remember right, Julia Morgan was his master architect at San Simeon."

"That's right, she was," Amy said.

"I see here," Jake continued, "that a codicil leaves Miss Davies the Beverly Drive house and its contents, but not a darn bit of money. I'm surprised. And disappointed. How come no money here for Miss Davies, Amy?"

"I don't know. Ed never said anything to me about that. I'm surprised too."

Jake jotted in his notebook, then handed the will back. Amy replaced it in the file cabinet. "Thanks again," Jake said. "I'll be on my way then. I'll get back to you about an interview with someone at the *Times*."

Amy gave him a little hug and he got a whiff of that

jasmine perfume, *nice*, before they walked off in different directions.

Nothing in the will for Marion Davies besides the house? he thought, going down the stairs. Even so, she was pretty well fixed. Handled her money well, made some good real estate deals. And in that trust she gets a big chunk of Hearst preferred stock and full voting rights in the corporation – *if* that holds up.

He was getting a little traction on the Marion Davies thing, but none at all on who killed Ed Franklin. He doubted it was Amy Noonan.

CHAPTER THIRTY-SIX

October 1944.

Peleliu was the worst. Kenny Nielsen had thought nothing could be more savage and terrifying than Guadalcanal, but then had come Cape Gloucester. The 1st Marine Division had been temporarily attached to the Army, which they'd hated. Marines under the Army? General MacArthur had sent them ashore on New Britain Island, close to Cape Gloucester. They were ordered to capture an enemy airfield so bombers could blast the big Japanese base at Rabaul, 200 miles away on the far side of the island.

It made no sense to Kenny. The U.S. by now had air bases within range of Rabaul and was already bombing the place. If you want to take an enemy base, *attack* the enemy base, don't lollygag around in the jungle miles away. A first lieutenant, Kenny commanded a company. He'd lost a lot of men there, and for what?

After the Cape, the division was blessedly detached from MacArthur's command and returned to the Solomons to rest and reorganize. Then had come the dumbest order of all: Invade Peleliu. Navy and Marine Corps strategists weren't any smarter than MacArthur after all. Peleliu was a Jap-held island in the Palau group, 300 miles east of the Philippines, America's next objective in the Pacific. Kenny didn't see what strategic value it had and neither could his CO, Colonel Harris.

In U.S. hands, Peleliu was too far away to be able to support the Army in the Philippines, nor could the Japanese threaten them if left to control the place. Leave the damn island alone!

But orders were orders, so the Old Breed, as the division was called, mounted up and invaded Peleliu. It was supposed to be an easy op, taking two or three days. Ha! The terrain was steep and mountainous, and the enemy had rugged defensive positions in the high ground. The slaughter on both sides became horrific, gains measured in meters, not miles. Heroic corpsmen were busy as hell with all the wounded. Resupply became a huge problem. Kenny's outfit was running out of ammunition and water. Almost dead center on the equator, Peleliu was an island wrapped in heat, the air so heavy with humidity he could almost chew it.

He could still smell the stench of roasted flesh when a flame-thrower team had burned out a Jap cave. He gagged whenever that horrible memory surfaced.

Kenny lost close to half his company, including too many good friends. One of them was Clint "Hoagy" Carmichael, a superb rifleman and a guy with a great sense of humor. He'd been one of Kenny's favorites.

The final objective was an eminence called Bloody Nose Ridge. Damn well named. When they finally took Bloody Nose and Peleliu was secured, seven weeks had passed. Two or three days? What a cruel joke that was.

Yep, Peleliu was the worst, tougher than Guadalcanal or Cape Gloucester.

Now Kenny was aboard ship, en route to the Solomons again. What horror would be next? Okinawa maybe?

Colonel Harris called him in and congratulated him on the leadership of his company. Congratulations? Hell, his casualties had been huge. Harris promoted him to captain and gave him command of a battalion. Kenny should have been elated, but he wasn't. His mind's eye kept seeing those hundreds of fresh graves back on that vile island, an island that had no value to America's war aims. One of the graves was Hoagy Carmichael's. At Hoagy's crude wooden cross Kenny's knees had given way and he'd fallen to the ground, sobbing.

He was visiting some of the wounded when the ship's klaxon blared and the squawk box bleated, "General quarters, general quarters!" An enemy sub was sighted nearby. What now? A torpedo attack? He felt the ship heel to starboard and pick up speed. As he scurried back to his quarters, he was nearly trampled by hordes of sailors scrambling to their battle stations.

Kenny was sick of this damned war. Sick in his heart, sick in his soul. He'd been married only fifteen months. Would he ever see Claudia again? Ever have a chance to settle down with her somewhere and enjoy some postwar years together?

Or would he get torpedoed in the next few minutes and end up swimming with the sharks?

CHAPTER THIRTY-SEVEN

I don't feel right asking for a day off to attend a funeral of someone I don't know," Valerie told Jake on Sunday night. "I'm still the greenhorn in my department, need to make a good impression on my boss."

So Jake went by himself the next day to the services for Ed Franklin at Holy Cross Cemetery in Culver City. He skipped the eulogies in the chapel but watched from beneath an oak tree as the casket was carried out to a black Packard hearse.

Recalling the bullet hole that marred Franklin's face, he doubted it had been an open casket ceremony. He wondered what Mrs. Franklin might have said in there. Two of the pallbearers were teenage boys, looking uncomfortable in black suits probably newly purchased for the occasion. They had to be Franklin's sons. Jake didn't recognize the other bearers, men in somber suits, probably attorney friends.

Once the casket was slid in back, a woman in black, including a veiled hat, came out and took a seat in the hearse as a liveried driver held the door for her. Penny Franklin, of course. Another woman Jake didn't recognize accompanied her.

The other mourners began coming out, twenty-five or thirty of them. Among them Jake spotted detectives Owen Wannamaker and Sam Sixto. Also Amy Noonan, walking with a woman Jake didn't know. Amy wore a charcoal-gray suit and a black pillbox hat. He didn't see Bill Hearst Junior.

The hearse started up and began a slow crawl to the

gravesite, about 300 yards away down a small incline. The others followed on foot. Jake strolled along behind them. It was a pleasant spot, surrounded by oaks, cypresses and palms, with headstones of all sizes situated on stretches of neatly mowed Bermuda grass.

Women in their heels stepped carefully, some tottering a little on the grass. One old lady was being pushed in a wheelchair.

Five or six wooden folding chairs faced the grave. When the hearse opened and the casket was carried over, Mrs. Franklin and some others took seats in the chairs. Everyone else stood around in a semicircle.

Jake took off his hat. He found a spot near the right end of the group from where he could see the widow's profile. She lifted her veil and looked somber — trying to, at least — as she gazed at the coffin. Behind it stood a marble stone maybe four feet high. Jake made out the words "Edwin P. Franklin, 1899 – 1951. Loyal Husband and Father, Faithful Servant of the Law."

A priest stood in front of Mrs. Franklin and intoned some words in Latin, then the familiar "ashes to ashes, dust to dust" and so forth. Penny Franklin held a handkerchief to her face, though she didn't seem to be weeping.

As the casket was slowly lowered into the grave, Jake scanned the crowd. Still no sign of Junior.

He felt a nudge at his arm. "Had to come and take a last look at the guy you offed, huh, Weaver?" said Sam Sixto. Jake felt like hammering the man's face with a hard right. He'd probably go right down, looked like he had a glass chin.

"What a dumb thing to say, Sixto. You know it wasn't me."

"Do I?" Said with an ugly sneer.

"Hello Jake." It was Owen Wannamaker, who'd come

up and taken Sixto by the arm. "Give it a rest, Sam. Come on, let's go, we have work to do."

Jake said, "Hi Owen. Yeah, keep this clown out of my face." When they walked off, Sixto scowling, Jake resisted an urge to go over and say something to Mrs. Franklin. What could he say that wouldn't sound phony? He didn't know the woman and she didn't know him.

He had a few words with Amy Noonan, then hiked back toward his car. He saw the two Franklin boys romping and playfully pushing at each other. *Real broken up, aren't they?*

Jake got back to his car and decided to go and see Marion Davies. Driving up Santa Monica Boulevard, still miffed at Sam Sixto for his dirty crack — at a funeral, no less — he pounded a fist on the steering wheel.

Jake checked the rear view mirror to see if he was being followed. He didn't think so. He'd been a little paranoid since the day Sixto had tailed him. He stopped at a Pure Oil station, went to the phone booth and called ahead. Miss Davies said, "Sure, I'll be glad to see you. Come on out."

Jake hadn't heard from Mickey Cohen in awhile. He wondered if his mobster friend really was looking into the Franklin murder. The car radio was tuned to Country KRKD and Roy Acuff was singing "Blue Eyes Crying in the Rain."

At the mansion on Beverly Drive, the maid answered the door and showed Jake in. She led the way to the library, where Miss Davies was waiting. The maid brought him coffee. Davies herself had a glass of something amber, maybe sherry.

"Miss Davies," Jake said, but she stopped him, saying, "Please now, it's Marion. How long have we known each other?"

"Okay then, Marion. The reason I came is, I wanted to let you know I saw W.R.'s will."

Anticipation widened her eyes. "Really? How did you manage that?"

"I talked his assistant, Amy Noonan, into letting me see it."

"Why would she do that?"

"She'd like to become a journalist, writing on legal matters, so I said I'd help her with some of my contacts."

"And this was her thank-you?"

"I think so. It couldn't have been my excessive charm."

"Oh no?" Davies said with a wink. "I imagine it could have been."

Jake let that pass. "Anyway," he said, "she let me read it, and you get this house and its furnishings but no money." Davies let out an audible gasp and sank heavily onto a chair.

"He left some small bequests to Julia Morgan and some charities, but almost all of it goes to Millicent and the family."

"I see." Looking sad and disillusioned, Davies took a sip from her glass. "I guess I shouldn't be disappointed but I am. Well, to hell with all of them. They had Willie's funeral in San Francisco the other day, you know. I'm glad I wasn't there. They'd have made me feel like a criminal." Jake was afraid she'd been about to say "a whore."

"I'm sorry to have brought you this bad news, Marion. You gave the chief the best years of your life."

"I sure as hell did." A tear trickled onto her cheek. She wiped at it. "Now why ever were you up at Franklin's office the night he was murdered? Were you hoping to sneak in and see that will?"

"Exactly. It was dumb of me. I should have tried Amy Noonan first."

"Yes, you should have. Well, thanks for telling me this, Jake. You've been very kind." Davies dabbed at her cheek again and said, "You know, one of the last times I spoke with him he got into one of his reminiscing moods. He grew very wistful as he brought up some of his laments."

"His laments?"

"Regrets. We all make mistakes — I sure have — and he talked about a few things he was sorry about."

"Such as, Marion?"

"He said he should have fought harder for us to be in the League of Nations, that our staying out critically crippled the thing. He liked Wilson. Then he had Mussolini on the payroll for awhile. This was in 1930 or '31 when little Benito was still admired in the U.S., before he invaded Ethiopia and bolted from the League. It was called 'The Duce's Views on Europe,' or some such thing. It ran once or twice a month for awhile."

"That's fascinating," Jake said. "I never knew that."

"When Mussolini asked for more money, Willie refused and put a stop to it, said he wished he'd never done that in the first place. Then in '34, before we found out what a monster Hitler was, Willie visited him on one of our big trips to Europe. Afterward he wrote in the papers that he thought Hitler would tone down his abuse of the Jews and all that would soon fade away. He got all teary-eyed when he told me that was one of his biggest regrets of all."

"Holy Moses, I'm sure it was," Jake said. "I didn't know that either. I didn't meet W.R. till I got to the paper in '38. He was always good to me."

"I know. He used to call you his favorite bloodhound."

Thinking again of Hearst's will, Jake thought whimsically, he could have left his favorite bloodhound a few thousand.

"Now, as to his will," he said, "I'm sorrier than I can say. You've still got your shares of preferred stock in the corporation, though, and full voting rights. If they challenge that, you've got to fight them."

"I don't know," she said. "Maybe."

Jake put down his coffee cup and insisted, "No, Marion, you must."

"We'll see," she said with little determination.

As the conversation wound down, Davies said, "Thanks for coming out and telling me this, Jake." She gave him a little peck on the cheek.

When he left, Jake said to himself, "Lady, don't you quit on this!"

Claudia Nielsen finished her day's studies at UCLA's School of Medicine and drove the Ford coupe she and Kenny had bought in Galesburg back to the apartment she and Ilse Weaver shared.

She'd done well in the anatomy session, had correctly identified the various organs and muscle groups. Working on cadavers hadn't bothered her, having seen so many dead men during the war. She'd been complimented by her instructor, Doctor Jennings, when they'd had coffee afterwards. That meant a lot to her.

As she drove along Westwood Drive, her thoughts turned to Kenny. He was a wonderful husband, had brightened her life after a bad experience as a teen in Ohio had plunged her into depression. She felt some guilt at not seeing him often enough. But she was so busy, was on a good road, a road to a fine career as a physician. *Doctor Claudia Nielsen.* That was her goal, the beacon she was striving for.

She hoped Kenny could cope with that. One day she'd

be a successful physician and Kenny would be what? What would he do after his recovery? Find some kind of a job, she guessed, maybe teaching. He had a great love of history, might make a good history teacher. Could they manage to do that in the same town? That might be difficult to arrange, but she hoped they could.

If I can, I'll go and see him pretty soon, she told herself.

CHAPTER THIRTY-EIGHT

Forty or fifty drama students, chattering expectantly, filled seats in a small auditorium at UCLA. Ilse Weaver was among them, seated in the second row. She had driven the speaker here.

A professor stepped onto the stage and quieted the audience with upraised hands. "Students," he said, "we are honored to have a special guest for our discussion today, and I know you're all eager to hear from him. May I present the celebrated actor, Mr. Bela Lugosi." He gestured toward one of the wings.

Lugosi waited several seconds for dramatic effect, then strode out from stage right. Gasps came up from the audience. He was completely dressed in black, and even wore his Dracula cape. His hair was slicked back and although two decades older now, he looked very much like the Count Dracula of the horror film.

He gave the professor a little head bob. As the man walked off, not quite hiding a surprised smile, Lugosi turned and bowed to the students. Enthusiastic applause broke out.

"Goot offternoon," he said, giving full voice to his eastern European accent. "And thank you. It iss my pleasure to be here. I understand that you have been shown my film, 'Dracula,' is that correct?"

Students called out "yes" and "sure."

"Splendid. I hope that you enjoyed it." A stagy pause. "Or perhaps were terrified."

With a flourish, he pulled out a small hand mirror and

gazed into it. Feigning shock, he quickly thrust it back in his pocket, trembling as if horrified. Students laughed.

"Couldn't see yourself, right?" someone called out.

"Turn into a bat," said another.

"I can only do that at night," Lugosi answered. "If you should wish to meet later, after dark . . ." He let that sentence die, then looking around, said, "It is good there are no windows here. I cannot cope with sunlight, you know." More laughter, including Ilse's. Lugosi was enjoying himself.

He proceeded to explain that although he was born in Romania, he grew up in Budapest and considered himself Hungarian. He said that he'd never been to the Transylvanian castle of Vlad the Impaler, around whom the Dracula legend had risen.

He went on to describe his early career, his drama studies and stage work in Budapest, his film work in Germany, and playing Count Dracula on stage in New York prior to the film. He didn't mention his later health and financial problems.

Then he took questions.

Are you a member of the Screen Actors Guild? What was it like working with Boris Karloff? Have movies today gotten better or worse? Why haven't you done many films lately? On it went; things like that.

"What advice do you have for us?" a young lady asked.

"Study hard, master your craft, and if you do manage to land a stage or film role, by all means obtain a good agent."

One kid rudely asked, "Do you do drugs, sir?"

With a stern, cold Dracula leer, Lugosi said, "Do you?"

In the front row, the professor turned and wagged an admonishing finger at the boorish lad.

A youngster asked if he'd worked with Greta Garbo.

"Quite briefly," Lugosi answered. "I was cast as a Russian

communist official in her film, *Ninotchka*. Billy Wilder directed. I had fourth billing, and yet appeared in only one small scene, in which I ordered her to go to Constantinople. I was paid very little for that, yet received fourth billing. It was most queer. I felt ill used. I enjoyed Miss Garbo, though. Splendid woman."

More questions, more answers.

A man who looked ten years older than the others, pencil poised above a notebook, raised a hand and said, "Larry Howard, *Los Angeles Mirror*."

Unhappy, Ilse turned and looked. Damn, she'd been assured no press would be allowed. Frowning, the professor glared at the man, too.

"I'm curious," Howard said, "as to why you were at that lawyer's office the night he was murdered. Can you explain that?"

Lugosi pulled the cape close around himself and fixed the reporter with an icy but somehow hungry stare. "You haff a handsome neck, Meester Howard." Hungarian accent thickening. "Yes, most nice. I might say inviting. Comm closer, please." Lugosi beckoned with an outstretched hand. "Comm here!"

It took a moment for the students to catch on. A second's shocked silence was broken by some cautious laughter.

Lugosi pulled the cape tighter, the evil smile still cemented on his face, turned abruptly, and vanished stage right in a swish of black linen.

Ed Franklin's widow called the man she'd been having an affair with. "I miss you, hon. When can I see you?" she asked.

"I miss you too but we'd better wait a bit till this thing dies down some more."

"Why?" she pleaded. "We can be careful. Last night I dreamed about us being together. I got all hot; my pussy got wet."

"Really? Maybe you were dreaming about Cary Grant."

"No, silly, it was you, you hunk of beef. Say, there's a motel in Santa Ana, Murray's Motor Court. We could meet down there. Nobody would know us."

"How the heck do you know about that place, Penny?"

"I saw it awhile back when Ed and I drove the kids down to Capistrano. It looked cozy."

"Hmm. Well, I guess it's unlikely we'd get recognized down there. That's way out of our territory. Murray's Motor Court, you say? How about tomorrow night then, say, eight o'clock?"

"Perfect, big guy. I'll get my sister to stay with the boys."

"Okay, baby. Bring that silk negligee, the one I like."

At UCLA, Ilse stood by as the professor thanked Bela Lugosi and handed him a check. "Very sorry about that newspaper man," the professor said. "I have no idea how he got in. That was grand how you stayed in character as you rebuffed the man. You can be sure I'll have a harsh word for our door monitor."

Lugosi hadn't told the police why he'd been up there and he certainly wasn't going to tell a newspaperman. That would be a dirty trick on Jake Weaver and he didn't believe in dirty tricks, especially on the man who'd paid his back rent for him.

After leaving the building, Ilse drove Lugosi back to his room in Van Nuys. Along the way she pondered how she could help her *Vati* find out who killed Ed Franklin. He'd said maybe she could do something with the Franklin boys.

The older one — Valerie said he was 17 — would probably be in high school. How could she find out what school that would be? *That's something I'll have to work on. It might be a kick to flirt with a boy who's a little younger than me.*

In the passenger seat, Lugosi, holding his folded-up cape on his lap, said, "You're very quiet, young lady. You seem deep in thought."

"Sorry. I was thinking about how I could help my father find Franklin's killer. But hey, you were great in there today. I loved what you did with that mirror. Very cool."

Lugosi smiled. "I considered smashing it as I did in the film but decided no, that would be over-acting, and I'm sure you wouldn't appreciate having broken glass on your stage."

He fell silent for a moment. Ilse glanced over and found Lugosi looking sad. She thought she saw a tear beneath an eye. "This meant a great deal to me," he said at last. "It's been a long time, a very long time, since anyone has cared to hear from me about my acting, or anything else for that matter." He dabbed at his eye. "But I thank you for arranging this today. I enjoyed it and I can use the fifty dollars."

Ilse was touched. *Don't spend it on drugs, you lonely old man*, she thought.

The next day after going over a city map, Ilse narrowed it down to three high schools Freddie Franklin might be attending: Los Angeles High, Hamilton, and Belmont. She called Hamilton High first.

"May I speak to the senior class counselor?" she asked, figuring that at age 17 the kid would be a senior.

Soon a woman said, "This is Miss Dexter. Who's calling, please?"

"Elaine Price with City Social Services," Ilse said.

"We're wondering how Fred Franklin is getting along and if he needs any counseling after his father's tragic death."

"Fred Franklin? You must be mistaken, ma'am. We don't have a Fred Franklin here."

Ilse disconnected. Next she called L.A. High and repeated the procedure, calling herself *Doctor* Price. What the heck, gild the lily.

This time a man came on the line. "I never heard of City Social Services," he said in a tone of suspicion. "What's that?"

Ilse hadn't heard of City Social Services either — it was something she made up. "It's a new program, sir, designed to help troubled kids. So, Fred Franklin then?"

"Freddie's doing fine, doesn't seem to have any emotional problem over that tragedy."

"That's good to hear," Ilse said, "and what time does school let out there again?"

"At 2:50 when sixth period ends."

Ilse said thanks and hung up.

She had seen the film of Dashiell Hammett's *The Maltese Falcon* and had started thinking of herself as a private eye.

She'd learned that Freddie Franklin went to L.A. High, wasn't particularly disturbed over his father's murder, and that school let out just before 3.

Ilse still had two problems. One, she didn't know what the boy looked like. Two, or if he had something extracurricular going on after school like baseball or track.

How in the world could she see a picture of the kid? She recalled her stepmother saying she hadn't seen any family photos in Penny Franklin's living room.

Ilse called Jake at the *Herald-Express*. "I just had a quick glance at the photo on Franklin's desk, *Liebchen*, didn't really get to study it. I did see two young pallbearers at the funeral — had to be his sons. The older one stood about five-nine with a slender build. He had curly hair, brown I think. Wasn't close enough to see his eye color or if he had freckles or anything like that. Doesn't help you much, does it?"

"A little bit, *Vati*, thanks."

Well, what's next, Sam Spade?

CHAPTER THIRTY-NINE

Jake's body was telling him it was time for a good physical workout. Instead of having a drink across the street at the Continental after work, he drove out to Howie Steinder's Main Street Gym at Third and Figueroa. Jake had been a pretty fair middleweight boxer in the Navy years ago and it would do him good to work up a sweat and forget about both the murder and Hearst's will for awhile.

He found a parking spot half a block away, fed the meter, and hiked over to the gym. Why a gym at Third and Fig was named Main Street he didn't know. Howie Steinder was eccentric that way.

Inside, he met Skinner Sanchez, a trainer and one of Howie's top guys. "Hey, Jake," Sanchez said, slapping him on the shoulder. "Long time no see. What can I do for ya?" The place was noisy and smelled of perspiration and liniment.

"Like to work out a bit, Skinner, but I didn't bring any gym clothes. Got a pair of trunks around here that might fit me?"

Before long Jake was working a punching bag, going at it hard. *Pow pow pow.* His hands hurt but his biceps, triceps and back muscles felt good. So did the sweat pouring down his face and chest. He pretended the punching bag was Sam Sixto. *Take that, you asshole detective.* Finished with the bag, he then spent a few minutes jumping rope.

Skinner Sanchez came up and said, "You're lookin' pretty good for an old fart, Jake. You plannin' on makin' a comeback?"

Jake laughed. "A comeback? Hell, Skinner, it's been years since I've been in the ring."

"Tell you what," Sanchez said, "Elmer Beltz is here, trainin' for his fight with Chiller Green. You know Elmer Beltz, dontcha? Middleweight contender, 'bout your size. Whyn't ya get in the ring with him and spar a bit?"

Beltz. Good name for a boxer, Jake thought. Valerie would hate him for this, but he said, "Okay, just a round or two. He's gotta take it easy on me."

Minutes later, having donned boxing gloves and a helmet, Jake climbed through the ropes and entered the ring. The boxing helmet covered the top of his skull and the temples, but not the nose and mouth.

"Pleased to meet ya, Weaver," Beltz said, touching his gloves to Jake's. "We'll go at it real easy."

"Good. It's been years for me," Jake replied.

Holding a stopwatch, Skinner Sanchez called out, "Okay boys, go." So Jake and Beltz went at it. Light jabs, mostly blocked by the gloves and forearms. An occasional tap to the chest or a hook to the ribs, nothing above the shoulders. Beltz throwing most of the punches, Jake mainly moving backwards. Geez, this guy is fast, he thought. Good thing this isn't for real.

The round seemed to go on and on. How long can three minutes last?

Sanchez eventually barked, "Time. Take a breather, then go one more, okay?"

Jake plopped onto a corner stool, chest heaving, breathing hard, drenched in sweat. Elmer Beltz came over and said, "You ain't bad, Weaver. Wish I coulda seen you back in the day."

"I won a . . . few fights . . . in . . . the Navy," Jake managed to say between gulps of air. "That was a long time ago . . . a looong time ago."

Sanchez gave Jake a cup of water, which he gulped down. Sanchez said, "Okay, you ready? Just one more."

Again it was mostly harmless sparring as the next round proceeded, a few light hits to the body but mainly just glove bumps. Beltz was taking it easy, basically working on his timing and footwork.

As before, Jake was mostly backpedaling, fighting defensively. But suddenly Beltz left himself open for a second. Instinct took over. Without thinking, Jake drove a good hard right jab to the man's chest.

Startled, Beltz took a step back. Then with lightning speed he sprang forward and hammered Jake in the jaw with a wicked right.

An explosion went off in Jake's head and he was down, just like that. Sparkles of green and yellow danced in his eyes. The lights hanging from the wooden rafters seemed to be moving around. Beltz entered his field of vision. Looming over him, he looked down and said, "God, I'm sorry man, didn't mean to do that. You okay?"

Dizzy, tasting blood in his mouth, Jake mumbled, "Yeah . . . I think."

Beltz started to help him up, but Skinner Sanchez said, "No, Elmer, his nose is bleeding. Let him lay there a bit."

Beltz pulled off his gloves, tossed them aside, then removed Jake's helmet and gloves. Sanchez came up with a wet cloth and held it to Jake's nose and mouth.

A few minutes later when the nosebleed stopped, Beltz hauled Jake to his feet. Jake wobbling, his legs not working too well. Beltz threw his arms around him and said "You were good, Weaver. You got guts, I'll tell you that."

"Maybe I shouldn'ta suggested you spar Elmer,"

Sanchez said.

"Naw, that's okay. It was probably my fault for the punch I landed. Guess I broke the rules, huh?"

Jake took a long shower, the hot water streaming over his head and body soothing him a little. When he finally turned off the water, he examined himself in a mirror. His lower lip was split and a red-orange bruise was beginning to blossom on his right cheek.

After he toweled off and dressed, Beltz came by and said, "I'm leaving you tickets for my fight with Chiller Green. Hope you'll come, Slugger."

Slugger? Jake laughed.

When Jake reached home, Valerie gasped and said, "What happened? You look terrible. Your lip looks like a bratwurst. Did one of the crime lords ambush you? One of Jack Dragna's thugs?"

"Naw, I was boxing over at the Main Street Gym."

"Boxing? You? Whatever for? You're too old for that."

"It wasn't actually boxing, hon. I just sparred a couple of rounds with a young pro. It would've been fine but I forgot myself, hit him a good one, and the guy retaliated. It was all my fault."

"You silly goof. Well, let me get some ice for that face."

"And a glass of Scotch too, Sweets?"

"One thing at a time, Sailor, first the ice, then the Scotch."

Jake sank onto his favorite chair and Valerie brought a wash cloth filled with ice cubes and held it to his bruised face. "Whatever am I going to do with you, Jake?"

"I wasn't planning on shparring," Jake said. That split lip was playing games with his pronunciation. "Jusht wanted to have a good workout, but one thing led to another."

Later, the cold cloth removed and a drink in hand, Jake told her about the funeral and his visit to Marion Davies.

"How is Miss Davies doing?" Valerie asked.

"She was a little shook up when I told her Hearst didn't leave her anything in his will."

"Nothing?"

"No money. Dirty trick if you ask me. But she's got all that stock in his corporation. If the widow and the boys contest that, and they sure might, she's got to fight them for what's rightfully hers."

Valerie took a drink of her own Scotch and said, "She certainly should. Well, boxer man, are you ready for some dinner? I picked up some enchiladas and chips on my way home."

CHAPTER FORTY

December 1944. Pavuvu Island.

Three kings," Kenny said, tossing his cards face up on top of the ammo box he used as a desk. It was after dark and a Coleman lantern lit his tent.

With a slight grin, unusual for the stoical Pawnee, Billy Ninetrees laid down his own cards. Skinny Wade had folded.

"Sorry, sir," Ninetrees said, "full house, jacks and fours." He scooped up the pot, dimes and nickels.

Now it was Wade's turn to deal. As he picked up the cards and began shuffling, he said, "I'm so sick of this goddamned Pavuvu." The 1st Division was staging here for its next assignment. There'd been no official word but Kenny thought they might invade Okinawa next.

"Gonna have to spend another Christmas out here on this crummy rock," Wade went on. He'd just begun dealing cards when the thunder of an explosion burst about half a mile away. None of the three even flinched. "Hope nobody got hit over there," Ninetrees said.

It couldn't be an air raid because the Japanese, who were being mauled everywhere these days, had no carriers left. The Battle of Leyte Gulf had finished off the last of them. They had no land air bases within hundreds of miles.

"Another nuisance shot from a Jap sub," Kenny said. "They surface out there, lob a shell at us, then scram fast as they can."

"And always at night like this to mess up our sleep," Skinny Wade said. "Them bastards. "Well, ante up, fellas." Everyone tossed in a dime.

It nagged at Kenny that he hadn't seen his wife Claudia in months. Not since her fleet hospital was moved from Guadalcanal to Saipan, hundreds of miles from Pavuvu here in the Solomons. Billy Ninetrees caught the look on his face. "Thinking about having to spend another Christmas away from your bride, sir?"

"Exactly," Kenny said, "you mind reader. I miss her like crazy." He rubbed at the scar on his arm where he'd been hit on Peleliu, luckily not a major wound. He picked up the cards he'd been dealt and studied them. A pair of fives, nothing much else.

I wonder where Claudia and I will live after the war, he thought. Maybe in my hometown, Galesburg? I'd like to go to Knox College there and get my degree. He knew Claudia didn't want to go back to Ohio; she had a lot of bad memories from there.

"I'll take two cards," Ninetrees said, jerking Kenny back to the present.

"I want three," Kenny said, tossing cards down, keeping the pair of fives.

"Just one for the dealer," Skinny Wade added.

Uh oh, Kenny thought. He's got something good. Still, Kenny didn't fold. "I'll open," he said, chucking down a mercury-head dime.

"I'll see that and raise you a dime," Wade said and supplied his dime.

"I'll see that," Ninetrees said, putting in twenty cents.

Wade dealt the additional cards, taking just one himself. Well well, three of a kind, Kenny thought, seeing that he'd got another five. The others examined their hands, too.

"Raise you," Wade said, throwing in his coin.

"I'll see you," Ninetrees said, matching Wade's input.

"Me too," Kenny said, adding to the little pot. "Call." He laid down his cards, saying, "Three fives."

"Got a straight here." It was Ninetrees. "Seven, eight, nine, ten and jack."

Wade folded. "You lucky Injun. I was bluffing."

Ninetrees raked in the coins.

Kenny suddenly shivered with a chill. He hugged himself to keep from shaking.

"Another malaria attack?" Wade asked. "I get 'em too, ever since the Canal. Fucking malaria. More'n half of us got it, 'cepting you, Billy. How comes that?"

"Mosquitoes know better than to mess with a Pawnee," Ninetrees said.

Kenny laughed. Still shivering, he sat back and said, "Just one more, fellas, it's getting late. Don't want you getting shot by any sentries out in the dark."

After the last hand was played — the *lucky Injun* won again — the two said their goodbyes and headed into the night.

The malaria attack over at last, Kenny brushed his teeth, then gazed at the picture of Claudia beside his bunk and said, "Goodnight, beautiful." He crawled in and pulled the mosquito net around him. "Dear God," he whispered, "please watch over Claudia, and if it's not too much trouble, make this war end. Amen."

Will this goddamned war ever end? A saying had been going around: "The Golden Gate in '48." He sure hoped *that* was wrong.

CHAPTER FORTY-ONE

At 2:45 Ilse parked across Olympic Boulevard from L.A. High's main entrance. She locked her Chevy Ridemaster coupe, the hand-me-down car from her father, and crossed the street. She was standing on the sidewalk when she heard the bell. Students soon began streaming down the stairs.

Ilse scanned the crowd looking for boys who might be seniors, ignoring girls and younger looking boys. Here came a possibility: a kid about five-nine, slim, with brown hair. Ilse approached him and asked, "Pardon me, would you happen to be Fred Franklin?"

"Gee whillikers no, ma'am," the kid said. Ma'am? That stung. Who calls a college girl ma'am? "I'm Dain Clay."

"Do you know Fred Franklin?"

"Nope, I sure don't," Dain Clay said, and hustled off.

Ilse tried it with a second boy. "Hello there, do you happen to be Fred Franklin?"

"Sorry, but Charles Manson is who I happen to be, and I don't like you, sister. Out of my way!"

Ilse stepped back. *Strange kid, has some problems.*

Maybe I'm out of luck, she thought, seeing the crowd of kids dispersing fast. Here's one guy, though. I'll ask him.

"No, ma'am," the boy said. "I'm Ronny Archer."

"Ronny, do you know Fred? Do you see him around here?"

Ronny Archer looked up and down the street. Few

students were still around. "Yeah, I know him but don't see him anywhere. Whadda you want with Freddie?"

"I'm in a class on opinion polling at UCLA. We're taking a survey. Fred was recommended as a good survey subject. You look like a good one too, Ronny." Ilse pulled her reporter's notebook from her purse.

"Let me ask you a couple of questions, okay? First, do you think the voting age should be lowered to 18?"

"Hadn't thought much about it, ma'am, but yeah I think it should. I'd like to be able to vote next year. Against Truman."

Ilse put a mark in her book. "That's one for. But Ronny, President Truman says he won't run again. We don't know who the Democratic candidate will be. Now secondly, do you think Mr. Truman was right in firing General MacArthur?"

"No, I sure don't. I think MacArthur's a good guy."

"That's one against. Thank you, Ronny." Ilse wrote something on a different page, tore it out and handed it over. "When you see Fred please ask him to call me. That's my phone number. We'd value his opinion too."

"Okay, I will," the kid said, tucking the note in a pants pocket. "I'll see him tomorrow, third period. So long, ma'am."

Ronny Archer trotted off down the street.

Fred Franklin called Ilse late the next afternoon. Luckily, she'd just reached her apartment after class.

"Is this the survey lady?" the boy asked.

"Right, I'm the survey lady. My name's Ilse Weaver. You've been recommended as a good subject so I'd like your opinion for a poll my class at UCLA is taking."

"Recommended by who?" he asked.

"I don't know exactly. My professor has a list of high school seniors who'd be good polling subjects. He hasn't said how the list was compiled."

"I see. Okay then, fire away."

"Sorry, Fred, we have to ask in person. Those are the rules. Could we meet someplace tomorrow? Maybe a soda fountain close to your school?"

"In person, really? If it's that important, well, gee . . . there's Jerry's Ice Cream at Olympic and Crenshaw. I guess I could meet you there about 3. How will I know you?"

"I'll be wearing a blue sweater and will be holding a notebook."

"That should be easy enough, Miss Weaver." Miss Weaver sounded better than ma'am. "Okay, I'll see you tomorrow."

After hanging up, Ilse thought, *Nice work, Sam Spade.*

The deteriorating neighborhood around the newspaper was becoming one of L.A.'s Skid Rows, though Jake found it exotic and colorful. Heading across the street to the Continental for an after-work beer he came across a woman confronting Jaime Garcia, one of the local hobos.

The woman handed him a pamphlet and said, "Repent! If you'll just listen to me I'll show you the way to heaven."

"Listen sister," Jaime retorted, "if you'll give me twenty cents for some muscatel I'll show you the way to paradise."

Jake grinned, entered, and took a stool at the bar. "I saw that little scene out there," Shaker said, reaching for a bottle of Falstaff. "We don't need these evangelical types hanging around here, tryin' to save our bums."

He put a glass in front of Jake and poured the beer. "Hey, you look kinda worried there, old pal. What's goin' on?"

Jake took a drink and said, "Bill Hearst Junior was in this afternoon talking with some of our editors. He'll be taking over as publisher pretty soon. He's likely to shake things up quite a bit."

"Your job's okay, though, ain't it?" Shaker asked.

Jake wasn't going to mention that his helping Marion Davies could jeopardize that. "I sure hope so, pardner. With that guy, you never can tell."

"Must've worried you a lot when Junior's old man cashed in, huh?"

"Yeah, quite a bit. W.R. was a good boss to me. Always considerate, at least with me. He wasn't universally liked, though. The old man was a night owl and in the Thirties, when he was living at San Simeon, he used to call our guys working the lobster trick, midnight to dawn. He had the papers flown up there every day and he would give those fellas strange orders on stuff to send up on the morning plane. He would say things like, 'I want twenty-four frankfurters, and twenty-four rolls, not the round kind, the long kind, understand?' 'Yes, Mr. Hearst.' "

"Musta driven those guys crazy, Jake."

"When the chief died, two of those night-crew boys sang a little ditty:

> He robbed the poor,
> He robbed the rich,
> And now he's dead,
> The son of a bitch."

Shaker snickered.

Jake said, "I guess it was pretty funny at that, but I couldn't bring myself to laugh at it. I could never mock the old man."

"Yeah, sorry." Running some hot water into a suds-filled

sink full of plates and glasses. Shaker said, "Hey, I heard a singer called Doodles Weaver on the Art Linkletter program today. Are you related?"

"Yeah, he's my long lost brother. I never told you about him."

Shaker snorted and said, "Bullshit, you don't have no brother. You told me you're an only child."

"Oh, that's right," Jake replied with a devilish grin. "Doodles does some acting and he sings with novelty groups like Spike Jones's band."

"You goofball," Shaker said. "Say, pal, you look like you got kind of a fat lip there. You get into a fight or something?"

"I was sparring the other day with Elmer Beltz at the Main Street Gym."

"Elmer Beltz, the middleweight? Jesus, man!"

"Yeah, it was something I never should've done. Just went there to work out a bit, but I let myself get talked into it. We were gonna do two rounds but I never finished the second. Elmer hit me with a damn good punch. Say, I've got two tickets for his fight with Chiller Green at the Hollywood Legion. Wanta go with me?"

"Sure, Jake, I'd love to. Thanks, man."

CHAPTER FORTY-TWO

Kenny was trapped in a cave. Had no room to move. He'd got himself jammed into a space less than a foot and a half high. Cold panic set in. A cool whisper of death crawled his spine.

After a while, he felt a hand on his shoulder. How could that be?

"Kenny, Kenny, wake up," a voice said. He began to realize it was the voice of Rosie the nurse. He was so tangled up in his sheets and blanket he could hardly move. That blanket knotted hard around his shoulders must have spurred his subconscious into that nightmare.

As he got himself unstuck from the bedcovers and turned, Rosie said, "You've got a visitor here, sweetie."

The hospital room slowly came into focus, and Kenny thought he saw Claudia standing a few feet behind Rosie. Claudia!

"Hello, Kenny. How are you doing, hon?"

"Claudia, I'm so damn glad to see you. You're a sight for sore eyes." He turned awkwardly — that bound-up leg was hard to move — to see his wife better. She looked great. Peach-colored blouse, gray skirt, high heels. Those hazel-green eyes he loved.

Rosie plumped two pillows behind his head, took hold of his shoulders, and helped him sit up. "I'll leave now, so you two can catch up," she said.

When Rosie was gone, Claudia leaned over and kissed

him. He caught a whiff of her lilac-scented perfume he liked so much.

She pulled up a chair and sat beside him. "I'm so sorry I haven't come to see you often enough. My studies keep me awfully busy."

"I understand," Kenny said, though it was a white lie. He didn't understand. He saw more of Jake these days than his own wife.

"Rosie seems like a nice nurse," Claudia said, "but where does she get off calling you sweetie?"

"Aw, all the nurses talk like that, hon. It doesn't mean a thing." But maybe it did, a little. He and Rosie had grown fond of each other.

"How long will you have to stay in this thing?" Claudia asked, touching the cast encasing his left leg.

"They say a few more weeks. It really got shattered in that snowy hell hole out there, you know. Took a long time for the specialists to piece it back together. Got a bunch of screws in there. Then I'll have to go through a lot of physical therapy. Sure hope I won't be walking with a limp the rest of my life."

"So do I, hon."

"So how it's going at med school, Claudia?"

"My instructors say I'm doing real well. In about a year I'll get my diploma and start a residency somewhere."

"Where would that be?"

"I don't know, but I hope it's in California."

"So do I. Wherever it is, I want to live there too, whenever I can get outta this darn place."

"Kenny, you were a hero in Korea, just like you were in the Pacific. And you're my hero too. You always have been and always will be."

That warmed him. "Aw, shucks," he said with a smile.

"What kind of doctor work do you want to get into after you finish?"

"I'm thinking general practioner, family practice. I want to help people, don't care to specialize in anything exotic."

"Good for you, hon. Caring for regular people sounds like the way to go."

Claudia reached into her handbag and pulled out a magazine and a book. "I know how you love to read." The book was *The Caine Mutiny.* "I hear this is good."

Kenny took it and studied the cover. "Herman Wouk," he said. "Thanks a lot. I'll look forward to reading this. Say, how was your drive down here?"

"It was fine, but that Ford is getting pretty old. Maybe I should get a new car."

Claudia saying *I* and not *we* bothered Kenny a bit. "Yeah, maybe we should," he said. He put the book on the side table and reached for a glass of water.

"Here, let me do that." Claudia lifted the glass and helped him take a drink.

"Thanks, hon. How's your roommate Ilse doing?"

Claudia said Ilse was fine and that besides her studies she was trying to help her father find out who killed that lawyer.

"Yeah, Jake told me about that murder, and that some darn cop thinks he did it. Ridiculous! Jake comes down here every now and then."

Claudia looked a little guilty. "More often than me, I guess. Well, I'll remedy that, Kenny. I'll come a lot more, I promise."

Kenny hoped she meant that. "Swell, Claudia. I sure do miss you."

"Miss you too, honey."

They chatted for almost an hour more. Things like Ilse's

doings with Bela Lugosi, how bad L.A. traffic was getting, and gang troubles on the south side.

When it came time for her to leave, Claudia gave him another kiss and said, "Get well fast, Kenny, and then we'll get on with the rest of our lives."

"We sure will, hon. Thanks a million for coming. Means a lot to me."

But when she was gone, a feeling of emptiness came over him. Claudia, Jake and everybody else he knew were out there doing things.

Ilse took a booth at Jerry's Ice Cream a few minutes before 3 the next day. She'd had to cut a lecture to keep this appointment, but she'd had perfect attendance in that class up to now and felt it was important to meet Freddie Franklin.

Quite a few high school kids were there, occupying stools at the soda fountain and booths, chattering away over Cokes and milkshakes. A few of them were smoking cigarettes. Les Paul and Mary Ford were singing "How High the Moon" on the jukebox in the corner, a big, brightly lit Wurlitzer.

The door opened and a boy came in hesitantly and began looking around. Figuring this must be Freddie Franklin, Ilse stood up, holding her notebook in front of her blue sweater. The boy spotted her, gave a small nod of recognition and headed her way. Halfway there a kid, one of three in a booth, called out, "Hey Freddie, sit with us."

"Can't today," he said, and walked up to Ilse. The three boys gave this pretty but unfamiliar young woman a good looking-over. One of them whistled.

Freddie looked back and said, "Aw shut up, you guys." Turning to Ilse: "I guess you're Miss Weaver?"

"That's me, Fred. She stuck out a hand. Freddie looked at it a moment, then gave her a shy, limp handshake.

"Thanks for coming, Fred. Have a seat."

Freddie sat, put his books on the table and said, "I'm glad to meet you, Miss Weaver."

"Come on, call me Ilse. Miss Weaver makes me sound like an old maid. What can I get you?"

"A cherry Coke, I guess, but I can pay. I've got some money."

"No, it's my treat. I invited you."

The paper cover of a drinking straw sailed up and landed on the table. Ilse laughed. "Those darn guys back there," Freddie said.

A waitress trotted over and said, "Well hi, Freddie." Her nametag identified her as Connie. She gave Ilse a bold, curious stare. Looking back at Freddie, she asked, "Where's Judy?"

"Doing homework, I guess. Gee whiz, Connie, this is a business meeting here."

Ilse said, "Connie, we'll have two cherry Cokes." As if the girl couldn't remember two cherry Cokes for a few seconds, she jotted that down on her order pad and left, glaring back once more at Ilse.

My presence here is causing a sensation, Ilse thought. "Is this embarrassing you, not being with your girlfriend?" she asked.

"Naw, and Judy's not exactly my girlfriend . . . well, sort of. We're not going steady or anything." Now the jukebox was playing "Come on-a My House." Rosemary Clooney. "So you go to UCLA?" Freddie asked.

"That's right."

"My dad went to USC. I was gonna go there too, but mom says we can't afford it now. Looks like it might be L.A.

State for me."

Reaching over and touching his hand, Ilse said, "You're a good looking man. You'll be cock of the walk at L.A. State." Freddie Franklin's face blushed a bright red. Ilse was enjoying herself — she'd never played this role before. "I'll bet Judy's not the only girl at school who's interested in you."

"Aw, geez, ma'am." *Ma'am again, darn it.* So much for being coquettish.

Ilse pulled her hand away and got out her notebook. "Okay then, let's do the poll." She proceeded to ask her two questions.

The answers were yes and yes, the voting age should be lowered to 18 and Truman did right in firing MacArthur. "My late father thought MacArthur was getting out of line over there, wanting to bomb Manchuria and all."

"Your late father? Hmm. Franklin," Ilse said, letting some fake puzzlement show as she pondered the name. "Oh my gosh, was that your father who was murdered recently?"

"Yes, ma'am. That was him."

"It's not ma'am. It's Ilse, remember? But that must have been really tough for you."

"Yeah, pretty bad . . . Ilse."

The cherry Cokes arrived and Connie put them down with another unkind glare at Ilse.

When she was gone, Ilse said, "Connie is one of the many girls who like you, isn't she? Look how jealous she is."

"I wouldn't know. We went to a drive-in movie once, Connie and me, before I started seeing Judy. Connie's been acting kinda weird ever since."

"A good thing got away from her and she feels bad," Ilse said. "But back to your father's death. It must have been a terrible blow to your mom too. How is she taking this?"

"Not that bad. You see, they weren't getting along lately, fought quite a bit." Freddie stopped himself and frowned. "Gosh, I shouldn'ta said that. I don't even know you. What's the matter with me?"

Touching his hand again: "No, it's okay, Freddie. It's good to get these things out. It's healthy to talk about your feelings."

"I guess." His face twisted in consternation. "But no, I said too much."

"That brings me to one last question," Ilse said. She knew she was taking a chance here. "This is about patricide."

"Patricide? What's that?"

"The killing of one's father. If a father was real bad, beat his son terribly, maybe even worse, was molesting his daughter, let's say. Would patricide be justified?"

"No it wouldn't!" Freddie suddenly slammed his glass down and stared hard. "What's going on here? Are you thinking I killed my dad?"

"No, no, of course not."

"I'm getting out of here, lady." Freddie jumped to his feet, picked up his books, and stormed toward the door. The room went quiet. People gawked. "Stuff it, you guys," Freddie said to the leering threesome who'd been staring. And he was out the door.

Guess I went a little too far there, Ilse told herself. She put a half dollar on the table and also left. *Okay, Freddie didn't kill his father but his mom might have.*

CHAPTER FORTY-THREE

April 1945. Okinawa.

Kenny Nielsen was dead. Must be dead. He was sure of it. The last thing he could remember was a sharp burning pain in his chest. Then, nothing. Now he couldn't feel a thing. Not his arms, legs, hands. Couldn't see anything either. It was total blackness. Just like that time he'd been trapped in St. Louis Cavern when he was a kid. God, he hated caves.

Is this what death was like? No heaven, no hell. Just total unfeeling blackness? Just a return to one of the worst moments of his life, back when he had an existence? Condemned to spend eternity in a black cave? Maybe this was punishment for something bad he'd done back when there were choices he could make. Like when he dipped Peggy McCallister's ponytail in an inkwell in third grade.

Funny, I can think, remember things, but can't move. Can't feel.

Why can't I see something!

I must be in a coffin. Sure, that explains it. I'm in my coffin.

He'd been commanding a battalion ordered to take out a Japanese machine gun nest. They'd had the high ground for once. Seemed like on Okinawa the enemy always held the high ground. This was better, though it was muddy and raining. Wasn't it always raining on Okinawa? The plum rains the Japanese called it. The attack was going well. We had them surrounded and outgunned.

He'd heard the coughing sound of an enemy mortar, then that sharp pain. What came after that? He couldn't tell, couldn't pull that up.

So here he was, doomed to remember things about his rather short life — for eternity. Alone and in the dark. Some afterlife. The clergy had been all wrong about that. No bright white light, no being wrapped in a glow of warm ecstasy.

No reuniting with all the buddies who'd lost their lives on Guadalcanal. Cape Gloucester. Peleliu. Okinawa. Or even his mother, who'd battled the cancer so courageously. Was she trapped in total blackness too? If so, screw you, God.

He thought about that baseball game where he'd fallen for the old hidden-ball trick. His friend Richard Lundquist had sure outsmarted him that day.

Getting laid in that whorehouse outside New River when he was a raw recruit.

Meeting Claudia in that hospital at Espiritu Santo. One of the best days in his life. The hurried wedding vows with her a year later under that flame tree on Guadalcanal. The pain of not being able to make love to her for two months because he had to get right back to base.

Pastor Zendt at First Christian in Galesburg. Nice man, Pastor Zendt, but he had it all wrong about heaven.

Meeting Jake Weaver, who'd become such a great friend. But now they'd never be able to write that book together.

Billy Ninetrees, the big Pawnee he'd taught to read and write. Billy became a friend as good as Jake Weaver.

The hell that was Peleliu. Peleliu was the worst. Had lost nearly half his men there.

The unopposed landing on Okinawa. What a blessed surprise that had been, although short-lived. The Japs were holding back on high ground in great defensive positions.

So this was what it was like to be dead. He stopped thinking. Mind went blank. Was it possible to sleep in this eternal prison?

It took awhile to realize that eventually some light was

seeping in. *Light! Really?* Maybe this wasn't a coffin after all. He tried to open his eyes. It took awhile. They were so heavy.

"Well, I see you're back with us, Marine."

Was that a voice? Who could have said that? Slowly a man bending over him began to come into focus. Eyeglasses, blood-spattered smock, white gloves, facemask lowered beneath his chin.

"Is this . . . heaven?" Kenny slurred.

"Nope. Field hospital, Kadena, Okinawa. You've got quite a chest wound, son. I believe you're going to be okay, but it'll take quite awhile. World War II is over for you, fella."

CHAPTER FORTY-FOUR

Claudia knew with some nagging discomfort that her lead instructor, Dr. Jennings, was showing a lot of interest in her — interest that was starting to go beyond her progress in med school.

In the morning, staring at herself in the bathroom mirror while brushing her teeth, she recognized that she was an attractive woman. Although 30 now, her skin was smooth, with just a few crow's feet — she preferred to call them character lines — crinkling around her hazel-green eyes, eyes that were bright and clear. Not a trace of gray in her ear-length auburn hair.

Kenny often said she was beautiful and so had that darn Dr. Barrett who'd propositioned her at Palomar Hospital a year or so ago.

Yeah, Dr. Jennings was interested. The two had had coffee together a couple of times and now Jennings was suggesting dinner. Just to go over some things about her studies, he'd said. *Yeah, sure.* Years ago Claudia had been pretty naïve about what men were thinking. Not now.

Dan Jennings could have some influence on where she would get a residency after graduating. He might be able to land her at someplace like Mount Sinai here in L.A. or Mercy in San Diego. If she offended him, it could be Barstow or Lodi, or even Aching Back, Arkansas.

Jennings was about 48 or 50, she guessed, trim and in good shape for a man his age. Some gray showed above the ears in his full head of brown hair, distinguished looking. Was he married? Claudia didn't know. The man didn't wear a ring.

"Are you through in there?" she heard her roommate call from the other room.

"Yes, Ilse, just about."

Claudia rinsed off her toothbrush and put it back in the holder above the sink. She loved Kenny, her poor busted-up Kenny. He was a terrific husband.

Why oh why did life have to be so darn complicated?

At Central Division, detective Sam Sixto pulled a chair up to Owen Wannamaker's desk. They would again go over the murder book, a detailed listing of what they had so far on the Franklin homicide.

"We're just not getting anywhere," Wannamaker said, slamming a fist on the desk. His gray coffee mug jumped. "Let's start at the top again. We know it wasn't suicide. There'd have been a gun in his hand or lying there. The only fingerprints we got were Franklin's, his secretary Edith Harris's, and that Amy Noonan gal. I still think the wife's our best bet."

"Naw, it was Weaver," Sixto insisted.

"You keep bringing that up. Why him, for chripesake? What was his motive?"

"Don't know, but the goddamn guy was there! Late at night. He admits that. The night watchman saw him. It's gotta be him."

"I don't buy that, Sam. Again, why? Weaver's just not the killer type. He's a family man. He was genuinely shook up when his daughter got stabbed by that fugitive Nazi. And the only gun he's got is an old Luger."

Firing up a cigarette, Sixto said, "He coulda dumped the murder weapon, easy."

"He could have, yeah, but in more than sixty percent of these cases it's the spouse. I still got the wife for this. She wasn't all that upset when we questioned her. Maybe she caught him fooling around, dicking some other girlie. We should grill her again. Maybe's she's got something going on the side too."

Sixto shook his head as if to say "Naw," and drove some smoke from his nostrils. "I doubt that," he said. "Wait now, Owen, back up. If it's not Weaver — though I believe it is — it mighta been that Noonan broad, maybe even that Edith Harris."

"Who knows, Sam. Secretaries sometimes get the short stick. He mighta been a rough boss. When it comes down to murder we've seen some mighty strange stuff. Damned unlikely to be that old lady, though." Wannamaker slammed the book shut and said, "Let's question the wifey again."

"Okay Owen, if you really want to, but we oughta grill Weaver again, too. In fact, I say we get a search warrant and give his place the works, a real good going-over."

Ilse came over to have dinner with her father and stepmother and to bring them up to date on her sleuthing.

She found Valerie in the kitchen preparing to roast a chicken. After exchanging cheek kisses, Ilse pitched in, chopping vegetables and wrapping potatoes in foil for baking.

Jake's lip was back to normal. He came in, hugged and kissed them both, then took a bottle of Mondavi chardonnay from the fridge, cut the foil, and pulled the cork. "I've been saving this for a special occasion and having my lovely daughter here sure as heck qualifies as that," he said. He got out wineglasses, poured, and said, "Here ladies, wet your whistles."

Glasses were raised, clinked against, and "Cheers" exchanged.

Jake asked, "How's everything at school, *Liebchen*?"

"Fine, *Vati*, but I have to confess I cut a class yesterday. Don't get mad, it's the first time I've done that. It was so I could meet with Ed Franklin's older son. I'll tell you about it over dinner."

This got her parents' attention. Valerie, who'd just placed the chicken dish in the oven, said, "It'll be awhile before dinner's ready so let's go out to the front room and hear about it now. Bring your wine."

Jake plopped onto his favorite easy chair as Valerie and Ilse took seats on the sofa. A newscast was playing on the radio. Something about a battle at a place in Korea called Pork Chop Hill. Jake got up and turned it off. "That damn Korean War has turned into bloody stalemate," he said. "Police action, my ass. That's a war."

Sitting again, he turned to Ilse and said, "So then . . . Franklin's son."

Ilse told how she'd gone to Los Angeles High and found a kid there who knew Freddie Franklin, and that he'd gotten Freddie to call her. She'd made up a story about surveying high school seniors for a class on opinion polling.

"A chip off the old block," Valerie said. "That's just the kind of thing your father would do."

Jake smiled in self-satisfaction.

"So I met Freddie at a malt shop yesterday," Ilse continued, "and we talked quite awhile. You know what? I'd never had a cherry Coke before. When I brought up patricide as one of my survey questions, he got real tense, said that killing a father would never be justified no matter how viciously criminal the man might be. I came away pretty convinced Freddie's not the killer.

"But he told me his mom and dad were having marital problems and fought a lot. He looked sad telling me that." Ilse took a sip of wine and added, "I think Freddie's mother might have done it."

"I think she may have, too," Valerie put in. "When I met her she also mentioned the problems they were having. She's not a happy woman. She thinks Franklin was probably playing around."

"You ladies are quite the pair of detectives," Jake said.

"Women can do almost anything," said Valerie, who was proud to be one of the few females in the U.S. working in rocket development. "Did you hear about that Florence Chadwick woman from San Diego who swam the English Channel the other day? First woman to do it from England to France."

"Yep, women are fantastic," Jake said. "Look at the two geniuses we've got here."

A bell sounded in the kitchen. Valerie jumped to her feet and said it was time to get the chicken out.

Jake got up and set the dining-room table, placing silverware at each plate, trying to remember which forks went where. Then he fetched the bottle of wine from the kitchen.

Over dinner he said he hadn't gotten any farther than they had. He didn't believe Franklin was killed by his assistant, Amy Noonan, and for sure not by Edith Harris, his secretary.

"It might be someone we haven't thought of," he said, "someone we don't even know."

Jake began to fret about Ed Franklin's older son having

Ilse's phone number. He kept that to himself because he didn't want to upset her — she'd done some good work. But what if Freddie Franklin told his mother about meeting Ilse and the woman got upset? Maybe she'd call Ilse and say, "What the hell are you doing?" Or tell Wannamaker or Sixto that she'd been questioned by Weaver's wife and her son by Weaver's daughter. The detectives would be mad as hell to know Jake's family was digging into this, against their explicit warning not to. Jake would look desperate to them. In their minds desperation could equate to guilt. This whole thing could start to unravel.

"Is the chicken all right, dear?" Valerie asked.

CHAPTER FORTY-FIVE

Ilse got to her apartment about 5 after school the next day. She found Claudia there at the kitchen with an anatomy book and a bottle of Pepsi in front of her. To her surprise, Claudia wore one of her prettiest dresses, a green sleeveless number. Ilse caught the scent of her roommate's lilac perfume, which she seldom used on school days.

Claudia looked up and said, "Hi. Doing homework."

Ilse put her own books on the table and said, "Me too. A couple of schoolgirls, aren't we?"

"Indeed we are. I have an exam tomorrow on the endocrine glands and need to be ready. How are things with you? Learned anything new on who might have killed that lawyer?"

Ilse took a bottle of ginger ale from the fridge and sat down across from Claudia. She told about the dinner she'd had last night with her parents and about meeting Freddie Franklin.

"You met this high school kid at a malt shop?"

"Yes, and it kind of freaked out a few kids there. They wondered what he was doing with an older woman. Ha. I'm three years older, four at the most."

"But a 21-year-old woman looks very mature to high school kids, Ilse."

"I guess so. The waitress was real upset, actually jealous. It turned out that she and Freddie used to go out. She stared daggers at me."

Claudia grinned and said, "That's priceless."

"To tell the truth I kind of enjoyed it. Freddie got all kinds of looks from his school friends and so did I. Anyway, he doesn't much like his mother. He says she and her husband fought a lot. I came away thinking the mom might very well be the killer. Valerie thinks so too."

Claudia drank some Pepsi and said, "A couple of great sleuths, you and your stepmom."

"It's been kind of fun. Important too. We've got to prove my *Vati* is innocent. Say, how did it go with your hubby when you went down there to see him?"

"Fine, but my poor guy is pretty messed up physically — his leg was very badly damaged — and maybe mentally too. He had some horrible experiences in Korea, went through a lot. My heart hurts for him."

"I sure hope he'll come out of it all right, Claudia. He's a great guy."

"Yes he is. I sometimes wonder if I deserve him."

Ilse's eyes widened. "Of course you deserve him. What a thing to say. After you get your medical degree and he gets fixed up . . . gee, you guys are for life."

"Sure," Claudia murmured, not meeting Ilse's eyes.

"Hey, why so dressed up? I love that dress."

"I'm going out to dinner."

"Oh, who with? I was planning to cook us up some spaghetti."

"Dr. Jennings, my lead instructor. He's asked me a couple of times and I figure I'd better not keep turning him down."

Ilse's brow puckered. "Isn't that kind of against the rules, you know, fraternizing with one of your professors?"

"Oh, I don't think so. We'll probably just talk about harmless medical things. I need to be nice to him. He could be of help to me when I go out for my residency."

"He wouldn't hurt your chances just because you wouldn't have dinner with him, would he? There are ethical standards. My instinct says don't go."

"Maybe you're right, Ilse, but it's too late. I already said I would. Can't back out now."

"I see. Well, be careful."

"Okay, Mom," Claudia said with a sarcastic smile. "I won't be out late. Wouldn't want you to ground me."

Ilse forced a small smile, finished her ginger ale, picked up her books, and went to her room.

CHAPTER FORTY-SIX

May 1945. Kansas, USA.

The Silver Streak rumbled past fields of wheat and corn, the corn low, just beginning to peek through the brown soil with little shoots of green.

Glancing out the window of their car, Claudia said, "Look at all those tall silos."

"Yeah, the skyscrapers of the prairie," Kenny replied. He had recovered from a chest wound suffered on Okinawa and they were en route to Kenny's hometown, Galesburg, Illinois, where they would settle and start their postwar lives.

"So you'll be going back to school?" Claudia asked.

"Yep, Knox College. Want to get my degree. I'll be the first man in the Nielsen line to be a college graduate."

"Good for you, hon, your dad will be proud. Meanwhile, I'll get some kind of job, a nurse in the local hospital, if possible. Hope they have some openings for an old Navy nurse."

"Old? You're not old, honey. You're young and beautiful."

Claudia ran a hand through her short auburn hair and said, "I'm older than you, Kenny."

"By one month. That's nothing."

"When we first met in the hospital at Espiritu Santo," Claudia said, "and I thought you were a pretty good guy, I looked up your birthday on your chart."

"No kidding? So from the start you were an older woman chasing a young stud, eh? Well, besides going to school I'll be working away on the book Jake and I plan to write. I'll have to buy a typewriter."

Trains were crowded these days, packed with servicemen and civilians alike. Kenny and Claudia had been lucky to get a private compartment. His rank as a lieutenant colonel probably helped with that.

They suddenly heard a commotion out in the corridor. Passengers were stomping and shouting. Kenny made out words like "hooray" and "hallelujah." He got to his feet and opened the door. Seven or eight soldiers and a couple of women packed the narrow passageway. One of them held up a portable radio.

"What's going on?" Kenny asked.

"Germany surrendered," a private shouted, holding a can of beer in his hand. "They surrendered! The Krauts tossed in the towel."

"Great news," Kenny said, "really great, but don't forget we've still got the Japs to deal with."

He went back inside and closed the door. "I heard," Claudia said. "That's terrif."

Kenny sat and abruptly felt a twinge of guilt. "Meanwhile, my old gang is still fighting on Okinawa. More of them will die before all that's over. Someday we'll probably have to invade Japan itself, the home islands. What a nightmare that'll be."

Claudia touched his hand and said, "You're lucky to be out of it. You were wounded on Guadalcanal, Peleliu, and Okinawa. You've done more than enough, way more than enough."

"Yeah, but those are my buddies out there — they're family. Skinny Wade, Billy Ninetrees." He slapped a fist into the palm of his left hand. "At least the Nazis are done for. That's great news. Let's have a drink to that in Topeka or

216

wherever we stop next."

"It can't be Topeka, Kenny. This is a dry state. Maybe after we cross the Missouri."

CHAPTER FORTY-SEVEN

Jake and his bartender friend Shaker got to Hollywood Legion Stadium just as the first preliminary bout ended. He found that the seats Elmer Beltz left him were at ringside. Darn nice of Elmer. He must have felt pretty bad about knocking him cuckoo when they'd sparred.

They found themselves seated next to Howie Steinder, owner of the Main Street Gym, and Skinner Sanchez, his right-hand man. Jake introduced Shaker and nice-to-meet-you's were said.

"I hear you and Elmer really got into it," Steinder said.

"Yeah, and it was my fault. I forgot myself and hit him a good shot and he fired back with a really good one. Man, I heard birds chirping in my head for a while. Never got hit like that in my Navy days. You should've seen the bruise I had."

Steinder laughed and said, "If you'd like to have a real fight I could match you against a rummy middleweight in a six-rounder one of these nights, a palooka I think you could take. You could bring home seventy-five bucks."

"Ha. No chance, Howie. I'm not gonna risk this face of mine in a ring ever again."

Jake then spotted Mickey Cohen on the opposite side, also front row. When Jake waved and caught his eye, Cohen motioned for him to come over.

"Excuse me a minute, fellas," he said. "Gotta go and say hello to someone." He got up and walked around to see

Cohen.

When he reached the other side, a gorgeous blonde sitting with Cohen said, "Why, Mr. Weaver, how nice to see you."

"Hello there," Jake said to Lana Turner. "Good to see you too." He'd been introduced to the famous actress at Musso & Frank's Grill awhile back. "I saw you in *The Three Musketeers* with Gene Kelly. Real nice."

"Why, thank you, Mr. Weaver."

"Jake," Cohen said, "I been looking into that Franklin hit for you."

"Aw, Mick, I asked you not to do that."

"You know how bad I am at taking advice, Jakester. Remember when Franklin represented you when Jack Dragna charged you with trespassing? Turns out Franklin impressed Jack that day, and he used him on a coupla cases."

"Dragna used Franklin? That's news to me, Mick. I never heard that."

Lana Turner sat there listening to all this.

"Yeah, he did," Cohen said. "Franklin and some lady lawyer he worked with, Amy something—."

"Noonan," Jake supplied.

"That's it, Amy Noonan. She comes off as some innocent creampuff, a goody two-shoes, but she ain't, not really. I got no proof of it, not yet, but I think maybe she offed the guy. Franklin got a little sideways with Jack, and I think Noonan mighta done it. Whacked him for Dragna, you know."

"Good God, Mickey. Amy Noonan? I don't see that at all, but you've sure given me something to think about."

The fighters for the next preliminary entered the ring to be announced. The bout was about to start.

"I better get back," Jake said. "Swell to see you again, Miss Turner."

"Same here, Mr. Weaver."

"See you in church, kid," Cohen threw in.

When Jake got back to his seat, Howie Steinder said, "So you know Mickey Cohen, huh? You're some character, Weaver."

"Aw, he knows everybody in town," Shaker said, "good guys and bad."

Eventually came the main event. As Elmer Beltz pulled off his robe he glanced down at Jake and gave him a big wink.

The bout began and droplets of sweat sprinkled down on them, one of the benefits — ha! — of ringside seats. Jake cringed at every good punch Beltz landed on Chiller Green. He also kept thinking about what Cohen had said. He had no idea Franklin did any work for Dragna and that it had turned sour. Amy Noonan? On Dragna's orders? Is that possible?

"Great left hook Elmer just landed," Howie Steinder said.

"Huh? Oh yeah," Jake replied. He'd lost focus on the fight.

Elmer Beltz kayoed Chiller Green in the seventh round.

Ilse was still up at 10:15 when Claudia came in from her dinner with Dr. Jennings. Ilse was lying on the sofa in her pajamas listening to music on the radio. She sat up, clicked the radio off and said, "How did it go, Claudia?"

"Oh, fine. We mostly talked about med stuff, how I'm progressing and so on. He said I was a little weak on the central nervous system and I need to brush up on that." Claudia tossed her purse on the coffee table. "Overall he says I'm doing real well."

"That's good. Did he get personal?" Ilse asked.

"Gosh, Mom" — mockingly — "here we go again with the questions. Well, sure, a little. He asked about Kenny and how he was doing. He also wanted to know more about the nursing work I did in the Navy, what my goals are, things like that. He didn't get fresh if that's what you want to know."

"Did you find out if he's married?"

"Yes, and he is. Didn't say much about his wife, though. He spoke more about his sons. He has two and he's very proud of them. One is a lawyer in San Francisco and the other runs some kind of business here in L.A."

"Did you talk about your residency after you graduate?"

"More third degree, huh Ilse?"

"Sorry, but I'm just curious."

"Anyway, no, that didn't come up. It didn't feel right asking him any favors. A lot of the time, I found myself sitting there thinking about Kenny and how frantic I was when he was missing in that Chinese civil war last year." Claudia then shook her head and said, "Think I'll have a glass of milk." She went to the fridge in the kitchen, asking, "You want some?"

"No thanks, I'm fine. Say, the rent's due this week."

"Already? Okay, I'll give you a check for my share in the morning," Claudia said, pouring herself some milk. She came back and sat in a chair next to the sofa.

Ilse got up and said she was going to turn in, had an early class in the morning. "Good night now. Glad it went well."

She was relieved to know Claudia still had her husband on her mind when out with that professor.

CHAPTER FORTY-EIGHT

August 1950. San Diego.

Kenny boarded a Military Air Transport Service C-121 at Lindbergh Field. He was about to fly to Japan for a council of war with General MacArthur's command. As had happened before during World War II, the 1st Marine Division was back under MacArthur, this time for use in Korea.

Part of the division was already in action there. Designated the 1st Marine Provisional Brigade, they were helping the battered and beleaguered 8th Army defend the Pusan Perimeter at the southeast tip of the peninsula. It was a savage fight but at last the Americans, who'd been so unprepared when the North first invaded, were no longer in retreat.

Kenny had heard about a terrible instance of treachery. At the Naktong River, ten South Korean soldiers, our allies, entered a U.S. position using the correct passwords, and proceeded to murder a tank crew with rifle fire and grenades. They in turn were promptly mowed down. At first it was thought these were enemy infiltrators, but that notion was discarded. It was unlikely that North Koreans could get their hands on ten clean, undamaged uniforms and learn the passwords, which were changed every day. No, this was a stab in the back by some of the very people we were there to defend. Awful stuff happens in war, awful stuff.

Pusan was a vital port. If we could hold it, more troops and supplies could keep coming in. If not and Pusan fell, it would be a disaster, an American Dunkirk, and all Korea would be lost to the Reds.

But Kenny had confidence in the provisional brigade. He'd been with many of its men during the Pacific war. They would hold.

He was sorry he wasn't with them now but as the division's intelligence officer, its G-2, he would be involved in the planning for something MacArthur was cooking up: an amphibious landing behind the North Korean army, somewhere close to Seoul. This was top secret and he was one of the few Marine officers who were privy to it. He was eager to learn more. All he knew was that the bulk of the division would do the landing.

Yep, the strutting old five-star general knew that when a big job had to be done it was the Marines who could do it.

After this Korea business was finished, maybe he and Jake Weaver could write another book. It was a possibility they had discussed. They could write about the mistake of drastically cutting down the size of our military after V–J Day, what we did right and wrong in Korea, and how the U.S. would lead the Free World to eventual victory over Joe Stalin and international communism.

His thoughts turned to Claudia. His wife, a nurse, would enter med school in a few weeks, starting on the road to becoming a doctor. He was proud of her. When they said their predawn goodbyes at their Camp Pendleton apartment, she'd said, "I hate to see you going off to this darn war, Kenny. It's not fair. You've done more than enough for Uncle Sam already."

"But duty calls, hon. I know you'll do terrific at UCLA. I'll write you as often as I can. I'll be back by Christmas." That would give the Marines four months to wrap up the Norkos. More than enough, he thought . . . he hoped.

"Be real careful, Kenny. Don't go and get yourself shot. You've had too much of that already."

Their parting hug was warm and intense, Claudia clenching him as if she never wanted to let go. Their kisses wet and ardent.

The plane took off and began climbing to altitude. Kenny looked back and saw San Diego Bay receding behind him. There was Broadway Pier, where he'd debarked for Guadalcanal eight long years ago. And that old lighthouse at the tip of Point Loma. Would he ever see these places again? Or Claudia?

Kenny Nielsen was going back to war.

CHAPTER FORTY-NINE

The killer surveilled the Weaver home on Saturn Avenue, driving past twice. The killer knew Jake and Valerie would be at work, and assumed Ilse would be in school, not aware that the daughter no longer lived there. The place looked and felt quiet.

The killer parked at the curb three houses down, got out and strolled casually back to the Weavers', checking windows along the way to see if any curious neighbors were peeking out. Didn't see any.

Reaching the Weavers', the killer strolled up the driveway, two strips of concrete with grass growing in between, entered the backyard, pulled on some cotton gloves, and tried the rear door. As expected, it was locked. Took out a ring of skeleton keys and tried several. The fourth one did the trick, the door opening into a laundry room behind the kitchen.

Listened warily. Heard nothing. The place had the feel of being empty. No cat or dog.

Took some time looking around the house. This person wasn't much interested in how people decorated their homes, but still took it all in. The sofa and chairs in the front room. The gooseneck lamp beside an end table. The Admiral TV set perched on an oak stand. A painting on the wall, a Sierra scene. Might have been Sequoia National Park.

Checked the two bathrooms. Snooped in the medicine cabinets, curious about what creams and perfumes Valerie

Weaver used. Saw a bottle of Bromo-Seltzer. Wondered who got the stomach aches. Careful to touch very little and not rearrange things.

Then the master bedroom. Big mirror on a wall. Double bed, neatly made. Small Philco radio on the wooden headboard. Spotted a pair of sparkly, expensive looking earrings on top of the dresser. Admired them, but left them alone. This wasn't a burglary. A boxing trophy on the dresser also caught the killer's eye. Hadn't known Weaver had done any boxing. Interesting.

Opened dresser drawers. Mrs. Weaver obviously used the first two, lacy things in there, panties, bras, scarves. The third drawer, men's stuff. The intruder pulled a .22 pistol from a coat pocket and nestled the weapon beneath some socks in that drawer. Listened closely. Still heard nothing. Pushed the drawer closed.

Mission completed, the killer retraced steps, locked the back door after stepping out. Removed the cotton gloves. Two minutes later, was driving away. Passed a Good Humor truck, its singsong tune tinkling away, the guy hoping to sell some ice cream bars.

When Valerie reached home she checked the garage and found it empty, so she drove in and parked. That was the arrangement with Jake: whoever arrived first used their one-car garage and the other parked in the driveway. She got out, unlocked the back door of the house and stepped inside.

In the utility room just off the kitchen she got a queer feeling. A shiver chilled her spine. "Is anyone there?" she called out. Silence. *Gee, I hope my mom didn't just die*, she thought.

Moving cautiously, she went on in, padded down the hallway to the master bedroom and set her purse on the dresser top. There were the earrings she forgot to put away last night, and Jake's old Navy boxing trophy. Everything seemed to be in order.

She kicked off her shoes, went to the kitchen and took a bottle of chardonnay from the refrigerator, poured herself a glassful, and took a drink. Ah, that helped. She carried the glass into the front room and sank onto the sofa. Took another drink and set the glass on the coffee table.

The odd feeling was gone now, or nearly gone. "You silly goose," Valerie told herself. She began reviewing what she'd done that day at Lockheed, preparing a comparison of the Viking and Atlas missiles. The Viking was Lockheed's, the Atlas, General Dynamics'. The Atlas had been fired in recent test launches, the Viking, not yet.

Before long she heard Jake's car pull in and stop in the driveway. She'd give her hubby a big hug and pour him some wine.

When Jake got out, the Good Humor truck that often cruised the neighborhood pulled up to the curb. Jake occasionally bought ice cream from the driver, an affable old fellow called Pops. People said it was short for popsicle.

Jake gave the guy a friendly wave. He'd almost reached the front steps when Pops called out, "Mr. Weaver, hold up."

Jake stopped and said, "I'm not really in the mood for ice cream tonight, Pops."

Pops approached and said, "That's okay. Got something to tell you. I saw somebody snooping around your place this afternoon. Thought you should know. Didn't look like he was from the power company or anything like that."

"Some guy prowling around here?" Jake said. "Thanks a lot, Pops. Just what did you see?"

"He walked up your driveway here and went around back. I drove on but when I got on this block again, oh, nine or ten minutes later, I saw him come back and drive off. Were you expecting anybody?"

"I sure wasn't, Pops. You keep saying he. So it was a man, then?"

"Well gosh, I assumed so, but then I wasn't all that close. Wore dark slacks and a coat. Now that I think about it, I s'pose a woman could've piled her hair up under that hat."

"Anything else you can recall, Pops?

"He or she was a little shorter'n you, maybe five-five or six. Slacks was dark gray, coat black or deep blue. With that hat on I couldn't see no hair color. That's 'bout all I can remember."

That didn't narrow it down much for Jake. "What kind of car was this person driving?"

"Black two-door. Couldn't tell you the make. Had one of those foxtails on the radio aerial. Popular with kids."

Why the hell was somebody skulking around behind my house? Jake wondered bitterly. If the prowler was out of sight nine or ten minutes, maybe got inside.

The front door opened at that moment and Valerie stepped onto the porch. "Hello there, Pops," she said. "What are you and Jake cooking up?"

"I'll tell you in a minute, Sweets," Jake said. Turning back to Pops: "Thanks a whole lot, pardner, sure appreciate it. I'm in kind of an ice cream mood after all." Reaching for his wallet: "Let me have half a dozen of those Eskimo pies, will you?"

CHAPTER FIFTY

Jake brought the ice cream bars in and put all but two of them in the little freezer section of the refrigerator. He gave one to Valerie just as she was about to hand him a glass of wine. "Ice cream bars and wine?" she said. "That'll be a first. How come you bought all these from Pops out there?"

"He did us a big favor, Val. I probably should have tipped him a few bucks besides buying these bars." Jake sipped some chardonnay, figuring he looked a little silly with an ice cream bar in one hand and a glass of wine in the other.

Valerie got out two small plates and set her ice cream on one to have a free hand and Jake did the same. "What kind of favor was this?" she asked.

"Now Val, relax and don't get upset, but he saw somebody prowling around the house today, someone who went around back."

"Uh-oh," Valerie said, her forehead scrunching into furrowed lines. She set her glass down hard.

"As Pops recalls it, when he got back on our block ten minutes or so later, he saw this person come back down the driveway and drive off. That was enough time for a break-in."

"I knew it, Jake, I knew it! When I went in I got a big scary feeling that someone was in here. Call it a sixth sense or whatever."

"You've always had good instincts, Val. Okay, you came in the back door as usual I guess?"

"Right."

"Did you see any damage, any sign the door had been forced?"

"I didn't look closely but it seemed okay. I just unlocked it like always." Still looking shaken, Valerie sank onto a kitchen chair.

"Somebody knew what they were doing," Jake said. "Maybe had a picklock or a skeleton key. Did you look around the place? Was anything taken?"

"Not that I could tell. I didn't check the whole house but the bedroom looked okay." Valerie got up and put the ice cream bars in the fridge, saying, "These things will melt if we leave them out." She sat down again.

Jake took another drink and said, "When you get calm and collected, let's go over the whole place and see if anything's missing."

Valerie finished off her wine and put the glass down. "Did Pops say what this man looked like?"

"He wasn't actually sure it was a man. Wore a coat and slacks, and a hat covered the hair, so he couldn't really say if it was a man or woman. Said the prowler was shorter than me." Jake was thinking Amy Noonan.

"Gosh, Jake, I feel so violated," Valerie said, making fists of her hands. "This is our home, our sanctuary. How dare they!" She was thinking Penny Franklin.

"Yeah, it pisses me off too, hon."

Moments later, after Jake gave Valerie a big, reassuring hug, they inspected the entire house. The front room, the spare room that once had been Ilse's, the bathrooms, and their own bedroom. So far there was no sign of something missing. Jake checked the back door too and found no damage, not a chisel mark or anything.

In the master bedroom, Valerie said, "My diamond

earrings are still here. Remember when you bought them at Buffum's for our anniversary? A burglar would have taken them." She checked her jewelry box and found nothing missing there either. She placed the earrings in the box as she'd meant to do the night before.

They began looking through their dresser drawers. Valerie first checked the top two drawers, which were hers. She no longer kept her pistol there, had put it above the closet with Jake's Luger.

Then Jake opened his drawer. Feeling through underwear and socks, he suddenly said, "Uh-oh." He pulled a handkerchief from his back pocket, wrapped it around his hand, and pulled out a .22 pistol.

"Oh my God," Valerie uttered. "That's not yours, is it?"

"It sure as hell isn't." He cautiously set the gun on the dresser top, still not touching it with his fingers. "Some clever bastard planted this on us," he snarled.

"Let's call the police, Jake."

"No, not just yet." Jake was now thinking Sam Sixto. Sixto was about the same height as Jake, maybe a little shorter.

The thought that Bela Lugosi had been a burglar briefly crossed his mind, but why on earth would Lugosi invade their home? Did he even know where it was? Besides, he was taller than Jake and he didn't have a car. No, Lugosi was on their side. It wasn't him.

The next day Jake bought a sturdy dead-bolt at the hardware store and installed it on the back door.

CHAPTER FIFTY-ONE

September 1950. Inchon Harbor, Korea.

What am I doing in the middle of the night in a small boat in an enemy harbor, Kenny thought. Madness! This was where the invasion would take place, thirty-some miles southwest of Seoul, and as G-2, Kenny had volunteered to scout the place himself. Yes, madness!

A sailor from the cruiser Mount McKinley, General MacArthur's flagship, piloted Kenny's little powerboat. A Marine machine gunner was also aboard. They'd entered the harbor through a slot called Flying Fish Channel. A warm and sticky breeze wafted over the water on this sultry night. Even in late summer Korea could be a hot place. He thought about Claudia and was glad she couldn't see the dangerous thing he was doing now.

The hydrographic specialists said Inchon had some of the highest and lowest tides in the world, varying more than thirty feet. Thus, the invasion would be trickier than any the Marines had made in World War II. They'd have to go in fast at high tide, then get the landing craft the hell out or else they'd be stuck in the oozing mudflats for half a day, till the next high tide. That was one problem. Another was that one of the targeted landing zones was not a beach, but a high stone seawall. Attacking Marines would have to bring ladders and there was no telling how much opposition they'd face when reaching the top.

Kenny hoped the harbor hadn't been mined. He was looking for mines but hadn't seen any so far.

He had pored over the maps and charts of the harbor, in the

middle of which sat a rocky lump called Wolmi-do Island. One of his objectives on this eerie night was to see if Wolmi-do was fortified, since Marines would probably have to take it before proceeding to the seawall.

He told the sailor to approach the island from the landward side, saying, "If the Reds don't already know about our ships out there we sure don't wanta tip our hand." He raised his binoculars and studied the island. A narrow concrete causeway led from it to the seawall, designated Red Beach, though that wall was anything but a beach.

In the murk of night Kenny made out a few small huts on the island and a couple of lights shining from poles like streetlights. "Put it in idle," he said, "and drift a little closer." That outboard motor clattered like an old Ford with a blown muffler.

Suddenly Kenny saw the outlines of three men appear. They seemed to be looking his way. A couple of shouted words pierced the night. Korean words. Must have been a challenge. Next a bright light blinked on, stabbing at them.

Kenny had no sooner shouted "Let's get out of here" than rifle shots sang out, some hitting close. Spouts of water jetted up close to the boat. The skipper gave the motor full power, spun the tiller hard, and the boat swung in a hard turn.

The boat's machine gunner returned fire. Kenny was about to say "Don't," but it was too late. Bright yellow tracers lashed at the island. The kid had acted on instinct; no point in reprimanding him. The three silhouettes ducked out of sight but the beam of light still shone.

"Haul ass toward the headland," Kenny ordered. "When we're out of sight of that damn light, get us back to the ship."

"Aye aye, sir." The boat zipped away from Wolmi-do as fast as it could.

The North Koreans now knew something was up, but what? Kenny hoped they would just think this had been a South Korean patrol, not a sneak and peek for a full-scale invasion.

As the boat skimmed through Flying Fish Channel, Kenny thought about the role of luck in war. It was bad luck that the task force had run smack into Typhoon Kezia on the Yellow Sea on its way to Inchon. The smaller ships were tossed around like toys and a few of them suffered damage. The good luck was that no seamen were lost.

The storm had passed and now the seas were calm. Kenny hoped that good luck would continue with the barometer holding steady the next few days.

Well, he'd been fired at for the first time in the Korean War. He knew it wouldn't be the last.

Back aboard ship, Kenny huddled with MacArthur, General Oliver Smith, the commander of the 1st Marine Division, and other officers. Charts of the harbor covered a table before them. White-coated mess stewards brought in coffee.

The officers got right to it. "Well, Colonel Nielsen?" MacArthur asked.

"First of all, sir, the harbor doesn't seem to be mined. We saw none at all, so our destroyers will be able to enter Flying Fish Channel. But we'll need to capture Wolmi-do before attacking the seawall on the mainland." He pointed at the island on the map. "We took fire from Wolmi-do. No telling the size of it, but the enemy has a force there. I suggest we take the island at high tide, wait twelve hours, then go and hit the seawall."

"You mean have Marines spend a night on Wolmi-do before proceeding to the main objective?" General Smith said unhappily.

Before Kenny could reply, MacArthur, imperious as ever, said, "That's exactly what he means, Oliver, and he's correct. I will not undertake the main landing with an enemy force in my rear." Not *our*, but *my*, typical of the man.

237

"Of course, sir," Smith said subordinately.

"All right then," MacArthur said, "we'll shell Wolmi-do and the seawall area tomorrow at first light. Throw everything you've got at them, Bill," he told a Navy officer.

"Aye aye, sir. We'll give them a good pasting."

"Then at high tide we land and take Wolmi-do," MacArthur went on. "That will give the enemy a day's notice of our intentions but it can't be helped. He's sure to have troops in the area, but I have full confidence that the Marines will take them. The bulk of his forces are far to the south near Pusan. Draw up your landing plans accordingly, Oliver. Colonel Nielsen, it wasn't necessary that you perform the recon yourself, a lower rank could have done it for you. Nevertheless, I'm pleased you did. Excellent work out there."

General Smith looked at Kenny for what seemed like the first time. "Yes, good initiative on your part," he said.

It was 3 a.m. when Kenny reached his quarters, feeling some relief and satisfaction. He'd done all right. He brushed his teeth, crawled onto his bunk and prayed for Claudia. For the Marines who would go into action tomorrow too.

CHAPTER FIFTY-TWO

At the office, Jake took a call from Marion Davies, who asked if he could come over, she had something to tell him.

"Sure, but I've got some things to wrap up here," he said. "I can be there between four and five." Jake then called Valerie at Lockheed and said he'd be late for dinner, that Marion Davies wanted to see him.

When he arrived at the Beverly Drive mansion the maid showed him in and took him to the library. Horace Brown, Davies' tall real estate friend who resembled old man Hearst was there. They each held crystal goblets.

"Thanks for coming, Jake. I believe you've met Horace."

"Nice to see you again, Mr. Brown," Jake said. They shook hands.

"How about a drink?" Davies asked. "We're having sherry, or would you prefer some Scotch?"

"Nothing, thanks, I'm fine."

Davies and Brown took seats together on the sofa and Jake settled in a chair facing them.

"Millicent and the boys are going to contest my corporate shares and voting rights," Davies said.

"I'm not surprised. Fight them for your rights," Jake replied.

"No, we've decided not to. Horace and I think that's best."

"I disagree, Marion. You've gotta stand up to them."

"No, that could get messy," Horace Brown said. "She's already fine financially, has several good real estate holdings."

Davies touched the man's hand and said, "Thanks to your good advice, dear."

Dear? Jake was surprised.

"Plus I own this house and everything in it," Davies said. "And I got a bundle when I sold the beach house in Santa Monica." Beach house? The sprawling place had seventy rooms or more. "My bank account is in very good shape."

"But Marion, it's a matter of principal. You shouldn't—"

"It's all decided, Mr. Weaver," Brown broke in.

Frowning, Jake said nothing to that. He didn't particularly care for this Horace Brown guy or the advice he'd been giving to W.R.'s loyal longtime consort. The thought crossed his mind that this guy could be a Lothario in the employ of Millicent Hearst on the nefarious mission of seducing the lonely woman and persuading her to back away.

Now holding the man's hand, Davies said, "Incidentally, Horace and I are going to be married."

Jake's mouth dropped open at this shocker. He managed to say "Congratulations," though he didn't mean it for a second.

Rush hour traffic was horrible and it took Jake an hour to reach home. Along the way Red Foley was singing "Chattanooga Shoeshine Boy" on the radio. Jake was thinking that if Horace Brown would go so far as to marry Miss Davies he probably wasn't an agent of Millicent Hearst.

Once home, he found Valerie in the kitchen marinating some steaks with Worcester sauce and lemon juice. "These look great," he said after a hug and kiss. "How'd you know I had a hankering for steak?"

"We've had a lot of chicken, fish, and Mexican lately, so I knew you'd be ready
for some red meat. How about a drink, Sailor?"

"Sure, I didn't have one at the mansion, so I'm ready." Valerie poured two glasses of Jack Daniel's, added ice and water, and handed him one. They sat in chairs at the kitchen table and clinked glasses.

"So what was on Marion Davies' mind?"

"She dropped two bombshells on me, Val. Hearst's widow is contesting her corporate shares and voting rights, and Marion's decided to give in without a fight."

"Really? That doesn't sound like her. Bad decision if you ask me."

"It sure is." Jake took a drink and added, "It kind of pisses me off. When Hearst died she called and said 'They stole him from me.' She basically begged for my help."

"Which you went out of your way to give her, Jake. You like the woman."

"Yeah, and I sure did try to help. It took some doing to find out what was in the trust and W.R.'s personal will. Gave her the best advice I could, told her to fight for what she deserved. Darn her. So, yeah, I'm upset and disappointed."

"Understandably." Valerie got up and turned on the oven to pre-heat. She sat again, took a drink, and said, "Two bombshells. What was the other one?"

"She's gonna marry Horace Brown."

"Horace Brown? Who's that?"

Jake told about the real estate mogul who'd been advising her and that he was tall and physically resembled W.R.

Valerie said, "She never got to marry the man she loved

241

because he couldn't get a divorce, so in haste she's gone and found herself a substitute Hearst. Silly woman."

"Silly is right, Val. Marion's an alcoholic, doesn't always think straight. I give them a year."

Valerie got up again, set the oven to broil, and slid the steak dish in. "Say, what have you done with that pistol some damn prowler planted here?"

"Dumped it down a storm drain on Slauson, way down south of the paper."

CHAPTER FIFTY-THREE

Sam Sixto badgered Wannamaker into obtaining a search warrant. The detectives showed up at Jake's house at 6:30 the next evening when he was likely to be home.

At the door, Wannamaker showed Jake the warrant and said, "Sorry Weaver, but we're going to search the place."

"Geez, Owen, I already showed you around. Why this?"

"Looking for evidence, pal," Sixto said before Wannamaker could answer. "Part of our investigation."

Valerie came in from the kitchen, looking worried, and asked what was going on. "Sorry, hon, these guys have a warrant. They're gonna search the house."

"We'll have to be thorough, ma'am," Wanamaker said, "but we'll try not to mess up things too much."

"Just keep out of our way, lady," Sixto snapped. Valerie frowned and felt a strong urge to give him the finger.

The search began, first in the front room, looking under cushions in the sofa, checking lamps and the radio-TV console, and going over every inch of the chairs.

Then came the kitchen, going through the cupboards, rearranging dishes, removing canned goods and jars of spices, thoroughly checking the contents of the refrigerator, even the ice-cube tray. Valerie knew she would have quite a job putting everything back in order.

Satisfied in the kitchen, the cops went to the bathroom, removing every item in the cabinet, sniffing at jars, aspirin boxes and so on. Sixto pulled the lid off the toilet tank and shined a flashlight down into the water.

Then came the spare bedroom. Tearing through the closet — it was completely empty — raising the mattress, feeling underneath. Pressing against the pillows. Sixto got down on his knees and probed the floor, looking for loose boards that might conceal something below.

"This is about as fun as a broken bat," Jake muttered under his breath.

The process was repeated in the master bedroom. Feeling through all the clothes in the closet, no doubt looking for guns. Searching shoeboxes.

Jake and Valerie stood in the background watching all this desecration. Seeing their visible dismay, Wannamaker said, "This is probably a waste of time."

Sixto again tapped the flooring, looking for hidey-holes that might be underneath. Next came the dresser. He rummaged through Valerie's drawers, messing up nighties, bras, scarves and underwear.

Then, Jake's drawer. When Sixto found nothing but underwear and socks, Jake thought he caught an expression of disappointment on the guy's face. *Huh.* Jake would always remember that stymied look.

The cops trooped out to the garage and spent several minutes looking over the lawnmower, rake, shovel, tool box, and oil cans. Jake watched. Valerie stayed inside trying to restore order to the kitchen.

They finished up in the utility room with the vacuum cleaner, brooms and mops. Looked into the washing machine, even poked fingers into the box of laundry powder.

Returning to the living room, Wannamaker at last said, "This place is clean. Hope you're satisfied, Sam." At the front door, Wannamaker apologized: "Just doing our duty, folks. Sorry for the disturbance." The two of them left,

Wannamaker sketching a salute with his hand. Jake heaved a sigh of relief.

Hands on hips, Valerie said, "Thank God you got rid of that gun, Jake. I was planning on cooking us a nice dinner but not now. It'll take an hour to get everything back in place. We'll have some sandwiches later."

Goddamn that Sixto, Jake was thinking. He'd noted that the man was an inch or so shorter than him.

CHAPTER FIFTY-FOUR

September 1950. Inchon, South Korea.

As a staff officer, the division's G-2, Kenny didn't get into action when the invasion took place. It was the first time he hadn't been a part of it when the "Old Breed" landed on an enemy shore. That felt all wrong. *Damn, I should be with them.* All he could do was stay on the Mount McKinley and take the reports radioed in from the various battalions and companies.

Kenny knew that battle plans usually flew out the window in the first few minutes when the inevitable surprises popped up. Just before sunup, after three hours of restless sleep, he stood on the bridge listening to the ear-numbing blasts of the cruiser and destroyer guns hammering at their targets. In addition to the American ships, two British cruisers were out there too, firing their eight-inch shells. This after all was a U.N. action.

The shells arced high in the air, reached their apex, then looped downward and exploded in flashes of white and orange. The sounds of the explosions reached Kenny several seconds later.

The bombardment was lifted as flood tide approached. Kenny realized the coffee mug in his hand was shaking as he watched scores of Higgins boats begin to swarm away from the troopships and head for Wolmi-do. He clutched the mug with both hands to steady it.

Kenny's friend Captain Billy Ninetrees, a company commander, was aboard one of those boats. A Pawnee Indian, Ninetrees had fought alongside him at Guadalcanal, Cape

Gloucester, Peleliu, and Okinawa. God, how Kenny wished he was with Billy now. Most people, including his wife Claudia, would say that was a ridiculous thought — he should be happy to be out of harm's way. But those people had no way of comprehending how combat Marines felt about one another. They were a brotherhood.

He told himself that after Inchon was taken and they advanced on Seoul, he would abandon the rear echelons and finagle an attachment to one of the regiments.

This time, happily, the battle plan held together for the most part. Wolmi-do was captured within two hours with only minor casualties. The small communist force there was eradicated in two fierce firefights. Most of the enemy were wiped out, but a few stunned Reds were taken prisoner and questioned.

The attackers settled down for a half-day's wait as the tide ebbed and the landing craft hustled back through Flying Fish Channel. Later the boats would return and carry more invasion troops to the mainland and that daunting seawall at Red Beach, and to lower ground to the south at Blue Beach.

At a little after noon, Kenny returned to his quarters and plopped down on his bunk. He hoped to take a nap but, nerves jangling from the field reports he'd taken and the strong Navy coffee he'd consumed, sleep proved impossible. He lay there trying in vain to push thoughts out of his mind, thoughts about firefights, about Billy Ninetrees, and about Claudia, thousands of miles away at med school.

Inchon turned out to be tough scrap but the Marines prevailed as MacArthur had predicted and as Kenny was sure they would.

At the next flood tide, Marines stormed ashore at Blue Beach to the south and scaled the seawall at Red Beach. There they were reinforced by those who'd taken Wolmi-do, dashing across that narrow causeway.

Red Beach was the toughest. Troops took casualties from enemy fire at the top of the seawall and from a concrete pillbox a few meters beyond. It took awhile to eliminate that strongpoint with hand grenades and machine gun fire. One surprise was that most of the defenders at the seawall used hand-held submachine guns. To many NK soldiers they, rather than rifles, were apparently the weapon of choice. They turned out to be Russian-made Shpagin Fours.

On the second day, with the port facilities at last firmly in U.S. hands, Marines advanced into the town of Inchon itself. That day, Kenny and the rest of the division command came ashore and set up headquarters in a captured house.

Kenny learned that down at the Pusan Perimeter it took U.N. forces two days to cross the Naktong River and push back the NKs there. Once they did, though, the enemy retreat became a rout. The Reds' casualties were enormous and their supply lines were overstretched. They had to be short of food, fuel and ammunition. Now as their battered remnants staggered northward, they were mercilessly strafed and napalmed by Air Force P-51s.

Meanwhile, the urban fighting in Inchon town was tough, street to street and house to house, but the Marines were winning. Kenny prayed that Billy Ninetrees was okay. His old friend was in the thick of that.

When the town was taken, Marines could sweep north toward Seoul and east to cut off enemy forces retreating from the south. Down there, the 8th Army now began streaming rapidly northward. A few detachments of British, Australian and Turkish soldiers were with them.

MacArthur had designated his units in the Inchon sector as X Corps. He now had two major infantry forces under his command, 8th Army and X Corps. Kenny heard scuttlebutt around the HQ that the old man was already dreaming of sending both of them across the 38th Parallel to capture all of Korea, which abutted China.

What were the Chinese Reds thinking about all this? Kenny wondered. They couldn't be happy about a friendly communist neighbor falling to "Western imperialists." He'd met their new premier, Chou-En-lai, last year when he'd been detained during the civil war there. He'd found him to be a tough guy.

Kenny hypothesized: If, say, Russian forces were driving north in Baja California, the U.S. would never stand for that — we'd do something about it. It was a fair comparison, wasn't it? Red China could be having similar thoughts.

For the moment, though, Kenny was elated that MacArthur's grand plan was succeeding. He could visualize the adoring headlines back home, idolizing the aging genius.

After Inchon town was taken, Kenny took an intel team out to inspect Kimpo airfield east of there. He was one of three men in a Jeep that bounced along terrible, war-damaged roads. They passed through a couple of Marine Corps checkpoints.

Finally arriving at the airfield, Kenny was surprised to see some recent construction. The runway had been lengthened and new revetments and concrete hardstands appeared. He realized this was fresh work, done since the NK invasion.

"Ominous," he muttered. "Someone was planning to put a modern air force in here."

"It looks that way, doesn't it, sir?" said a captain who'd been driving their Jeep.

"Sure does, Baker. That control tower looks new, too. Fresh lumber. This is sophisticated stuff. I'll report this to MacArthur right away."

* * *

Which Kenny did later that afternoon.

"It's nothing to worry about," the commanding general said, laying a fatherly hand on Kenny's shoulder. "If this was the work of the Reds, they'll never get to use Kimpo, but we will. Nice of them to do this for us. I can put some of our new jet fighters in there. I will have this little war wrapped up in the next couple of months."

Kenny wasn't so sure about that. The discovery at Kimpo still seemed a bad omen to him. The plan may have been for some Russian-built MIGs to enter the war.

The next day, calling on a favor from a Marine Corps general he'd known for years, Kenny was able to get himself assigned to his old regiment, the 5th. MacArthur could spare him; the general had his own Army G-2, Major General Charles Willoughby.

Glad to be detached from MacArthur's headquarters, Kenny joined the 5th Marines for the northward push to Seoul and the 38th Parallel beyond. He was given command of a battalion.

CHAPTER FIFTY-FIVE

Ed Franklin's widow had another tryst with her lover, this time at a motel in Downey where they felt no one would know them. Before hopping into bed they drank champagne.

"I hope you're not worrying too much, babe," he said.

"Well, I *am* worrying. I hope this doggone investigation will be over pretty soon. Then we can do these things at your place. We can't do them at mine — the boys, you know."

He put down his wine flute, opened her negligee and fondled her breasts, then licked the nipples with his tongue.

"Oh, you get me so hot." Penny reached for his belt buckle and helped him get out of his pants.

Soon she was straddling him. "I love to ride that big thing . . . Oh, sweet Jesus, oh!"

Later in the afterglow they shared a cigarette, Penny taking a puff then handing it to him. Her late husband Ed never crossed her mind.

A few miles north, Valerie and Jake at last had their home back in order after that obnoxious search those detectives had made. Soon they were in bed doing the same as Penny Franklin and her lover.

"You've still got it, Sailor," she said huskily.

"With Ilse gone we can make all the noise we want," Jake said. They'd been doing this more often since his daughter moved out.

Afterward, Valerie murmured, "I sure needed that. It was so darn upsetting today."

Meanwhile Jake's daughter and her roommate had just returned from a movie at the Egyptian Theatre. *A Streetcar Named Desire.* Ilse and Claudia settled around the kitchenette table with glasses of pinot noir. A pot of geraniums occupied a ledge above the window.

"What did you think of the film?" Claudia asked.

"Enjoyed it. Marlon Brando was great and so was Vivienne Leigh. She played that sad character real well."

"I agree," Claudia said. "It's good they filmed it in black and white. Technicolor would've spoiled the mood."

That topic finished, she said, "We're both a few months away from graduation, Ilse. What then? What are your plans?"

"Mr. Hearst promised me a job at the *Herald-Express* after that exposé on Standard Oil *Vati* and I wrote. But he's gone now and I doubt if Hearst Junior would honor that. I'm sure he doesn't even know about it. I do want to become an investigative reporter, though, or a police reporter. It's been fun looking into that murder, questioning Freddie Franklin and so on. I might apply at the *Times* or maybe one of the San Francisco papers. It'd probably be best if I wasn't on the same paper as my father anyway. What about you, Claudia?"

"After my residency I'd like to set up a family practice somewhere, in one of L.A.'s suburbs or maybe San Diego. I want to be close to Kenny."

"Sounds good." Ilse sipped some wine and said, "You got a letter from him, didn't you?"

"A postcard, actually, showing some palm trees along a beach in La Jolla. He thanked me for coming to see him and said he loves me. Made me feel good."

"That's great. He's a swell guy."

"He sure is. I'm going to go see him again real soon. I thank my lucky stars he showed up at Espiritu Santo."

"Espiritu Santo?"

"Yes, a French island in the New Hebrides. That's where our fleet hospital was in '42. He was wounded on Guadalcanal, you know. As we got to know each other he helped me get over some bad stuff that happened in Ohio when I was in high school. He turned my world around. I owe him a lot."

"I didn't know about Guadalcanal," Ilse said.

"Yes, he was wounded there and again at Peleliu and Okinawa and now this bad stuff in Korea. How much can one body take? The poor guy."

"He needs you, Claw."

"I know. I've reached a decision: no more dinners with Dr. Jennings. My grades are good and I'll graduate even if I disappoint the guy."

Ilse felt better about her roommate when she went to bed that night.

Jake stopped by Mickey Cohen's haberdashery on Wilshire the next day. Two beefy punks with gun lumps under their jackets looked him over real good when he stepped in. Mickey always had some muscle around.

The goons chilled out when the boss entered from the back room, grinned and said, "Hey, Jakester, glad you come in. Let me show you a suit that'll make you look real spiffy."

"No thanks, Mickey, all I wanta do is buy a tie. Spilled

some damn chili on this one at lunch."

"Cheapskate," Cohen said. "You know something, it turns out I was half-assed on who killed that lawyer guy. Franklin did some work for Jack Dragna, sure, but that Amy Noonan broad didn't waste him. I was off base on that. She ain't the Easter lily she claims to be but she didn't ice the guy."

"Then who did?"

"Don't know, maybe the wifey. I stopped looking into that stuff, got troubles of my own. The grand jury's been sniffin' around."

One of Cohen's bulls had been standing close, listening in. "Deuce, don't you got somethin' to do?" Mickey said, swatting the air with a "shoo" motion.

Jake was glad to hear Cohen had called himself off on the Franklin murder business. "Let me see some neckties," he said.

CHAPTER FIFTY-SIX

September 1950. South Korea.

Scouring the personnel lists, Kenny found that Gunnery Sergeant Eddie Cooper was with the 5th Marines. This was the tough kid who'd been his companion during his imprisonment and subsequent escape last year from Red China. Kenny pulled rank and got Cooper assigned to him. He had high regard for the gunny.

When Cooper reported, he saluted and said, "Gosh, sir, I didn't know it was you when I got those orders. Darn good to see you."

"Likewise, Eddie. I'm putting you on my staff. Want to have you at my side again." He shook the sergeant's hand.

"That's swell, sir. Glad to hear it."

"How's your girlfriend, Angela?"

"Just fine, sir. We got together after China and we're engaged now."

"Congratulations."

The Marines of X Corps soon advanced on Seoul, where they found some fight still left in the weakened North Koreans. All the Han River bridges had been blown so the engineers built pontoon bridges to make the crossing to the capital.

Advance platoons had crossed at night to eliminate any enemy that could fire on the main force in the morning. They'd mostly succeeded in some fierce nighttime firefights, but still the morning crossing took some fire from two hills as they raced across the pontoon spans

Kenny's battalion was among them. An artillery shell whined in and exploded nearby in the water, dousing him with an unwelcome shower. "That was close, sir," Eddie Cooper said.

They reached the other side, clambered up the bank and moved toward the city. Enemy fire was sporadic. Kenny got his first sight of Seoul and found it to be a tragic mess. Fires burned here and there among shattered buildings. The town had taken a terrific beating in the Reds' June invasion, and suffered again in the past week from U.N. artillery fire.

Hungry civilians in tattered clothing seemed to be everywhere, begging for food and water. It was a hell of a nuisance — Marines had a war to fight. "Give 'em a few K-rations if you can spare them," he told some of the men around him.

He found a mostly undamaged two-story brick building and commandeered it for a temporary battalion HQ.

Kenny was heavily involved in the ensuing recapture of Seoul. He was saddened at the charred masonry, looted stores, burned-out homes and shattered government buildings he saw.

Before long he was standing in the background in the badly damaged capitol palace and watching as MacArthur made a ceremony of turning the city over to South Korean president Syngman Rhee. Civilian and military cameramen were busy taking still photos and newsreel footage.

"By the grace of a merciful Providence, our fighting forces under the standard of the greatest hope and inspiration of mankind, the United Nations, have liberated this ancient capital city," MacArthur said in soaring rhetoric that almost had Kenny gagging. "I now leave you to the discharge of civil responsibilities," the general concluded.

None of this was a surprise to Kenny. MacArthur had always been the consummate showman, making sure he was center stage at all times.

The North Koreans had fought hard for Seoul but now were in headlong retreat. U.S. forces had little trouble pushing on to the 38th Parallel. Kenny wondered, what now? Would MacArthur send them into North Korea? Would President Truman or the U.N.Security Council authorize that? He was pretty sure that was just what MacArthur wanted to do, even though the original mandate was simply to defend the south, and that had been accomplished.

Three days later, Truman okayed a National Security Council paper that told MacArthur, "If there is no threat of intervention by Peking or Moscow, you are to extend operations north of the parallel and plan for the occupation of North Korea."

This was all the general, who saw no such threat, needed. The war would move north.

That night Kenny wrote a letter to Claudia. He said he was fine and that she needn't worry about him. He added that the 5th Marines would enter North Korea and that this gave him some concern. He wondered if the censors would cut out that part.

CHAPTER FIFTY-SEVEN

Owen Wannamaker and Sam Sixto went to see the widow Penny Franklin again. At the door, Sixto was more apologetic for the unannounced visit than Wannamaker, which surprised the lead detective. Wannamaker gave him a look.

Once inside the woman said, "Here we go again, huh, boys? I'll go make coffee while you think up some nasty questions."

"I'll help you with that, ma'am," Sixto said. Another surprise. Wannamaker didn't want coffee, wanted to jump right into the questioning. He sat in a chair and wrinkled his brow watching them go to the kitchen. When did Sixto become such a gentleman?

They were back a few minutes later, Sixto carrying a tray holding cups, saucers, spoons, and bowls of cream and sugar, which he set on the glass-topped coffee table. Mrs. Franklin took a seat on the sofa facing it. Sixto perched on a chair close to Wannamaker, who ignored his cup and jumped right in.

"Mrs. Franklin, we've asked you this before, but where were you the night your husband was killed?"

"Still here with the boys, same as before. They've confirmed that."

"Yes, and what time did they go to bed?"

"At 10, that's their bedtime."

"Even the high school senior, Freddie?"

"Even Freddie, officer. He's a good student and knows it's important to get his sleep."

"I see, and what did you do then? Did you go out for awhile after they were asleep?"

Sixto, holding his cup, said, "Aw, Owen."

"No I didn't," Franklin said. "I watched TV awhile waiting for Ed to come home. When he didn't, I went to bed about 11. So you see, I sure as heck didn't kill him."

"Were you worried by his absence? Did he often work late?"

"He often did . . . if it was really work."

"What do you mean by that, ma'am?"

With a sardonic grin, the woman said, "I think you know, detective. Boys will be boys."

"Yes, some boys will. I think you knew he was cheating on you and so when you were sure your sons were asleep you went out, drove to his office, and gave him what you felt he deserved."

"Aw, Owen," Sixto started but Penny Franklin cut him off: "I most certainly did not! How dare you. I'm grossly insulted. Besides, I didn't think he was in his office, more likely in the arms of some floozy somewhere. And we're sick and tired of having people badger us about this."

"People, ma'am? What people have been badgering you?"

"The wife of that newspaperman, Weaver. She came over and questioned me. And his daughter gave Freddie the third degree too."

Wannamaker slammed a fist into his other hand. "His wife and daughter? Really?"

"They sure did, detective." She picked up her cup defiantly and sipped some coffee.

"I told that darn Weaver to keep out of this. I'm gonna give that guy some serious hell."

"He's probably your killer," the woman said. "Weaver."

Sixto: "I think so too, ma'am."

"Come on, you two. If Weaver was the killer he wouldn't send his wife and daughter sniffing around to see if it was you."

"Why not?" Sixto said. "Lay a red herring, send us in the wrong direction."

Wannamaker shook his head. "Back to you, ma'am. We believe your husband was killed after midnight. Do you have an alibi for after the boys were in bed that night? A maid or neighbor, anyone?"

"Ha. We don't have a maid and no neighbor came over. It was just me and Milton Berle . . . on the TV, you know."

The detectives wrapped it up and left soon after that. At the wheel in the car, Wannamaker said, "You were out of character in there, Sam. Why so solicitous of the woman?"

"Cause she didn't do it. Weaver did."

Wannamaker drove off in silence, still not buying that. But he was going to have some harsh words for Jake Weaver.

CHAPTER FIFTY-EIGHT

October 1950. Wonsan, North Korea.

Another landing on a hostile shore, but this time not an amphibious one. Aboard troopships, the 1st Marine Division debarked on the piers at Wonsan, a port city on Korea's east coast, a few miles north of the Parallel.

North Koreans had heavily mined the waters around Wonsan and the landing had been delayed several days while minesweepers cleared a channel. The town had been mostly secured by an ROK (Republic of Korea) division. Supplied and trained by the U.S., a few South Korean units were now performing well.

Despite the ROK presence in Wonsan, Marines encountered some light resistance, a few snipers and rifle teams, which were soon cut down.

While the task force had sailed from Inchon around the tip of Korea to this deployment, Kenny prayed for Claudia, hoping she was doing well and that he'd be back with her before long.

When he and Sergeant Cooper descended the gangplank, each carrying their gear, Kenny caught sight of numerous port facilities, including storage tanks and large cranes for the loading and unloading of ships. The harbor had been cleared of local craft — nothing here now but Navy vessels.

Kenny gave Eddie Cooper the lowdown: "MacArthur's sending X Corps, which includes us, up Korea's east side and 8th Army up the west, on the other side of the mountains."

"Think we'll wrap up the Norkos pretty fast, sir?"

"I hope so, Eddie, they're badly worn down and disorganized. In war you never can tell, though. Plans don't always work out the way you want. I'm not too thrilled about dividing forces like this. If I had my way we'd consolidate and push right up to the Yalu River, all of us together." Kenny laughed and said, "But MacArthur didn't ask my opinion on that. If we did it my way, the enemy in the northeast side of the peninsula would get starved out and collapse."

That is, if the Chinese don't come in, he thought. That would be a whole different ballgame. He was thinking of his analogy of Russians in Baja getting close to California. Kenny kept that to himself. Eddie Cooper didn't need to know of that concern.

They piled their gear in a waiting Jeep and climbed in. Kenny was planning to set up a bivouac for his battalion north of town. There they'd get organized and replenish their supplies before driving north.

The Jeep chugged through Wonsan town, passing columns of Marines toting their weapons, field packs on their backs. Overhead, Corsairs from the carrier Essex offshore in the Sea of Japan flew cover.

The Jeep passed buildings of all sizes, including Buddhist temples, pagodas, and office buildings. Quite a few were damaged. Bewildered civilians were everywhere, most of them in conical hats and baggy black trousers. Some of them stuck out their hands, begging from the Marines.

A frosty breeze chilled Kenny. September had been warm, sometimes hot, but perhaps the Korean winter was getting ready to pounce. He said, "Eddie, one of our objectives is a reservoir up there, someplace called Chosin."

Four days later.

The North Koreans stopped and fought at a ridge thirty miles northwest of Wonsan. Kenny's battalion was in the thick of it. Over heated protest from his aide, Eddie Cooper, Kenny picked up an M-1, slapped a helmet on his head and said he was going out to join the company Billy Ninetrees commanded.

"Sir, that's totally unnecessary," Cooper said. "You shouldn't expose yourself."

"I'm just gonna have a look-see, Eddie. Want to assess the situation up close. You stay here with Lieutenant Keyser and take the reports."

Kenny rode a Jeep to the front and found Ninetrees' company hunkered in foxholes a quarter mile from the enemy-held ridge.

After asking where the skipper was, he crawled up to the Pawnee and put a hand on his friend's shoulder. Surprised, Ninetrees said, "What the devil are you doing here, sir? I mean Kenny. We're taking enemy fire."

"Need to see how we're doing, Billy. Just like Okinawa, isn't it, the bad guys with the high ground again?"

"Dammit, Kenny, I see you've got a rifle. You stay out of this. I won't have you getting hurt. Keep behind me and stay down. I'm in command here. Do as I say."

"Aye aye, sir," Kenny said.

Just then he heard the cough of an enemy mortar fired from the ridge, its whine as it sailed downward, and its concussive blast as it exploded several meters away. Rocks and dirt showered over their helmets.

"Anybody hurt over there?" Ninetrees called to the nearby foxholes.

"One guy's arm's hit, sir, everybody else okay."

"Get him to a corpsman, Sergeant."

"Sure thing, sir."

"What's your idea here, Billy?" Kenny asked.

"Looking for a way to flank 'em. I won't go frontal against that hill."

"Good."

"The left doesn't look promising but I see a slot over there to the right between this rise and the next one. I'll send a platoon in there to see if they can get enfilade on them."

Kenny would have done the same but didn't say so. Ninetrees was in charge here.

Billy called a platoon leader over, a second lieutenant, and gave him the orders. As the platoon moved out in that direction a rifle shot zinged off a rock two meters from Kenny, tossing shards of granite in the air.

Kenny hated war but when he was in it an inexplicable enthusiasm came over him. This was where he should be, with his brother Marines. He slipped lower in the foxhole and watched.

An hour later the platoon had gone into the slot, climbed a hill lower than the enemy's, but close enough to hit them from the side. And they did, pouring rifle and machine gun fire on the Norkos. The attack caught the enemy by surprise and had them looking in that direction.

Ninetrees stood and shouted, "Now, men. Forward. Take that hill." In a lower voice: "You stay back here, Kenny. I mean it." And off he jogged, keeping low.

As the charge began, Kenny stayed somewhat in the rear, but not much. He trotted forward too. A minute later an enemy soldier about forty meters off suddenly looked his way. Kenny fired. A crimson blotch materialized on the soldier's chest.

As he toppled backward, Kenny caught a glimpse of his face. He was just a kid, an Asian teenager. Well, this is what I do, Kenny told himself. I'm a Marine.

Getting hammered now from the front and side, the enemy soon collapsed and the survivors rushed pell-mell to the north. The ridge littered with torn bodies, Kenny inspected the blood-soaked ground and told Ninetrees, "Good work."

"Thanks Kenny. Now get your ass back where it belongs."

Kenny slapped the Pawnee's shoulder and did as he was told.

"Sure relieved to see you, sir," Eddie Cooper said when he arrived at his HQ. "You shouldn't have gone out there."

"So everybody keeps telling me. It was a good scap, Eddie. Ninetrees' company carried the day."

"Sir, here's something you need to hear. Third Batt, a little west of here, took some prisoners last night. One of them was Chinese."

Outside, some snowflakes were falling.

CHAPTER FIFTY-NINE

Jake sat at his desk going over a story Marko Janicek had just written about an armed robbery at the May Company. The police reporter was on vacation and Marko had filled in. Just then detective Wannamaker appeared in his doorway.

Surprised, Jake said, "Owen, come in."

Wannamaker closed the door before taking a chair in front of Jake. Without preamble he said, "Dammit, Weaver, didn't I tell you to keep out of this?"

Oh-oh. "Yes, and—"

"But you sure as hell didn't, even though you gave me your word. I find that your wife and daughter stuck their noses in too, questioned the widow and one of her sons."

"How did you . . . well, never mind, you're a good detective."

"Penny Franklin told me. Sixto and I questioned her again and she told us about it. It pisses her off, as it sure as hell should."

"I'm darn sorry about that, Owen. They were just trying to help prove I'm not your killer. I'll put a stop to it right now, slam the door on that."

"You'd damn well better. They could be charged with interfering in a police investigation, you know."

"Aw, you wouldn't do that, would you?"

"No." Pointing a finger at Jake. "But I sure could."

"Now don't bite my head off on this," Jake said, "but the gals think Penny Franklin is your killer."

"Between us and the fencepost, and don't tell a soul, so do I, but that's beside the point. Any more of this meddling and I will press charges."

The door opened and city editor Aggie Underwood came in. "Oh, sorry, didn't know you were busy. Let me see that Janicek piece as soon as you're done," she said, nodded at Wannamaker and left. Closed the door behind her.

"That was Aggie Underwood, wasn't it?" Wannamaker said. "Used to be your police reporter. Had a good rep with all the cops."

"Yep, that was Aggie. I'm hearing you loud and clear on this, Owen. There'll be no more digging by any of us. Nada."

"Okay then, Jake. Message delivered. This time keep your word." Another menacing jab with a finger. "So long." Wannamaker left. No shaking of hands.

Jake sat there feeling blue. He didn't enjoy being called on the carpet like that, although he'd deserved it. He was proud of Valerie and Ilse for the digging they'd done. It took guts for Valerie to call on a woman she didn't know and more or less ask if she was a murderer. Ilse tracking down that Franklin kid and meeting him at a soda fountain was great investigative work too.

But he'd have to call them off. Wannamaker meant it when he said he would charge them if any more of that happened.

The conversation with Mickey Cohen sprang to mind. Jake sure wasn't going to tell Wannamaker that Cohen had been looking into this. Cohen thought Amy Noonan was the killer, carrying out a hit job for Jack Dragna. That sounded way far-fetched. Should he pay another visit to Miss Noonan? Jake didn't like the idea of being seen at the *Examiner* building again. Well, maybe a phone call. He had a reason to talk with her anyway.

He picked up his phone and called Noonan's office. Edith Harris answered and put the lady lawyer on the line. "I got hold of one of the features editors at the *Times*," he told her. "Take down this name."

Noonan thanked him, wrote down the name, and said, "I've got that piece I wrote for the law journal to show you if you're still willing to look at it."

"Sure, that's fine, Amy. Come on by." Jake said so long, then: Holy cow, Janicek's robbery story! Jake read it closely, found it fine and changed only two words. He got up and took it to Aggie Underwood.

CHAPTER SIXTY

October 1950. North Korea.

K enny wondered how it could be so cold. October was usually a fine month back home in Illinois, the days soft and warm after the midyear heat, sometimes with four or five days of invigorating Indian summer. The nights chilly but rarely freezing. But here in Korea old man winter was already starting to make himself felt.

Kenny took to wearing his heavy coat and made sure his men did too. Supplies, including winter gear, were now coming in from Hungnam, a port north of Wonsan. The Navy out there on the Sea of Japan was doing a good job.

The 5th Marines had advanced several miles beyond that battle north of Wonsan two weeks ago. They'd had a couple more scraps with the enemy since then but nothing major, just skirmishes. Thankfully, casualties had been light.

No more Chinese soldiers had been identified, just that one. Kenny thought he was probably an observer for the generalissimo Cho-En-lai. Would more come in, perhaps actual fighting forces? Kenny fervently hoped not.

He'd learned that 8th Army on the other side of the mountain spine that bisected North Korea was advancing well, just as X Corps had done here. MacArthur's divided-force plan seemed to be working. So far.

Alarming news came that night from the Air Force. U.N. air supremacy was being challenged for the first time. Russian jet fighters had appeared in the far north, just below the Yalu River, and had engaged in dogfights with American Saber jets. Kenny and three of his staff were huddled around an oil-burning stove in his HQ tent when that troubling report came in.

"I doubt if those NK fliers are very good," Lieutenant Keyser said. "I think our flyboys can handle them."

"How do you know they're Koreans, sir?" Eddie Cooper asked, rubbing his hands above the stove. "Maybe some Russian pilots are flying those MIGs."

"I hope not," Kenny said. "That'd be a major provocation."

They went on to discuss the battalion's positioning, the condition of the vehicles, and the amount of fuel and ammunition on hand. A C-47 cargo plane had flown low over the bivouac that afternoon and dropped some additional supplies by parachute.

Kenny wrote out orders for the next day's actions and handed them to Keyser. His battalion was to reconnoiter in force along a Korean rail line and take a town called Oro-ri. After that, the 5th Marines would consolidate all battalions and attack farther up that line to secure the towns of Sudong and Kagaru-ri. Then they'd be close to the Chosin Reservoir where they would set up a strongpoint. That reservoir's dynamos generated electricity for much of North Korea and even parts of Manchuria.

Snuggled in his sleeping bag that night, Kenny prayed for Claudia and hoped her medical studies were going well. Outside, a frigid wind rattled the tent.

CHAPTER SIXTY-ONE

Amy Noonan showed up at Jake's office within an hour of the phone call. As she took a seat in front of his desk and pulled a manuscript from her purse, Jake studied the woman, looking for any sign she could be a killer. Pretty face with a trace of toughness in it — after all she was a lawyer in a rough and tumble town — light makeup. Nothing he saw said killer to him.

"Awfully nice of you to do this, Jake," she said, handing him five pages of mimeographed copy, stapled in the upper left corner.

Jake gave it a speed-read, found a few run-on sentences, overlong paragraphs, and some lawyerese where something simpler would have sufficed.

Finished, he said, "This reads well, Amy. There are a few unnecessary adverbs in here, and newspapers prefer shorter paragraphs, but overall this is good copy. Be sure to show this to Hollister at the *Times* when you see him."

When he handed it back, Noonan took a small package of mints from her purse and popped one in her mouth. She extended the packet and asked if Jake would like one. He said yes, slipped one in his mouth, and said, "Say, I heard through the grapevine that Ed did some work for Jack Dragna. I was surprised to hear that. Is it true?"

"Wherever did you hear that, Jake?"

"Reporter's secret."

Noonan laughed and said, "I remember those anti-crime stories you wrote about Bugsy Siegel and all. You've got contacts in the underworld, don't you?"

"A few, yes."

"Well, it is true. Ed said he didn't like doing it but that Dragna paid him well. We could always use some extra money sometimes, couldn't we?"

"Yep. When I was a low-paid rookie here I did some moonlighting at MGM in publicity. That was kind of fun and it helped put food on the table."

Noonan asked what stars he'd met and what they were like. Jake mentioned Olivia de Havilland, Myrna Loy, and a couple of others. He said he found some to be high-hat and vain, others insecure, and some to be just plain folks.

Remembering what Mickey Cohen had said, he asked, "Did that work out okay for Ed? Did he have any trouble with Dragna?"

Noonan squinted and took a moment before saying, "Why no, not that I know of. Ed didn't mention anything like that. Why do you ask?"

"I don't know. Reporters ask a lot of questions, sometimes dumb ones."

"Are you thinking Dragna might have killed him?"

"I don't know what I'm thinking, Amy. Just throwing darts in the air here."

"I see. Well, thanks again for reading my article and setting up Mr. Hollister for me. I'll be sure and watch those adverbs." Noonan got to her feet and extended a hand, which Jake shook. "I'd better be on my way, have a client coming in at 4."

"Appreciate your stopping by, Amy. Good luck at the *Times.*" Jake watched as the attractive woman walked away, nice fanny, and knew the guys in the city room would be ogling her too.

He sat and wondered if Mickey Cohen was off base

on this. He'd said Amy wasn't the goody two-shoes she appeared to be.

Jake and Valerie sat in the front room that night drinking Scotch and water. He told her about detective Wannamaker stopping by, that he'd found out about her visiting Penny Franklin and was damned angry about it. "I promised him we'd stay out of his way from now on."

"Okay, I guess," Valerie said. "I don't know what else I could do now anyway. How did he find out?"

"He and that Sixto guy questioned the Franklin woman again and she told them."

"Darn her." Valerie swirled her glass. The ice cubes tinkled. "Well, what about you? Will you stop snooping?"

"Except for asking Amy Noonan some questions today I'm out of it too."

"You saw Amy Noonan today?"

Jake said Noonan had brought in a story she'd written for the law journal and that he'd arranged for her to meet a man at the *Times*. She hoped to be a law writer for a newspaper. He said he'd asked her about Franklin doing some legal work for Jack Dragna. "I told you Mickey Cohen thought Miss Noonan killed Franklin on Dragna's orders, didn't I?"

"Yes, Jake, and that sounds really far-fetched."

"I think so too, Sweets. But now Cohen's keeping out of this."

"That's good, but he did help us when those Germans tried to kidnap Ilse last year. Had some of his men watching out for us."

Jake took a drink and said, "Right, and I'll always be grateful, but this is a different thing altogether. We can't afford to get sideways with Wannamaker any more. I'll tell Ilse to keep out of this too."

"Good. She needs to concentrate on her studies and not skip any more classes."

"Yep, I'll tell her that right now," Jake said, and went to the phone.

CHAPTER SIXTY-TWO

October 1950. Oro-ri, North Korea.

Kenny's battalion captured Oro-ri, a humble little town with colorful buildings, a Buddhist temple, and a quaint town square featuring a statue of some fierce, helmeted Asian wielding a big sword. A steam engine stood idle and cold in the little train station. Marines had encountered no traffic as they'd advanced up that rail line. Korean trains weren't running, at least not in this part of the country.

Marines gathered around two ornate fountains in the square and filled their canteens. Kenny's stern order against looting was mostly obeyed. A light snow drifted down.

One of the town elders approached in a black, robe-like gown, rope sandals on his feet. He seemed to recognize Kenny as an authority figure. He spoke to him through an interpreter, a Korean-American corporal from Los Angeles. The old man said that a North Korean army unit deserted the place the day before, after cleaning out most of their food stores.

Kenny had Eddie Cooper give the elder a cigarette. When the sergeant lit it for him the man puffed on it and bowed deeply.

"Our village has seen many foreign masters," he said via the translator. "Mongolians, Japanese, Chinese, and Japanese once again, but this is the first time we have been occupied by white men. Your land is far away, is it not? Why do you come here?"

"To free you from communist rule," Kenny said.

"I do not understand this. We are a small country, many would say insignificant. Why should you care how we are governed?"

"That's a good question, sir. You'd have to ask someone

higher up than me."

The old man offered a thin smile and bowed again. "Gautama Buddha be with you," he said, and shambled away. Kenny stood there, reflecting on the simple profoundness of the guy's observations. Why indeed was he up here above the 38th Parallel?

Raggedy civilians began to gather around, begging with outstretched hands. Although Kenny's men had little food to spare, some of them handed out a few K-rations. Kenny watched awhile and then rode a Jeep to where his HQ tent was set up at the edge of town.

More bad news came that night. His radio man said 8th Army had captured nine more Chinese soldiers, men in Chinese Red uniforms who couldn't speak any Korean.

Kenny had some bad dreams that night. One of them featured an old man in black brandishing an evil-looking dagger. Another involved being trapped in a cave.

CHAPTER SIXTY-THREE

Aggie Underwood came into Jake's office and said, "It's our lucky day. Junior is coming in to address the troops. I've no idea what he's going to say, maybe some changes or layoffs. Who knows?"

Jake grinned. "I'd better make sure my tie is straight. Gotta look good on my last day of work."

"Bullshit, Jake, he's not going to fire you. But if he does, I'll quit, will go out the door right beside you."

"Don't be silly, Aggie. If it comes to that, don't you dare quit. This old rag needs you."

Aggie laughed and left.

After the second edition was put to bed and before the deadline for the third, Bill Hearst came in wearing an immaculate charcoal suit with a burgundy tie. He spent a couple of minutes in managing editor John Campbell's office, then came out and climbed on top of a desk in the middle of the city room. Jake came in and pulled up a chair beside reporter Richie Millsap. Junior's thin black hair was brushed back and he still didn't much resemble his father.

Voices quieted and typewriters stopped as the man raised manicured hands. "Hello everyone," he called out. "As of today I am your publisher, having the honor of succeeding my late father. I've spoken with most of our editors and a few others, and I'll look forward to meeting individually with the rest of you in the days ahead. As was the case with my father, I will not be here every day but I'll watch the papers closely and will come in here every so often."

Jake knew he'd bought a home in Bel-Air.

"For the time being," Junior went on, "it will be business as usual, no changes in personnel. Later, though, there may be a few." Did he glance at Jake at that moment? "Our editorial policy will be unchanged for the most part, although I want less sensationalism. The *Herald-Express* needs to be more dignified."

"Like the *Times*?" Richie Millsap muttered under his breath.

"Shh," Jake mouthed.

"I also want more emphasis on world news," Hearst continued. "There's a war on in the Far East to stop communist aggression. We don't have a war correspondent at the moment but I'm thinking of sending someone out there to cover it." Now he *did* glance at Jake.

"Soon I will meet with the sports, features and society editors. That's all for now. Carry on, people." Junior stepped down without asking if there were any questions and left the room.

A dozen conversations began buzzing the moment he was gone.

Jake shrugged, went back to his office and slammed a fist on the desk. Last year his story predicting the outbreak of the Korean War caused a sensation and was a nice feather in the paper's cap, but he wanted no part of that war now. *Does that clown want to send me there?*

He noticed for the first time a note from the city desk lying there. Edward R. Murrow of CBS had called and wanted him to call back.

Balboa Naval Hospital, San Diego.

Kenny was drifting in that twilight region between sleep and marginal awakeness. He'd been dreaming or thinking, he couldn't tell which, about first kisses. It was the day he and Jacqueline Lundquist rode bikes out to Lake Storey to go swimming. That was their junior year at Galesburg High. He'd got up his nerve that day and kissed her for the first time.

His mental meanderings then turned to a better and more important first kiss. He'd been recovering at Espiritu Santo from his Guadalcanal chest wound, with the help of that lovely nurse Claudia Chase. They'd become friends and were strolling in the hospital gardens near the Coral Sea. Hand in hand for the first time. The sun up and warm, sparkling waves dancing in the sea, birds singing their morning songs.

That's when he found the nerve to kiss her. It was a tentative little brush of the lips at first, but it grew deeper, warmer, more meaningful. "What took you so long?" Claudia asked. He had no good answer to that. His childhood shyness surfacing, perhaps. He kissed her again.

Kenny still couldn't discern whether this was a dream or memories encoded in his subconscious when the image vanished. He sensed that someone had snuck into his room. That someone was Rosie the nurse, he realized, catching the scent of her lavender perfume.

Rosie crept up, put a hand on his forehead and whispered, "Shh. Checking for fever."

Kenny liked Rosie; great nurse and she'd become a friend. But why was she here in the middle of the night? She'd never done that before.

"Kenny," she said softly, "you're a wonderful guy, brave,

courageous and handsome as a movie star."

Had this gal lost her mind, coming in here and saying things like this at whatever time this was? Maybe she'd been drinking. To Kenny's further surprise, now she was drawing back the covers and pulling away his sleeping gown. *What the hell?* Next, she tossed off the robe she'd been wearing, slipped naked onto the bed and began to straddle him.

"What are you—?"

"Shut up, Kenny," Rosie said, putting a finger to his lips. She leaned forward and began kissing him. Her body was soft and warm against his and Kenny felt arousal rising in his groin.

"We both need this," she murmured. "It will do you good, relieve some of your tension. God knows, I need it too."

Her exposed breasts loomed just above Kenny's face. He began to kiss them. Rosie moaned in pleasure.

Somehow fighting off primal instinct, Kenny burst out, "No, stop! We can't do this. I belong to Claudia."

Rosie sat up and began to pull away. "I'm glad you said that."

"You're glad? I don't get it, Rosie. You come in here and then . . . was this some kind of a test?"

"I guess maybe it was. You always seemed like a decent guy, devoted to your wife. I knew I didn't have a chance but I wanted to be sure. I hope she realizes what she has in you."

"Jesus, Rosie, you had me going there for a second."

"I know. You're as good a man as I always thought. If things were different, though . . ." She let that sentence hang, pulled on her robe, and padded out of the room.

Sure glad Claudia couldn't see that, Kenny thought. That was some test, if it had really happened, that is. Or was it just part of a dream? But if it was a dream, why is that lavender perfume still lingering? And a wet tear on my cheek?

Kenny had trouble getting back to sleep. Couldn't recapture that day with Claudia beside the Coral Sea.

CHAPTER SIXTY-FOUR

November 1950. Kagaru-ri, North Korea.

Taking Oro-ri had been easy enough for the 5th Marines and so had Sudong, but all that changed when they fought for Kagaru-ri, the last town on the drive to the Chosin Reservoir.

Temperatures plummeted and a heavy snowfall whistled down. Enemy resistance was heavy and bad visibility only worsened the battle situation. Kenny wished his men had white coats as the Finns had in their war with the Russians in the winter of 1940. He'd heard the adage that General Winter was a brilliant commander and now he seemed to be with the North Koreans. Some of Kenny's men had taken to painting their helmets white.

Marines were suffering many casualties at Kagaru-ri, both from enemy fire as well as frostbite.

Again he took his M-1 and, over strong objections from his staff, went out to the front to see what he could do. Picking his way over rocky, icy ground, he headed in the direction of gunfire and explosions. He passed artillery teams and an aid station, where corpsmen were busy, too busy, tending the wounded. A tarp covered what had to be a sad pile of dead Marines.

He found a sergeant who pointed to a hill where he thought Billy Ninetrees' company was in action. Kenny found Ninetrees' unit dug in on a small snow-covered rise overlooking an enemy position below. At least Marines had the high ground for once.

Ninetrees spotted him trudging up in a crouch and said, "Dammit Kenny, why do you keep showing up like this? You belong back at your HQ."

"Yeah, Billy, but you know me, just had to assess the situation."

"Well, goddamn it, keep your ass down. Crazy fool."

The old familiar sounds of battle melded into one loud din of noise as he saw Marines hammering the enemy with rifle and machine-gun fire as well as mortar bursts. Kenny fired a few shots at the NKs below, having no idea if he'd hit anyone but feeling some satisfaction at participating. He ducked when an enemy shell whistled in and exploded several meters off to his right.

The NKs eventually began to crumble under the heavy onslaught and were starting to pull out, at least those who were alive. Countless shattered bodies littered a grim landscape that was now both white and red. Death was oh so greedy.

Ninetrees ordered his men down the hill to mop up.

Satisfied at this victory, Kenny left and hiked back to the rear, struggling through snowdrifts. He fell once and pushed himself up, brushing snow from his arms and legs. Damn, he was cold. He saw a raggedy dog chasing madly round and round in circles, howling, kicking up snow, made crazy by the thunderous artillery blasts. Poor creature.

Passing a field kitchen where battle-weary Marines were getting some welcome chow, Kenny thought he caught sight of Clint "Hoagy" Carmichael among them. But that was impossible. His friend Hoagy had died years ago at Peleliu. God, now he was seeing things.

When he arrived at last, the warmth of the HQ tent was a gift from the gods. He put his rifle aside, removed gloves, and began rubbing his hands above the stove to bring them back to life.

"Sure glad you're okay, sir," Eddie Cooper said. "You've gotta stop doing things like that."

"Yeah, yeah."

"Did you see any of those Chicoms out there?" Cooper asked.

"Chicoms? No, what are you talking about?"

"A whole company of Chinese Reds are out there with the NKs, sir. Definitely identified as Chinese."

CHAPTER SIXTY-FIVE

Jake and Valerie went to dinner at Perino's. She was taller than Jake in her high heels as they entered, but he didn't mind. He was proud to be seen in the company of his tall, lovely wife.

The maître d' greeted them and led the way to a leather-ette booth. After Valerie fluffed a napkin on her lap, silvery wheeled chafing dishes rolled by, one of Perino's features she found charming.

A busboy came up and placed glasses of water on the table while Jake scanned the wine list. Before long he ordered a bottle of 1943 Sonoma cabernet sauvignon from the som-melier.

Then came a waiter. "We'll order later," Jake told him. "We're in no hurry tonight."

When the man walked off, Valerie asked, "How was your day, Sailor?"

"Hearst Junior came in, stood up on a desk like Moses on Mount Sinai and addressed the troops."

"Oh-oh, what did he say?"

"Not a whole lot, Val. He let us know he's now the pub-lisher and that he wants less sensationalism and more world news. Wants us to be more dignified, if you can imagine the *H-E* being dignified. Says there'll be no personnel changes, at least for the time being."

"That's good. You must have felt relieved."

"I guess I did." Glancing at the menu, Jake asked, "What are you in the mood for?"

"Their famous prime rib, of course. You?"

"Same thing." Jake took a drink of water and added, "Oh, Junior also says we need a war correspondent again. He glanced at me at that moment."

"You buried your lead, Jake. That was the most important thing he said. But, shoot, you're all through with that going-to-war sort of thing, aren't you? You're an editor now."

The waiter reappeared and asked, "Have you decided, folks?"

"Yep. We'll both have the prime rib, on the lean side."

The man nodded his approval and left, soon replaced by the sommelier, who showed Jake the bottle of cab. When Jake said, "That's it," the man removed the cork and poured a small amount in a wineglass for Jake to taste. He swirled it a moment, tested the bouquet with his nose, and pronounced it ready to pour. When that show was over, Jake and Valerie clinked glasses. "Here's to you," Jake said. "Best wife a man could ask for."

"You old charmer, you."

"Where we were?" Jake asked.

"The war correspondent thing."

"Oh, right. Junior says he wants us to cover the Korean War. There's no way I'll do that, Val. I'd quit first. If he asks I'll tell him to send Marko Janicek. He's a former Army Ranger and a good reporter. Marko would do a good job for us."

"What if Junior insists on it being you? Would you really quit?"

"Darn right I would. I'd hate to leave the jolly old *Herald*, but I can get a job anywhere. *The Times* would take me but I've been thinking about the *Daily News*. It's a real hustling little rag and I like their main guy, Matt Weinstock."

"I see. That'd be an interesting change for you."

The conversation drifted into the Ed Franklin murder and detective Wannamaker's insistence that they stay out of it. Valerie brought up her notion that Penny Franklin was the killer.

"Maybe," Jake said, "but I'm starting to think Sam Sixto. He mighta been the one who planted that pistol on us."

They each drank some wine and then the meals were wheeled up. The waiter placed baked potatoes slavered with butter and sour cream on their plates, and made a performance of slicing prime rib for them.

Later, as they enjoyed their meals, Valerie said, "I wonder how Kenny Nielsen is getting along down in San Diego. Why don't we go and see him one of these weekends?"

"Good idea, hon. Let's bring Ilse and Claudia with us. Kenny would be happy to see us all."

CHAPTER SIXTY-SIX

November 1950. Chosin Reservoir, North Korea.

For Kenny and the rest of the 5th Marine Regiment the Korean War had gone to hell in a hand basket, a very cold and bitter hand basket. The Chinese Reds were in, no doubt about it. General MacArthur had been dead wrong when he assured President Truman they wouldn't intervene.

The 5th and 7th Marines reached their assigned positions near the Chosin Reservoir and quickly found themselves in action against the Chinese. They seemed to be everywhere. After winning the Chinese civil war, Cho-En-lai's People's Army was battle-hardened and stronger than ever.

Outmanned and outgunned by the ceaseless hordes of Reds, the Marines were fighting for their lives. MacArthur's dream of quick victory uniting all Korea under the U.N. had gone up in smoke, or rather the cold mists of a bitter winter.

No sooner had Kenny's battalion and the rest of the 5th Marines taken up their position here than they were attacked. A savage, vicious attack like no other Kenny had faced in the Pacific war.

So far, each wave of enemy assaults was fought off, but at a terrible cost. Casualties were enormous. Engineers had managed to scrape out a landing strip to the south at Hagaru-ri where courageous C-47 fliers, always under fire, were able to bring in supplies and fly out with loads of wounded. Most of the planes got through, but not all.

Marines were trained to fight, and fight they did, regardless of rank. Kenny fought along with his men and so did most other officers, except of course for commanding general Smith and his staff. Kenny placed himself that day with Baker Company, which was trying to fend off an enemy breakthrough on the left flank.

Red soldiers charged them, swarming out of a white mist. When they were in range, Kenny and everyone else opened fire. He took a bead on a soldier rushing pell-mell toward them and squeezed the trigger. A scarlet splotch blossomed on the man's chest and he toppled, his rifle flying in the air. Then another. And another. Kenny was glad Claudia couldn't see him at this moment.

Machine-gun fire was riddling these attackers. More of them kept coming, though, many of them using the bodies of fallen comrades for cover. Kenny nailed two more, then had to pause and reload.

After thirty minutes that seemed an eternity, the attack was repelled and the Reds, their numbers greatly diminished, began to vanish in the mist. They left behind countless bodies that soon would be frozen stiff in grotesque angles of death.

Kenny knew the enemy would be back, though, later today or tomorrow for sure.

The hideous scene now calm, Kenny shambled back to his tent. He hated killing people but that was his job, everyone's job. Face it, he was a trained killer.

Back in his tent he checked himself for wounds and miraculously found none. Maybe Gautama Buddha had been with him, he thought, recalling what that Korean elder had said. As Kenny sank onto his cot, his body began to shudder uncontrollably. It was delayed reaction. He'd had this before. All he could do was hug himself until it passed, which took several minutes.

No one said anything about it, not Lieutenant Keyser or Sergeant Cooper. They understood. They'd been through hell too.

CHAPTER SIXTY-SEVEN

December 1950. North Korea.

There was nothing to do but retreat. The 5th and 7th Marines had no choice. They were encircled by overwhelming numbers of Chinese Reds, so they had to fight their way out. It would be a long, tortuous trek down the long road to Hungnam harbor. They'd be opposed almost every step of the way before they could be evacuated by the Navy.

"Retreat, hell," one Marine declared. "We're just attacking in a different direction."

Hordes of Reds surrounded the road to Hungnam. All day long, Marines had to fight them off on both sides. Casualties soared for attackers and defenders alike. Reds fell by the hundreds but more always replaced them. "How the hell can there be so many of those bastards?" Kenny said. "Half of China must be out there fighting us."

A shell whined in and hit a truck laden with wounded Marines. It blew up in a gush of flame and body parts flew every which way. Kenny said a little prayer for their souls. He had called Guadalcanal a green hell. This was a white hell.

After dark the 5th Marines managed to reach the landing strip at Hagaru-ri and dug in for the night. Kenny saw a bloody wrapping on Eddie Cooper's left arm, a dent on Lieutenant Keyser's helmet. Sporadic gunfire rattled throughout the night, the Reds messing up attempts to sleep. The temperature fell below zero, freezing up tank and truck engines and batteries.

Sleep being impossible, Kenny twisted and fidgeted in his sleeping bag that night. Home for Christmas? Hah, what a joke that was. He conjured up a vision of Claudia's face, her soft auburn hair and warm hazel-green eyes. He hoped she was fine and doing well in med school. He ached to be with her. When he got out of this damned Korea he would resign from the Corps and do something else with his life, maybe become a history teacher. He never wanted to kill another human being, ever.

He thought about his hometown, its shady brick streets and elegant old homes. Galesburg's Knox College, where he'd earned his degree after the war. Old Main, the school's stately brick building where Lincoln and Douglas had debated in the last century. His Sunday School days at First Christian Church on North Broad Street.

Palling around as a kid with the Fearless Foursome. The mysterious Indian talisman they'd found. The ballgame where Richard Lundquist fooled him with that hidden-ball trick, one of his most embarrassing moments ever. He'd heard that Mikey was in the Army, and wondered what the other fearless ones were doing now.

He thought of Chou-En-lai, the generalissimo who was now China's premier. He'd met the man last year when he'd been imprisoned after helping to evacuate the U.S. Embassy in Nanking. He pictured the man now, saying, "Away from our borders, you damned imperialists."

Outside, the wind howled and random gunfire crackled.

Morning came at last. Kenny saw another C-47 take off with a load of wounded, despite the Reds firing at it. Before the order came to mount up and continue the retrograde south, the enemy attacked. Again.

Kenny fought with Billy Ninetrees' company, this time with no complaint from the Pawnee. Every man was needed. A cluster of Reds in gray quilted coats was trying to advance on them. Ribbons of tracer fire flashed in both directions. Kenny picked off three or four Reds — he was still killing human beings — and somehow managed not to get hit himself. Maybe the Good Lord was saving him for something. Eventually the enemy pulled back, leaving many fallen bodies behind. The calm wouldn't last.

Before long, as a big enemy mortar barrage swept in, Kenny found himself crouched near a boulder, his M-1 in hand ."Quick, into this cave, sir," Eddie Cooper urged. "You'll be safer in there."

Kenny turned and saw the mouth of a cave several meters behind him. He hesitated. Suddenly he was seeing St. Louis Cavern in Illinois where years ago he'd been trapped and was convinced he would die. Christ!

"No, I'll be okay behind this boulder," he said.

A sudden whine filled the air. This would be close. He made sure his helmet was in place and hunkered down as low as he could.

A bright white explosion! A split second of wicked pain. He felt nothing more.

CHAPTER SIXTY-EIGHT

On Saturday all four of them — Jake, Valerie, Claudia and Ilse — went to San Diego to visit Kenny. Jake drove them in his Chevrolet Deluxe. Valerie rode shotgun and the apartment mates had the back seat.

As they passed Camp Pendleton, Claudia pointed and said, "Kenny and I used to live right over there."

Farther south, Valerie exclaimed, "Look at that gorgeous field of flowers. What lovely colors. That must be a flower farm."

"My uncle, who's a farmer in Ohio," Claudia said, "would call that a waste of good land, that it should be in corn or beans."

When Jake finally parked at the naval hospital, they heard sounds of cheering coming from Balboa Stadium just south of there. "Some football game is going on," he said. "Somebody just scored."

Soon they entered Kenny's room and found him on his feet practicing with crutches. "Gosh it's great to see you all. Thanks for coming." He took an awkward step toward Claudia and stumbled. She wrapped him in a bear hug to steady him. "It's wonderful to see you up," she said, and showered him with kisses to a background of broad smiles on Valerie's and Ilse's faces.

The kisses over, Claudia said, "Honey, I'm so sorry—"

"You don't have to say it," Kenny stopped her. "I'm just

glad you came." He sank onto a chair, pointed at the crutches and said, "It's only been a day or two with these things but I'm making progress, see? In a little while I'll be walking with a just a cane. Maybe eventually I won't even need that."

"How does the leg feel, sweetheart?" Claudia asked. *Hurts like the devil.* "Not bad," he fibbed. "What's going on with you three? Tell me all the news." The women sat in the remaining chairs and Jake perched on the edge of the bed.

They proceeded to bring him up to date. Claudia was getting close to graduation and so was Ilse. "We've both got good grades," Claudia said. "We're a pair of study-holics."

Valerie told about her work on the Viking rocket. "We've solved some problems with the gyroscope and it's about ready for a test launch."

Claudia then pulled a small wrapped box from her purse, handed it to Kenny and said, "A little gift for you, hon. Open it later." Kenny thanked her and put it in his lap. He asked Jake about the murder investigation.

Jake told him all he knew, including the break-in, the pistol that was planted in their bedroom, and the cops' search of their home.

"Good thing you dumped it," Kenny said. "You say this Sixto guy looked surprised when he didn't find it. You think he's the killer then?"

"Don't know, but the Good Humor man who saw him, or her, said the prowler wasn't very tall and that fits Sixto. If it was him, he's probably the killer."

Valerie jumped in: "But since we don't know the prowler's gender for sure, I still say Penny Franklin is our killer." She described her meeting with Franklin's widow, saying that she sounded unfaithful, had probably been cheating on her husband. And was sure he'd been playing around too.

"Hmm," Kenny said, tossing all this around in his fertile

mind.

Ilse then told about tracking down Freddie, the older son, and questioning him at a soda fountain. Kenny asked several questions about that.

"You sound like an investigative reporter," Jake said. "You've always been good at figuring out tactical situations."

"I guess. Now tell me more about this Franklin kid, Ilse. How did he act? What were his facial expressions?"

"When I brought up patricide he got real angry, said a son would never kill his father no matter how bad the man might be. He accused me of saying he killed his dad, said I must be nuts. He got up then and there, and bolted out of the place."

"I see," Kenny said. He fell silent, taking all this in. Finally he leaned forward and said," He did it. He killed his father."

Jake, stunned, said, "Really?"

"Sure, he considers himself straight arrow, a do-gooder, maybe was a Sunday School star. He sounds schizophrenic. When he said nobody would ever kill his father he might have meant just the opposite. He couldn't deal with the thought of his father cheating on his mother so he got rid of the guy. Furthermore he knows his mother is a cheat too. The kid has snapped. Thinks he's the avenging angel. He's liable to kill her too."

"Holy shit," Jake blurted. "If you're right we've gotta do something about this. Fast." *God, this Kenny is a smart cookie.*

CHAPTER SIXTY-NINE

December 1950. North Korea.

The next thing Kenny knew he was opening his eyes and beginning to see, as through a haze, a corpsman leaning over him. "Let me give you another shot of morphine, sir."

Kenny's sluggish mind wasn't working well, but he caught sight of the aluminum ribs of a fuselage and realized he was on a plane. What did this guy just say? Was it morphine?

"Sir? Another shot?"

"Shot? What do you . . . Oh, you mean morphine?"

"That's right, sir. It'll help you rest easier."

"How many have I had?" Kenny asked. His fingers were cold. He couldn't feel his feet.

"One or two, I think."

"No more then."

"Are you sure, sir?"

"Very sure," Kenny said. "Where are we?"

"Aboard an evac plane, sir. We'll be landing at Hungnam pretty soon."

Kenny's ears made out moans and cries of pain around him. This must be quite a big load of wounded.

His groggy head shut down again. All sorts of hazy, wacky dreams appeared. He was flying upside down in an open-cockpit biplane. Claudia floated by on a cloud, waving to him. Then Jake Weaver was sitting on a huge typewriter floating in a lake. He spoke into a telephone that had no cord. Kenny's old high school flame Jacqueline Lundquist was laughing. He fell out of that plane and was falling, falling. Was he ever going to hit ground or water? The dream stopped right there.

His eyes opened and the corpsman was back. "Hi. You're not floating on a cloud, are you?" Kenny said.

The corpsman laughed. "A cloud? No sir, what I'm floating on is a C-47 Dakota."

"How bad am I hurt, fella?"

"Pretty bad, sir. Luckily you have no frostbite like a lot of the boys here, but your left leg is real messed up. I hope the docs can save it."

Save it? Am I gonna lose my leg?Will I be able to survive this or am I just chasing after the wind?

Kenny closed his eyes and drifted back into sleep. He dreamed he was being pushed in a wheelchair. He had no left leg. People in clown masks were laughing.

CHAPTER SEVENTY

Although he knew he'd be chewed out again for interfering, Jake called detective Wannamaker and told him Kenny Nielsen insisted that Freddie Franklin killed his father and might kill his mother too.

"Jesus, man, how many times do I have to tell you . . . Well who the hell is Kenny Nielsen?"

"The coauthor of our book about World War II. The guy has a brilliant mind. He's always drawn great conclusions on battlefield situations."

"He has, huh? If you think I'm going down that road on a hunch by some soldier boy I don't even know, you're full of it."

"Owen, you're a professional detective investigating a murder. It's your duty to follow up every lead."

"Now I'm getting lectured by a typewriter jockey on how to do my job."

"And what if he's right, Owen? You wanta take that chance with a woman's life?"

A long pause, then: "Well shoot, Weaver, the captain will have my ass for this but okay, I guess I'll go to the well again, haul him and his mom in for another go-round."

The next day, Wannamaker, Sam Sixto, Penny Franklin and her older son were sitting around a metal table in an interrogation room at Central Division. Sixto and the woman exchanged an uncomfortable look. Puzzled, Wannamaker noticed Sixto shake his head very slightly at her.

"Thanks for coming in," Wannamaker said. "One more thing to clear up. Let's get right to it." Staring hard at Freddie Franklin's eyes, he said, "Young man, did you kill your father?"

Panic crossed the boy's face. He said nothing for a long moment. Then, lightning fast, he grabbed for Sixto's service revolver. Managed to get a hand on it. "Damn right I did, and you're next, Mom, you cheating bitch!"

Wannamaker lunged at the kid but not before he aimed at his mother and squeezed the trigger. There was nothing but an audible click. Wannamaker swatted the gun from Freddie's hand. "Thank God he didn't know to palm the grip safety."

Shaken and red with anger, Penny Franklin whined, "Dammit, Sam, you said nothing like this would ever happen. Why did I ever mess around with you? Some lover you turned out to be."

Freddie bolted for the door but Wannamaker leaped after him, grabbed him by the shoulders and wrestled him down. "You're not going anywhere, kid." Breathing hard, he looked up at Sixto: "You and this woman?"

Penny Franklin spoke first. "Yeah, we were having a fling. How dumb could I be, screwing a cop."

Shoving Freddie onto a chair, Wannamaker said, "You've got a lot to answer for, Sam. We'll get to that later, but first things first. Fred Franklin, you are under arrest for murder. Anything you say can be used against you." He added that he had a right to a lawyer and so on.

"Damn it, Mom, you've got no right to live," Freddie the avenging angel stormed.

CHAPTER SEVENTY-ONE

December 1950. Over the Pacific.

From Hungnam, Kenny had gone by hospital ship to Japan. Now he was aboard a plane bound for the States. He'd been examined over and over, poked and prodded countless times by doctors in face masks who muttered to each other, sharing opinions. Nurses had popped all sorts of pills in his mouth.

Why in hell didn't he go into that cave with Eddie Cooper? For that matter, why did he join the Corps in the first place, twelve years ago?

As the plane droned onward, yet another doc was now examining his leg. The man had wispy gray hair and looked to be about 50. He wore white gloves speckled with drops of blood. He pulled back the dressing and touched bone and cartilage.

"Ouch! Jesus, doc."

"Quite a bit of pain, right, son?"

"God, yes. Is there any hope? Am I going to lose my leg?"

"I hope not, fella, but the tibia and fibula bones down there are shattered. We've braced it up as best we can for now with splints and straps. They'll have to put it back together in the States with some screws and such. I see no gangrene and that's a good thing. Very little infection either. The specialists in San Diego will be able to tell you more. They're doing marvelous things there now."

Kenny asked if the other Marines had reached safety in Hungnam.

"Yes, most of them. They tell me it was a terrible fight. What brave men they were."

311

"That's for sure, doc." Kenny hoped Billy Ninetrees and Eddie Cooper were among the survivors. He would pray for them.

The doctor put the dressing back in place and left, saying, "Rest easy, son."

Rest easy? Ha. Kenny had been sleeping a lot, usually with frightening nightmares. Sometimes stuff about caves. Sometimes covered in bitter snow. Sometimes the hell that was boot camp at Parris Island.

He'd completely lost any sense of time and place. The last he could remember it was December. Had Christmas come and gone? Had Claudia been informed of his condition?

After awhile he realized he was on the ground somewhere. Maybe Hawaii? He hadn't been aware of the plane making a landing. The hatch was open and fresh air wafted in. This was a welcome change after smelling what? — ether? other chemicals? — and the stench of putrefied infection for so long.

He knew some Marines had died on this flight. He'd seen several covered bodies carried off on litters. Sad sight. Maybe it would be best if he just died too. Wouldn't be fair to burden Claudia down with a crippled old man. Let her create a good new life for herself.

Stop that! Am I insane? I want to live.

A cheerful nurse came by. Kenny liked her, she'd always been nice. He couldn't remember her name. She gently touched his forehead, checking for fever.

"Colonel," she said, "if you had one wish for anything at all, just one wish, what would it be?"

Kenny lay silent for a long while. At last he murmured, "Just tomorrow."

CHAPTER SEVENTY-TWO

Nine months later.

It was September and Rams football was under way. The Trojans and Bruins too. Relaxing in his easy chair at home, Jake was thinking not about football, but what a journey his life had been. He'd started his newspaper career at the *News-Journal* in Longview, Texas, was briefly married there to Dixie Freitas, a cocktail waitress. That turned out to be a whopper of a mistake.

Then going to L.A. where his news career really began to flourish. As the paper's military writer he'd met President Roosevelt and sneaked into Nazi Germany during World War II. Twice! Thought about how he'd tracked down the rocket man Wernher von Braun and got him into U.S. hands. Was awarded Britain's George Cross for that exploit. A great honor.

More scraps of memory. Coauthoring a book on that war with his friend Kenny Nielsen. Meeting young John F. Kennedy, a congressman from Massachusetts. The exposé he and Ilse wrote on illegal wartime profiteering by Standard Oil, which had raised the ire of the Rockefeller family. His looking into the still unsolved murder of mobster Bugsy Siegel, and the friendship that developed with another underworld figure, Mickey Cohen.

He was starting to ponder his own new journalistic endeavor when Valerie came in the room and said, "You look deep in thought, dear."

Jake looked up and said, "I was just reminiscing about all that's happened, especially the great good luck I had in meeting and marrying you."

"I feel exactly the same, Sailor." She leaned down and kissed him. "And I'm sure glad things are working out for Kenny and Claudia."

"Me too, Sweets."

CHAPTER SEVENTY-THREE

Everyone had graduated from something, everyone except Valerie. Ilse from UCLA, with honors. Claudia from its school of medicine. Jake from the *Herald-Express*. Kenny from San Diego's naval hospital.

Ilse and her stepmother had put together a big picnic reunion in L.A.'s Griffith Park on a warm September Saturday. Tubs of fried chicken with plenty of side dishes were laid on a long picnic table. Beer, wine and soft drinks in coolers. An ice cream maker, too, where the men would take turns cranking the handle.

Even Bela Lugosi was there. This was Ilse's idea. She'd driven to Van Nuys to fetch the old actor.

The women and Jake wore shorts and gym shoes. Kenny was in jeans concealing his scarred leg, while Lugosi wore a long-sleeve white shirt, pinstriped black pants and dress shoes.

Jake had brought a bat and softball. There weren't enough people to have an actual game, but soon they were taking turns hitting the ball around on a long expanse of grass.

To start, Ilse lobbed a ball to Jake. He swung and drove it to the "outfield," where Claudia caught it on a bounce and tossed it back in to Ilse.

Kenny was next. He'd been walking with a cane, limping a little. He took an awkward swing and missed. "Are you okay?" Claudia called out.

"Sure I am. Throw me another one, Ilse." Kenny steadied himself, resumed his stance, and hit a sharp grounder up the middle. He retrieved his cane and said, "Sorry, but I can't run the bases."

"Hey, you're doing fine," Valerie said. "How about you, Mr. Lugosi?" she asked.

"Oh, I'm afraid that . . . well, I will give it a try." He swung feebly twice, missing each time. He glared at the traitorous bat and said, "We were not meant for each other, were we?" The others laughed.

Claudia came up to bat next and Ilse pitched. Her former roommate swung and hit a looper high in the air which Jake ran down and snagged.

Valerie told Ilse to bat next and she would throw. Her first toss was bad and arrived on a bounce. Ilse, a fine athlete, nevertheless reached down and, red ponytail twirling, drove the ball over everyone's heads. Two kids riding by on bikes whistled and hooted. "Way to go, Ilse, that's my girl," Jake called out as he trotted out to relieve the ball.

"I'm the last one to bat," Valerie said. "Does that make me the cleanup hitter?"

Jake came in and got ready to throw to her. Valerie took her stance, waggled the bat once or twice and said, "Lay it in here, Sailor."

She swung and hit a popup toward Bela Lugosi. He staggered toward it, saw it bounce off his hand, but managed to reach out and clutch it before it hit the ground.

"All right, Bela," Kenny shouted. "Nice catch."

Jake said, "Ilse's the winner. Let's gather round the table now and drink to our student-athlete." And they did. White wine for the women, Pepsi for Kenny, a beer for Jake, and Lugosi had a cup of red wine.

"I thought vampires never drank wine," Jake kidded him.

"First of all, sir, I am not a vampire, and secondly, do not believe everything you see in the movies."

"This was a swell idea today," Kenny said. "Thanks for putting this together, ladies. Here's another idea. Let's all tell what's been going on with each of us. You first, Ilse, champion slugger."

Ilse raised her plastic cup high and said, "First, a toast to all of us. We're doing great."

"To all of us," the others chimed in.

"Okay," Ilse went on, "I guess you know I graduated pretty high in my class" — cheers interrupted this — "and am now a reporter with the *Pasadena Star-News*. I really like it, it's a good paper. If I'm lucky maybe they'll let me cover the Rose Bowl game. You next, *Vati*."

Jake said, "Can you imagine me in television? Ed Murrow offered me a job as the West Coast man with CBS News and I took it. I'll be working with some good people on his team, like Eric Sevareid, Douglas Edwards and Walt Cronkite. Sevareid was with me at the liberation of Paris in '44."

"Wow," Kenny chirped. "My coauthor goes big time."

"I quit the *Herald*," Jake went on, "after Hearst Junior ordered me to go and cover the Korean War. This'll be a refreshing new start for me, though I'll miss our watering hole, the Continental, and my pal Shaker the bartender. Your turn, Kenny."

Ilse noticed happily that Kenny and Claudia had been holding hands.

Using his cane, Kenny stood and said, "As you can see I'm getting around on my feet but I won't be running the hundred-yard dash anytime soon. One day, though, I won't even need this thing." Wiggling the cane. "I'm in grad school at San Diego State to get my teacher's certificate. I plan on teaching high school history down there somewhere, maybe even coach some basketball."

Jake felt a surge of pride at the progress Kenny was making.

"Claudia honey?" Kenny said.

Claudia said she was doing her residency at St. Mary's Hospital in Long Beach, was proud to have her M.D., and planned to open a family practice in San Diego. "I've got my eye on a place in La Mesa, nice little town."

Next Valerie put down her wine cup and said, "I'm proud to say my Viking rocket just had a perfect test launch at White Sands. I say *my* because I did a lot of work on it." She turned to Bela Lugosi.

"All I can say is that I am humbled by the friendship you have extended to me, especially from you, Ilse. I too am a graduate, from a drug-treatment center, and now I hope that I can find the strength to remain clean. I am also hoping at my advanced age to still land a film role. One can never tell."

"I'm pulling for you," Jake said. "Okay, the speeches are done, let's eat. They sat around the table and dug in.

"I saw in the paper," Valerie said, "that Marion Davies filed for divorce from that Horace Brown. You were right when you said you'd give them a year, Jake."

"Course I was."

"Say, I got a letter the other day from my old friend Billy Ninetrees," Kenny put in. "He's left the Corps too and is back on the Pawnee reservation in Osage County."

Scooping some potato salad on her plate, Ilse said, "*Vati*, whatever happened to Freddie Franklin?"

"He was convicted of killing his father, attempted murder on his mother, too. After all, he'd confessed to Wannamaker. He avoided San Quentin and is now doing time under guard at the Patton Mental Hospital out in San Berdoo. Very troubled kid."

"And that Sam Sixto person?" Ilse asked.

"He was placed on administrative leave while Internal Affairs looked into the misconduct of having an affair with an actual suspect in the middle of a murder investigation. He's been let go and works as a security guard somewhere, El Monte I think. Say, this fried chicken is great, Val."

"Thanks, Sailor," Valerie said. "Now let's forget about all those things and enjoy the rest of the day. We're together and we're happy."

■